SHADOW

TIMBER-GHOST, MONTANA CHAPTER

DEVIL'S HANDMAIDENS MC
BOOK 2

D.M. EARL

© Copyright 2023 D.M. Earl
All rights reserved.
Cover by Drue Hoffman, Buoni Amici Press
Editing by Karen Hrdlicka
Proofread by Joanne Thompson

All rights reserved. No part of this book may be reproduced in any form or by any electronic or mechanical means, including information storage and retrieval systems—except in the case of brief quotations embodied in critical articles or reviews—without permission in writing from the author.

This book is a work of fiction. The names, characters, and places portrayed in this book are entirely products of the author's imagination or used fictitiously. Any resemblance to actual events, locales, or persons, living or dead, is entirely coincidental and not intended by the author.

The unauthorized reproduction or distribution of this copyrighted work is illegal. Criminal copyright infringement, including infringement without monetary gain, is investigated by the FBI and is punishable by up to five years in federal prison and a fine of $250,000.

If you find any eBooks being sold or shared illegally, please contact the author at dm@dmearl.com.

ACKNOWLEDGMENTS

Karen Hrdlicka and **Joanne Thompson** my editing and proofreading team. I'm blessed to be working with both Karen and Joanne. Between these two women they make my stories shine. With their eyes on my books I feel you're getting the best book it can be due to their experience and knowledge of how I write.

Debra Presley and **Drue Hoffman** of **Buoni Amici Press**. Talk about handling everything as my two publicists work endlessly to handle the social media aspect and so much more so I can concentrate on my writing. They are angels and I'm thrilled to have them be part of my team.

Enticing Journey Promotions and **Itsy-Bitsy Book Bits**. These two promotional companies help me with every new release and are very professional and always on top of everything.

Bloggers every single one of you. What you do for each and every one of my stories I can never repay you. Please know how much appreciate each share, mention, post and video.

My **DM's Babes** (ARC Team) and **DM's Horde**

(Reader's group). The women in these two groups have become part of my family. I'm blessed to know each and every one of them.

READERS without each of Y'all I'd not be able to live out my life's dream of writing books that make people feel. Your support fills my heart and feeds my soul.

TRANSLATIONS

Navajo Translations

nizhoni-Beautiful
anii'- Face
ma'iitsoh-Wolf
zhį'ii-Raven
ch'įįdii-Demonic Spirits
atsoo'-Tongue
Hózhó-Balance and Beauty
Biligaana-White
Aho-Thank you
Yah Ta Hey-Good
Ayóó'áníínishní-I love you
chahóółhééł naabaahii t'áá sáhi – Dark Warrior Walking Alone
nitsaa yikah tsintah - Big Walking Trees

Blackfoot Translations

Áápi- White

Italian Translations

Puttana- Whore
Occhio per occhio, dente per dente- An Eye for An Eye, Tooth for a Tooth.
Figlia- *Daughter*

ONE
'SHADOW'
ZOEY

As I push my bike as hard and fast as I can in the starless, ebony abyss we call Montana nights, the guilt is overwhelmingly crushing down on my shoulders. Every time I get this particular call and leave immediately, without a word of explanation to Goldilocks, I feel like total shit and a sneaky-ass bitch. We're besties and share everything. Though gotta say, tonight couldn't get the hell outta there fast enough. Noodles asked her to marry him. What the ever-lovin' fuck? What have they known each other... five fucking minutes, for Christ's sake? I hate to even think this, but it's bad enough Hannah's back and gonna live in the house with us. I did spend some time with the kid and she's all right in my book. Hannah's got her head on straight most of the time. Sharing my bestie with her long-lost daughter/sister is gonna be hard enough at times, but now add a fiancé, who eventually will be her husband. Shit, my girl Goldilocks ain't gonna want my kind of freaky hanging around, damn, especially if those two are even thinking about having babies someday. Like one look at my fucked-up face won't scare the tyke for the rest of his or her life, for Christ's sake.

With my head up my ass, I barely see the movement on the side of the road. Pulling in my front brake slowly and consistently, while my foot pushes down with some serious pressure on my rear brake, my attention at this precise moment is on the herd of mule deer moving silently through the dense forest toward the road. Somehow, and by the grace of God, I manage to pass their asses before they decide to leisurely cross the road to the other side. Slowing down even further, I take the next curve like a pansy-ass new rider, but between my heart beating like a drum and my body trembling, that shit for some reason just freaked the fuck out of me. Knowing I don't have time to act like a goddamn baby, when the dimly lit shoulder area for accidents is in sight, I instantly pull over and shift my bike into neutral before giving my kickstand a good kick. Once my bike is stable on the stand, I can't get my ass off my bike quick enough. Son of a motherfuckin' bitch, that was too goddamn close. If that slight movement hadn't caught my eye, I would've been spread out all over that road with either some serious road rash or maybe missing a limb or two along the asphalt. Or just a shattered skull. That thought gives me a shiver.

What the hell is my problem today? Shit, I know the answer to that, just don't know how to fix it. I did this to myself and now have to pay the damn consequences. There's not one person who can help me. Again, not true, but don't want his asshole help. Got in this goddamn mess 'cause of his bullshit to start with. I'm such a dumbass and this situation proves it one hundred and fifty percent. How the hell am I gonna tell my club sisters that I—Shadow, their badass tough as fuck enforcer—fell for one of the oldest cons ever? To make it worse, when that jerk filled me in on himself, I could have shit my pants and puked at the same time. Well, until I pictured what I could do to him and how much I could make him squeal in agony. My one saving grace, I can escape into my head.

When my nerves settle down once again, I get on my bike, start her up, and continue on my night ride. Don't have much farther to go, but from this point on, my attention has to stay on where I'm at and if I'm being followed by anyone. This could be life or death kind of shit. And as much as that motherfucker pisses me off, I don't want to be the reason why he disappears unless I'm the one making that happen. Leaning into the curve, I glance in my side mirror to see a car, a dark sedan, hanging back a bit. That doesn't sit well so I downshift, hoping this jerk will pass me and go on his merry damn way. Well, of course, they fuckin' don't do that, but they are now lingering behind me, trying to look inconspicuous. Dumbass shouldn't be driving a jacked-up, older model sedan then. Seeing my turnoff straight ahead, I pass it, then gun the throttle and race down not even an eighth of a mile and make a crazy as fuck turn onto the hidden gravel road he showed me in case of any "trouble." As soon as I can, I turn off my bike and the headlight, scrunching low behind a tree-lined area with large old trees and some bushes, trying to wait while sitting still and not breathing like someone is chasing me.

Hearing the car first then smelling it, I smile to myself. This asshole is burning oil—stupid ass—his engine is either gonna seize or with any luck, blow up. Barely breathing, I watch as they speed by. *Thank Christ*, I think to myself but stay put. Not gonna rush and miss them either turning around or worse, coming at me on foot to follow me.

My head is all over the fucking place. I almost panicked when Goldilocks said that Hannah was gonna move in then dropped the bomb about getting engaged. For a split second, I felt sharp, agonizing, all-consuming hysteria start to rise up. The horror of not having anywhere or anyone to live with almost brought me to my knees. Then Goldilocks demanded I not only still live in her home but maybe would be able to help her with

Hannah. That right there calmed my nerves but also made me feel like I was good enough and could be useful.

Not seeing those assholes, I slowly push my bike outta the tree line and, with one more look around, I start it up and quickly make my way down to the turnoff. Shit, this ain't barely a road, and in the past, there have been times when I almost dropped my bike.

I've thought about driving my shitty old cage but whenever the weather permits, I'm on my bitch of a bike. Turning one last time, just to be careful, I manage to make my way down the half mile death trap of a driveway to the house. Damn, if ya could call it that. More of an obstacle course, not sure why he hasn't at least filled the damn huge potholes. Stupid fucker that he is.

Seeing the log house, I let out the breath I've been holding on to. Damn, can't keep doing this bullshit for so many fucking reasons. Shit, I'm part of the Devil's Handmaidens MC and one thing our club doesn't ever do: we don't keep secrets from our club sisters. Loyalty in our club is everything. More importantly though is keeping this shit from my family—Goldilocks, Pops, Momma Diane, and now including Hannah. Shit, better start adding Noodles to the goddamn list too. A small smile hits my lips briefly 'cause I have a growing family, the one thing I've always wanted. One thing I'm not gonna do is add this motherfucker 'cause I might kill him before this night is over.

Seeing the pole barn open, I pull into it, off to the left side where his bikes and cages are. I get off the bike shaking my limbs, not only from the ride but from tensing up my muscles. Not a good night to ride for me, I'm guessing. Too many almosts happening.

Removing my travel bag, I drop it to the ground. Then grabbing my thick braid, I remove the band and let my long raven hair loose. Running my fingers through to my scalp, I give it a quick scratch. Feeling a little bit more like myself, I turn. He's standing in the doorway, leaning against the wood frame, one ankle crossed over the other, that goddamn sexy smirk on his beautiful high cheekbone face. He fits his jeans like no man I've ever known. And in my type of business, I've seen my share of men and also killed quite a few. My eyes follow his scuffed boots up his long length of legs to his thick thighs, which catch my attention, as I work my way up and over the area that is highlighted by his low-riding jeans. His flat as fuck abs lead up to the sculptured chest that has my mouth watering. When I get to his face, I stop breathing. That face always takes my breath away. Long ebony hair, almost to his ass, is currently half up, half down. His chiseled jaw and cheekbones show his bloodline. But the eyes pull me in. Expecting brown or even black ones, nope, his are as green as the trees in the forests of Montana. Nothing like my own ice blues, which look cold and dead, his are—shit—the only thing I can compare them to is what I've seen on television and in pictures. His are a true gemstone forest green. Those are his weapons. One of many. I just stand here staring at him like a smitten young girl. His smirk gets wider, but he never moves. After what seems like hours, but isn't even a few minutes, he tilts his head and studies me. Doesn't take him long to read my body language and figure out something is wrong.

"Nizhoni, *beautiful* get your fine ass over here and tell me what the hell's going on. Something's got ya freaked, what's done it? Goddamn it, come on, Zoey, talk to me."

Hearing my name from his lips when I told him, time and time again, only my family calls me that, I feel the panic and intense anger take over. A man doesn't get that privilege. Not after all the ones who used and abused it and me.

"I told you not to use that name. You don't get that name. Hear me, motherfucker, 'cause I ain't gonna tell ya again. Next time might have to cut that tongue of yours out of your mouth and shove it up your fine as fuck brown ass."

He outright laughs then slowly stands up and walks into my space but doesn't put a hand on me.

"All right. Now, I know you're a sexy badass woman but remember one thing. If you cut my tongue out, you know what that means. No more…"

"No, don't say it. You suck big time."

"Won't be able to without a tongue. So now that problem's solved, can we move on to what's weighing on your mind and has your shoulders tense as fuck? You're going to tell me before I explain why I called you for your expertise and help."

As I explain to him about everything that has gone on with Goldilocks or Tink, as he knows her by, Noodles, Hannah, and then the ride from hell over here between the deer and that strange car, he watches me closely, trying to read me. Not gonna happen. After so many years, I've learned the hard way, gotta keep some shit close to the chest. Only way to protect myself.

"So, what was so fucking important that you had to demand I ride over here tonight in the pitch dark, you crazy asswipe? What couldn't wait until tomorrow, for Christ's sake?"

He shakes his head slowly while his hand goes around my waist gently, pulling me closer to him. My hands automatically land on that defined chest of his and when his unique scent hits my nose, all I want to do is climb him so he can hold me tight with those arms of steel. Instead, I sniff then smell him and I wait for his answer.

"Did you just scent me? Anyway, I got a call tonight, said they might have found me the two to four toys that I've put a request in for. They want a meet, but at a different spot, and the price went up another thirty grand each. Not sure if they made me or if something popped in the system. I was told my backstory was solid but there is always a better hacker out there, right? Thought some backup would be a good idea to keep my ass breathing, and you being my secret *badass weapon*, don't trust anyone more than you to have my back. Oh, I made a call and also have Avalanche on his way."

"Shit, dude, why do you always call him in? He not only hates me but belittles me too. Every goddamn time. One of these days, I'm gonna put a bullet right between his dopey-looking eyes, swear to God."

"Come on, *beautiful*, he's my brother and one of the few I still trust. Give me that, all right?"

I just nod and agree, knowing he's very close to losing it. He's been trying for a couple of years on and off to demolish this menace to society jagoff's sick ring, with no success. This filth can get whatever anyone asks of them, for a price of course. And he's worked so hard and has gone in so deep. He gets so close then just like that, they're gone. It's like someone is warning them, or worse, informing on him. I've been trying to figure out why he trusts the big dumb lug who's on his way.

Reaching down I go to pick up my bag, but he gets to it first and grabs it. Then he reaches for my hand and together we move out of the pole barn and toward the house. Once inside, I tell him to just drop my bag anywhere as I'm dying of thirst. Walking into the kitchen, just as we are about to grab something to drink, I feel him before I hear his irritating voice.

"Hey, boss, whatcha need? Am I going with ya or staying behind to keep an eye on them? Either way, just let me know, I'm good with either. At least I won't scare the fuck outta the little ones."

He laughs and I look his way, shooting him the finger.

"Whatever, Big Bird, watch your mouth, not in the mood for your childish bullshit tonight."

"Oh, I'm feeling sorry then for my man here 'cause he called you just for that, ya know. Might as well leave, little skull anii' *face* before you get yourself hurt."

Walking right up to him, I have to lean back to look up at this enormous jerk. When I raise my hands, he flinches, so I grin like the lunatic I am. Moving my upper body which has his attention, when I lift my knee and make contact with his balls, he goes down instantly.

"Next time think twice before calling me names, Big Bird. As the old saying goes, the bigger they are, the harder they fall, asshole."

Then without thinking, I pull my leg back and as I go to kick him again in the nuts, I'm grabbed from behind and lifted high in the air.

"Enough of this stupid petty bullshit from both of you. Goddamn idiots. Not sure what the problem is between the two of you but that's it, no more. You're pissing me off and we have too much at stake, so suck it up, try to act like adults for once in your lives."

When he goes to put me down, he pulls me close to his chest, so I feel the length of his body, including the hard as steel cock behind his zipper, telling me he's thrilled to see me. My mood switches instantly. Again, with the confusing feelings. I feel my nipples getting hard as my center and core clench, wanting what I can't handle. This is becoming a pain in my ass. Then I hear Big Bird's irritating voice.

"Goddamn, you two horny assholes need to get a room already. It's disgusting how neither of you can keep your hands off each other every time you're together. Get your minds outta the gutter, we got serious shit to do."

With that comment, I first giggle then outright laugh, which helps me release the tension in my body. At least that dick is good for something.

TWO
'PANTHER'

CHAHÓÓŁHÉÉL NAABAAHII T'ÁÁ SÁHI
DARK WARRIOR WALKING ALONE

Watching Zoey and Avalanche do their usual assholes dance around each other brings a small smirk to my otherwise stoic face. Rubbing my hands over my face, I feel my anxiety taking over. This never gets easier. Now with this woman kind of in my life, at least when she wants, I think—no fucking pray—to the Great Spirit for some form of uncomplicated and maybe even a peaceful life that's trouble-free, eventually. Yeah, I'm a dreamer. What can I say though, not that any of my dreams have ever come true. Yet. But there is always a first time.

Hearing the two of them laughing, I lift my head to see them both looking at me. Shit, I must have zoned out and missed what one of them asked me.

"Okay, which of you misfits said something and, yeah, I wasn't paying attention to this episode of *Sesame Street* so forgive me."

Avalanche shakes his head, but his eyes stay glued to me. We grew up on the reservation as brothers and entered the military together. I reclassified and he went for the discharge so each of us went our separate ways, and we lost contact for a long length of time. Not sure how, but when I was desperate and in trouble he found me at the precise time I needed him the most. Together we've built this horse ranch into what it is today. Best horseflesh out there in this part of Montana. Not to mention our studs, which have made a name for themselves, and we are lucky enough to make money off of each breeding season. We know each other inside out and have at times read each other's thoughts. Some may call it bullshit, but being almost full Navajo I would never disrespect it and call it that. It's more like our life's meaning and connection. And for Avalanche, he grew up harder being only half Navajo and half white.

"Boss, we were discussing this beyond bullshit idea you're trying to sell us. Don't care what you think, this don't feel right to me. I have all kinds of dark clouds surrounding it and that tells me it's a definite no. Our skull anii' over here agrees for once."

Before he can keep goading her, Zoey pulls back and punches him in his arm, which has Avalanche howling in pain. What a fucking wimp, for Christ's sake, she's a girl. Not that I'd ever say that out loud or in front of her, she'd probably kick my ass too.

"Big Bird, I told you not to speak Navajo around

me unless I know what you're saying. And quit calling me skull face already. The joke is worn out, for Christ's sake. And as much as I hate to admit it, he's right, we both agree you should call off tonight. I don't have a good feeling and as I've told you, time and time again, I always listen to my gut instinct. It's saved my life a dozen times at least."

"If you know what anii' means then what the fuck are ya smacking me for, you freak? I'm getting sick and tired of always being your punching bag, bitch. And he talks in our language all the time and you don't beat on him, for Christ's sake."

"Goddamn it, enough. The two of you are going to make my hair turn gray. Avalanche, no more name-calling and, Zoey, no more punching. Nod if you agree. NOW."

It takes them a minute of glaring at each other, and I think Zoey actually growled, but eventually they both give me a very short nod. Well, thank God for small miracles. Now to the business at hand.

"I hear both of you and have a similar forbidding feeling. Hold up—shut your mouths and listen. We've been at this for what... how many sons of a bitchin' months? And this is the first time they've ever tried to fill one of my *special orders*, so even though it might blow up in our faces, I've got to try. After what went down on that reservation in South Dakota don't ask me not to make every attempt humanly possible to catch these sick motherfuckers and put them six feet under."

I see the intense anger enter Avalanche's eyes right before he gives me a slight nod. Well, damn, that was easier than I expected. Looking at Zoey expectantly, I wait, knowing to rush her is to sign your own death warrant. Avalanche and I say nothing and wait quietly until Zoey throws both of her arms up in the air. This tells me we are about to see a famous Shadow temper tantrum, so I try to prepare myself. The differences are huge between her when she's Zoey to when she turns herself into Shadow, who is a very unique and magnificent creature, while at the same time beyond scary and makes the hair on my neck tingle. I also never take my eyes off her when she's in her Shadow mainframe.

My mind strays for a second as I remember the first time I ever saw Zoey. I'd walked into my buddy's tattoo parlor for my next session, and there she was in all her glory. Nothing, not even me banging the door into the wall when I opened it and slamming it shut against the winds from hell, intrigued her enough to open her eyes. Lying still as fuck on that bed, eyes closed, letting that little crazy-ass female tattoo artist tattoo and fill in the skull on her face. It fascinated me that a woman as hot as her would do that to her face. I was so intent on staring at what was being done, I never noticed Zoey opening her eyes until the heat from her own stare had me looking into the most stunning ice-blue eyes I've ever seen. Knew in that goddamn moment that no matter what, even if it killed me, I was gonna make that woman mine. And I didn't even know her name. Just thinking about it brings a smile to my face because Zoey has not made my life's mission easy on me at all.

"Are you fucking kidding me, stud? You have a death wish or something? Right now, there is just the two of us so there's no way in hell we can keep eyes on you all the time, plus protect the innocent tender ages who are involved. And from what you guys told me about South Dakota, these motherfuckers don't have a conscience and would have no problem murdering these kids in cold blood. Come on, find a way to stall them even 'til tomorrow morning so we can call in some cavalry. Why take the chance, you dumbass? We're too close to fracturing this circuit of motherfuckers and bringing the jagoffs to their knees, so don't fuck this shit up trying to be the almighty savior again. Remember what happened the last time you thought you had it in hand. If not for Big Bird here, you would have been dead. Thank Christ he has the tracking skills he does or your body would be decaying and no one would have ever known. Never thought I'd say this, but I'm thankful for your connection with Big Bird."

Hearing Avalanche snort and pat himself on the back just when Zoey flips him off, I take a moment to actually think about what both of them are trying to pound into my head. Zoey's right, that last interaction almost killed me, literally. If not for my best friend, I wouldn't be breathing, and I still suffer aftereffects from my many injuries. That group was brutal, and I can't even spare a moment's thought to what we found at that abandoned house. The nightmares are enough.

"Okay, okay, I give up. I'll do my best to make the meeting tomorrow sometime after noon. That way we can get some of the guys on board and have Black Widow do her thing. Are you happy now, beautiful? If so, maybe I can persuade you to spend the night with me."

When she barely nods her head, I laugh out loud at the disbelief on my man's face because he's shocked beyond belief how easily she gave in to my request. Just as I go to talk smack and give shit, my phone starts ringing and vibrating. Game on.

"Yeah."

"Listen, got no reason to talk that way to me. I don't disrespect you; I expect the same. Hey, don't say that again, you motherfuckin' bastard. I'm Native not a dumb Indian. Say that to my face and you'll learn about my native ways while I'm cutting off your scalp, then I'll pull your tongue out of your mouth and remove it permanently. Next your eyelids will go and I'll leave you staked to the ground outside with honey on your face. How long until the ants come looking for their next meal, you crazy as fuck bastard?

"Now back to business, I can't make it tonight, not possible. How about tomorrow? Whatever works for you, I'll do my best to leave my schedule open. Yeah, I can try to get ahold of her but why do you want that one there? She's a pain in not only mine but everyone's ass, without even considering she's lethally insane. Well, I can't help it that your boss is infatuated with the bitch, but I'll do my best. Yeah, let me know in the a.m. where and when. Later, you prejudiced cocksucker."

While shoving my phone in my back pocket, I glance around to see Avalanche smirking my way. He says nothing, just gives me a chin lift, turns and walks toward the hallway. Great, one down. Here we go with the most difficult one. When my eyes meet hers, she gives me a very rare grin. When I start walking her way, she stands her ground until I'm within an arm's length. Then she moves past the great room to the office/library and strolls in, taking one of the seats against the wall. I follow slowly, not sure what she's up to.

"Zoey, they want you there tomorrow. Is that even possible on your end? Have you broken your code of silence to talk to Tink yet, or your club sisters, about what's going on here and how you're involved? If not, no worries, I'll do my best to bullshit my way around you not being there."

She continues to stare at me, with those dead eyes of hers never moving at all. When she acts like this, with all of her tattoos and her bad-as-fuck attitude, my entire body becomes aware and very watchful because sometimes—in the very dark part of my mind—I do think she's beyond fucking insane. And to explain my own insanity, I'm actually getting excited and harder by the minute with all that is her. So, to speed things up this time she wins, and I sit down on the other chair after moving it to face hers. Zoey runs her fingers through her long as fuck black hair and again it hits me, she has to have Native blood running through her veins. Might explain my unconscious obsession with her.

"Panther, what's your endgame here? Sooner or later, they are gonna catch on that you aren't a sick cocksucker like them and don't have the insane tendencies that lean toward the inhumane and dark side of humanity. Then what? They'll torture then kill you and by the time they're done, we won't even find your DNA."

"Aw, Nizhoni, are you worried about me? I'm touched, but you know they are escalating with this shit, so I can't sit here while they do what they do to the innocents of the world. Especially since they seem to be escalating with their ability to fill whatever orders are thrown their way. I told you about when I walked into that circuit party last month, seeing all those dog cages filled with not only their fighting dogs but also human beings. I almost puked on the spot. They were all filthy, covered in their own shit and piss, looking half starved. If I could have saved them all that day I would have, but the timing was off. To see them trying to fight humans as they do their dogs, while in the corner a bunch of them were trying to make kiddy porn, made me promise to get whoever is on top, running this group. And that person seems to have some major trust issues with not only those working with him, but those he is dealing with. I want that person more than my next breath. But for tonight, let's not talk about his sick bullshit. You're here with me so we might as well make the most of it, don't you think?"

Watching Zoey's eyes close for a brief second then when she opens them, I see the signs of wanting and even a little bit of lust in them. As much as she fights 'us' she feels it just as strongly as I do every time we are together. Her head drops down for a brief second then she lifts up and looks directly into my eyes. I just sit here, my emotions and heart open for her to read my feelings for her—all of her. Finally, after what feels like hours but was probably minutes, she stands, reaching for my hand, and leads me out of the library toward my bedroom. Yeah, she's come a long way since those early days when she couldn't even touch me, let alone let me touch her. She'd go into either a survival mode or just shut down. Both were beyond difficult to see. Not to mention I never was sure after one of those episodes what kind of mood she'd be in. Would she want to try and have sex or just cut to the chase and castrate me? Back then, that was a serious concern and worry, and even now, sometimes I'm not too certain which way she's leaning.

When we make it to my room, she walks through the door, almost dragging me in behind her, then shuts and locks the door. Another one of her crazy ways. If she's in a bedroom, the door has to be locked and sometimes barricaded. Still have no fucking clue why, though I can guess, but whatever makes her comfortable. Each time we come together is so different than the last. I always let her have the lead. We go where she wants, needs, or can go. Both of our pasts still haunt us, though I think I've dealt with more of my demons than she has. Well, most of the time, as she's very closed mouthed about her life and experiences. I hope one day she is comfortable enough to share with me what's she's been through. If I let my brain imagine what's happened to her, I'd want to kill half the male population I'm sure.

Her hands tentatively reach for my shirt, which she pulls up with my arms going with it so she can take it over my head and throws it to the floor. Next, is the button on my jeans. She's careful not to rip the zipper down, thank Christ, as I'm hard as a length of steel pipe. Her fingers gently whisper over the length of my cock before she pushes my jeans over my hips and down to my ankles. She bends down, lifting first my left then my right foot, pulling my boots off then my pants, leaving me in my briefs and socks in front of her. Feeling foolish in my socks, I toe them off, kicking them to the side.

Zoey's eyes move up and down my body as she licks her lips, liking what she sees, I'm hoping. I know that my body is appealing because I work it like a pack mule. Between keeping the ranch running and my regular workout sessions, including weights that I lift daily, I'm packing a six-pack while my arms are sinewy and ripped. Fingers on my chest bring me back as her fingers pinch my nipples. The sensation that sends to my balls feels like molten waves running through me instead of my blood. When her mouth reaches my chest, I let out a moan because her lips on me have an effect no other has been able to cause. Somehow my cock lengthens even more as precum coats the top of my briefs, including the waistband that it is sticking out from.

When I reach for her, she steps back, waving a finger my way, shaking her head at the same time. Shit, it's one of those nights. I hate these types of evenings. Zoey doesn't ever want to be touched, which is why I've yet to feel her heat wrap around my cock. It's driving me crazy. Son of a bitch is this going to make it hard—no pun intended. I want to feel and taste her. See how wet she is for me. Fuck, need to have her weight on me so I can finally take her rough and fuck her, then slow it down and make love to her while making her mine.

Instead, it's the start of our usual tug-of-war, the fight for dominance. For me it's getting old, but if I want her I know this is the only way it's going to happen. Her way that is, for now.

THREE
'SHADOW'
ZOEY

I can feel his intensity and how much Panther wants to put his big, callused hands and gorgeous mouth on me. Goddamn, I wish for one night my brain would shut off my demons so I could be like every other hot-blooded woman and let her man have his way with her.

Wait, what the ever-lovin' fuck, *her man*? When did he become more than an occasional guy I messed around with? I swore off any type of relationships years ago. Who in their right mind would want to hook up with the freak that is me? It's not only my tattooed face but all the baggage I've not been able to get outta my head. And I'm a bit unusual in bed. Then add all my triggers, and damn, it must be fun to have sex and fuck me. NOT, if what the last guy I let in a few years ago told me was true. Said it was like fucking a few different women, all at the same time. If memory serves me right, that was after he suggested anal and I throat punched him. Last time I ever saw him.

Knowing I can't keep pushing him away, I reach down, grabbing his one hand and plop it on my tit. Yeah, just like that. Since I still have on my clothes, I'm hoping I should be able to let him do this without losing my shit, mainly because he won't feel all the scars and burns. Well, at least I hope he doesn't feel them and that I can handle his hands on me.

Panther is the only man who's ever been inside of me, well, with his mouth and fingers, who has given me an orgasm. Why he keeps trying to, as he puts it, make me his. And even with our limited sexual contact, he makes it a mission that he won't come until I do at least two times. Sometimes I feel raw down there, but I'll never tell a soul how much his determination and attention mean to me. Makes me feel cared for, and that's something I've never felt during sex.

Trying to keep my mind on what's happening at the moment is hard for me. Especially, with this kind of intimacy. Back in the day, any person in my past could fuck me and I'd be able to actually disassociate myself from any of the feeling or emotions that should be involved. Funny thing is, I've not done that with Panther, not once. Not that we've had intercourse, but for what we've done, if I was a normal woman; I'd say I've found my soul mate.

That's a fantasy dream for me as it will never happen. Not like it did for my best friend, Goldilocks, and her new fiancé, Noodles.

I feel his hands squeezing both of my tits, then they slowly and intentionally start moving downward toward, I'm guessing, my promised land, I take a very deep breath. Panther is a good man, better than I deserve. I've been used, beaten, then broken but he doesn't seem to care at all. I know it's just a matter of time, when one day, he'll wake the fuck up for sure, look at me, and vanish, taking what's left of my broken damaged heart.

"Nizhoni, come on, let all that bullshit go for tonight. I want you to just be here in my arms with me, no ghosts or demons, okay? Just you and me. I know we need to have that dreaded conversation we keep pushing off, but not now and definitely not tonight. Zoey, I want to be intimate with you, Nizhoni. Damn, woman, come closer, feel me, and see how rigid my cock is for you. Zoey, my body is craving you desperately. Please? I won't push you if you can't, but I want to see all of you in the light. No, don't go there, you know I don't give a rat's ass about your scars and shit. I've got my own that you've seen and had your hands on how many times?"

Hearing the desire and naked want in his voice, it hits me hard right in my chest. Either I have to take a chance and be real about what we're doing, or just do what I always do when things get hard or complicated; walk—nope—run away. Knowing the later won't happen, I pull back enough to reach down and grab the hem of my shirt, pulling it up and over my head, leaving me in a very sheer black bra. Looking into Panther's eyes, I feel like I'm being pulled into the greenest of his abyss.

His hands immediately caress the front of me then start to work both of my tits at the same time. My head falls back as he gets a bit rough, which is just how I like it. The rougher the better. I feel his fingers pulling on my nipples through the cups of my bra until that slight burn becomes real pain and I moan. Yeah, he's it for me. I can't dream of forever with him because it's not fair to Panther to be tied down to a fuckup like me. He deserves only the very best, and that sure as fuck isn't me. I'm far from that.

"Zoey, look at me, feel me, listen to me breathing. Be with me in the moment, Nizhoni. I need you tonight, need to feel your heart and mine beating and intertwining together."

He continues to pull on my nipples until they are elongated and reddish. When his hands go to the underside of my tits and he starts pumping them upward, I sigh and kind of whine. His hands are huge and callused from hours of working on the ranch. They feel so good on me and I tell him that.

"Shit, Panther, that feels so good. I love the way your callused fingers feel on my sensitive skin. Please don't stop."

With just those few words, he pulls me even closer, his hands moving all over me. When he lowers his head and his lips are just about touching mine, he waits for a second or two to see if I'm going to pull away. Instead, I tiptoe up and my lips hit his as I nibble his bottom lip. When his mouth opens for me, I take the invitation offered and push my tongue in and start the sensual duel between lovers. I know his taste intimately, but for some reason tonight his flavor has me craving him even more. I can't get enough. Fuck, finally.

My fingers go to his waist, holding on tightly as my mouth savors his unique tang. As our kisses get more wild and hungrier, my hands go over his shoulders and into his long, thick black hair. I love the way it feels like silk gliding through my fingers. He has me plastered to his front as both of his hands have grabbed my ass cheeks hard, pulling me as close as possible to the solid thick cock, throbbing and hot, as it's pressing into my stomach. I'm desperately trying to stay in the moment for once and just feel. Panther must feel something because his kisses become gentler, and his hands aren't squeezing me as firmly.

Not wanting to stop using my fingers on his scalp, I pull his head closer, so his lips are right in front of me. Before my lips can even press on his, he pulls back slightly, holding me now at the shoulders. Looking up, I see that look: not pity but sadness all over his face. Son of a bitch, somehow, he felt it, even though I tried to hide it. Fuck, I hate that he's so in such harmony with me.

"Zoey, it's okay. Really, Nizhoni, we don't have to do anything. Let's just lie together in bed, relaxing, chilling, and enjoying each other's company. I'm totally good with that, as I've told you this time and time again. Never will I pressure you into something you aren't up to or ready for. We've got all the time in the world. Tonight isn't our last time together so take a breath and calm down. Relax."

Shaking my head, I step back while pulling my hair out of my face, pushing it behind my ears. I can feel the weight of my depression start to settle on my shoulders. As always, I'm a failure. Those words repeat all the time in my mind.

"Fuck, Panther, I'm so goddamn sorry. Come here, I'll at least try to take care of you."

He moves quickly, picking me up, and walking to the huge bed in the center of the room. Placing me in the middle of it, he lies next to me without touching me at all, except one hand on my hip.

"Zoey, hear me, I get it. Take a minute, and no, you don't have to take care of me. What am I… a little bastard teenage boy, humping his high school girlfriend under the bleachers? Uh no, we're fucking adults who each have had horrific pasts, so like I said, no worries. Whatever happens or doesn't happen is cool with me. I like you being around with all that sarcasm you give Avalanche and me. Love watching you interrogate the assholes we find and capture without any feeling. Your ability to freeze out the world while you work amazes and enthralls me. I adore that little girl in you, and yeah, there's still one who's always fighting to hide, and the woman who makes me want to be a better man."

Damn him, his words leave me feeling mushy inside and cared for. As much as I crave it, I don't like these emotions because they leave me vulnerable, something I can never be. So, needing control, I move closer to Panther, putting my head on his chest and my hand on his cock. Feeling him grow even more as the rest of him tenses, I use his words against him.

"Relax, Panther. Just feel and enjoy."

For a minute he gives me nothing, but then I hear it. The almost silent breath he lets escape out, then his body relaxes into the bed as he moves so he's lying on his back. I very carefully lean up and put one hand in his briefs, pushing them out of the way, down past his balls. He lifts his ass and then his hands come into play, and he pushes the material down the rest of the way until they hit his ankles and after taking one out, he flips them off his foot to the floor.

Using his precum to lubricate his shaft, I slowly move down then tighten on my way back up. His moans tell me he likes the feel of that, so on the next downward stroke I barely shift my wrist, so the movement allows my fingers to almost touch his balls. He lifts his entire pelvic area, wanting my fingers on his sack, but I glide my hand up quickly once again, tightening my hold on his gorgeous, thick, long cock. We settle into a rhythm that allows me to have the power, which for some reason works tonight.

Shifting, I move my head a little, so my mouth is right above his nipple. I take a mouthful and bite down just a bit too hard. The sound that comes out of him has me smiling against his body. I feel his cock jerk in my hand so when I hit his root, I release his member and grasp on to his balls, stroking them with light pressure then harder. His hips are moving up and down as he lets me hear how turned on he is. When his hips land on the bed, I let his testicles go and grasp his cock by the root and immediately continue on with my version of a hand job. With just a few tight, hard jerks he's leaking like crazy and losing his battle with fighting for control.

Knowing what I need to do, I release his nipple with a pop, lean farther down, and when I have the mushroom head held tightly in my hand, I lightly blow on the top of his cock. He lets out a string of curse words as my hand drops down then immediately back up in quick succession, and when I'm on my way up again, I feel it. Panther's entire body goes tense as he holds his breath and time seems to stand still. Then I feel the pulsing as his cock shoots stream after stream of his cum out as he trembles beneath my hand. He grunts then takes a gulp of air into his lungs, trying to find his breath again.

When he's finally back to himself and I'm holding his softening cock in my hand, which is covered in him, I kind of smile to myself. At least I was able to do this for him tonight.

"Feeling pretty sure of yourself, Nizhoni, right about now, aren't you? Zoey. Ahéhee' *thank you*. I'm feeling so relaxed but please don't ever feel pressured to take care of me, that's my job for you. Now, don't get all pissy, just lie down. I'll grab something to clean you off with after I take care of myself. Be right back."

Watching him stroll into his bathroom, I know the time is getting closer to when I'll have to disappear so I can let him go. This will never work because I won't let it. Can't, or else he'll be in more danger than he can ever imagine.

FOUR
'SHADOW'
ZOEY

I feel like a major bitch sneaking out of Panther's bed and house, but I need to take some time away from him before the club Chapel meeting later today. Needing to check in with my Devil's Handmaidens sisters is on the list and to see if Goldilocks needs anything from me. We've been kind of doing reconnaissance on some news we've heard about some trafficking happening around our hometown of Timber-Ghost. I know Tank and Goldilocks have had multiple conversations about this and want to end these groups of assholes.

Riding balls to the wall on my bike from hell, pipes screaming down the highway, I finally have that feeling of freedom I craved when I woke up. The walls were closing in on me, and lately on my bike is the only place I can obtain this relaxed warmth throughout my body. With my mind all over, I still try to keep my eyes and ears open for any kind of danger. Turning on the ramp that will lead to our working ranch, I hope luck's on my side and I catch Goldilocks and some other sisters before they leave.

Knowing they'll realize I've not been home all night when I arrive on my bike in yesterday's clothes is probably going to require me to explain to at least my best friend about Panther. It doesn't help that she's in la-la land with her newfound fiancé always around and attached at her hip. Fuck, I sound like a jealous lover and that's not it. My own insecurities are running around like crazy in my head. I've dealt with these ups and downs of my own mental health for years, so I've come to recognize how to deal with the ebbs and flows.

Pulling up to the front of the ranch, I drop my kickstand then shut off the bike, leaning back for a minute, just looking around and listening. The peace of Montana, especially this hunk of land Goldilocks bought, always surprises me to no end. This is literally paradise on earth.

Hearing the door open, I look that way to see Noodles standing in the doorway, barefooted, drinking a cup of most likely coffee. What shocks me is the worry written all over his face as his eyes never leave my face. Holy fuck, this sappy son of a bitch is actually concerned for me and is going to try and get in there with me, I can feel it. Another person for me to worry and fret over. Being so deep in my own thoughts, I don't hear him until his voice startles me almost to my own death.

"No, Shadow, don't go there. You don't and are not responsible for me, not now or ever. I'm a grown-ass man and an ex-Navy SEAL so get over yourself, sister."

Smirking to myself at his confidence, I walk directly to him.

"Noodles, unless either of us wants to break Goldilocks's heart, we are now each other's responsibility. No other way to look at it, brother. So, let's not play this game, and promise to do what's best for that tiny and mighty bitch who's wearing your ring."

He looks at me, I mean, really stares forever like he's trying to read into my darkened soul. Then suddenly his eyes twinkle as he takes me in, and then I'm blinded by his white as fuck smile.

"Wait a goddamn minute, are you just getting home? Holy shit! Maggie is going to lose her mind when I tell her I caught Zoey doing the walk of shame. This is ridiculous, and if you tell any of the guys I'm a gossip, motherfucker, I'll deny it, but tell me who the lucky bastard is? A biker, rancher, trucker, or hmm, who could it be? Maybe a tattoo artist?"

He's got his hand to his chin and is tapping his finger against his face, smirking my way. Oh shit, just what I don't need, especially from Goldilocks's new man. No matter what, I've got to shut this down with this pain in my ass bastard of the devil.

"Knock it off, you motherfuckin' troublemaker. Keep your trap shut or else!"

I watch as he throws his head back and laughs. Laughing at me, Shadow the enforcer of the Devil's Handmaidens MC. But for some reason I'm not getting mad or wanting to tear his limbs off his body. This jerk has already wormed his way in my blackened heart, and I'm guessing now I'm stuck with his ass.

"Hey, Shadow, just joking with you, no worries. Your secret is safe with me, promise. One of the only times I won't share with Maggie because it's not hurting anyone, especially you. I feel you, Zoey, sometimes my girl forgets you are your own woman, grown and able to more than take care of yourself. So get your ass in there before she loses her mind. Looks like you're late and that right there is a red flag, as that's something you never are."

Not letting his words register in my brain, I give him a brief nod and make my way around him into the house. I can hear noise coming from the kitchen, so I walk directly into that area. Swinging the door open, I stop dead in my tracks. Goldilocks is on the top step of the step stool, trying to reach something in the highest cabinet above the stove.

"What in the ever-lovin' fuck are you doing, Goldilocks, trying to break that skinny-ass neck of yours? That man of yours needs to rein you in, for Christ's sake. Get the fuck down and tell me what you want, I'll get it."

Slowly, like she either rode a horse all day yesterday or was bucked off one, she steps down. When she turns, the look of rage is written all over her face. Yeah, here it comes so I prepare myself.

"Really, Zoey, not only could your bellowing have scared me to death, making me fall backward off that awful stool, but we both know you wouldn't even attempt to catch me, so I'd probably end up breaking a bone or two. And where in the hell have you been? I've texted you all morning. Lose your phone, too much to drink, or are you putting those sexy undies to good use?"

Can't help it, I laugh because she's ranting like she always does when her mind is running all over the place. I know the club's been researching trafficking circuits around this area between Montana, Idaho, Wyoming, and South Dakota. From what Raven, Taz, and Glory found out from those record books of purchases taken at that ranch of Janice DeThorne's with the Grimm Wolves MC, this particular circuit is huge. Goes down to New Mexico and from Oregon clear to Chicago, Illinois. There were some comments about the East Coast and down South but nothing concrete.

"Take a breath, Goldilocks. Sorry, didn't see your texts, my bad. And you're outta your mind if you think I'd let ya fall off that stool standing here with my hand up my own ass. You weigh less than my leather jacket, so no worries, would have caught you easily. Remember when I became the club enforcer? I took an oath to protect you to the death. Now, tell me what's really bothering you. First though, explain to me why your walking that way. Did you have another one of your klutzy accidents? Come on, I could use a good laugh this morning."

Watching her face turn pink as her eyes look down for a brief second, I'm confused until Noodles strolls past me, walking right to my bestie and pulling her close. Then it hits me like a brick right in the face. Holy fuck, lil' Goldilocks and Noodles must have been pounding the bedsheets last night. Oh, this is gonna be fun.

"Oh, I get it. Noodles over there wasn't limp last night from the way you are stumbling around, Goldilocks. Apparently, he took real good care of you."

Before my bestie can spew her nastiness at me, the door opens and in walks Hannah looking extremely tired and pissed off. What the fuck, this kid better be following the rules of being a new prospect.

"Prospect, why do you look like shit this morning? Someone give you a callout last night? Or did you prospects do something really stupid like get together and get drunk off your asses?"

Hannah looks around the room before her eyes

stop at Goldilocks and she squints first, then actually glares at our prez. From the look, it's directed at both Goldilocks and Noodles. Did they have words yesterday? Maybe Hannah got an order from Goldilocks she didn't like? Or could be our newest prospect tried using her connection to our prez to get out of doing something, which I seriously doubt, but who the hell knows what goes through this girl's head? Fuck, I hate being out of the loop like this. Gotta keep a better eye on Squirt.

"Damn it, Maggie, I totally need a different bedroom. Please don't. I can't have another night of you and him bumping nasties, making all those gross moans, groans, and noises while the headboard is making a racket against our shared wall until the early morning hours. I'll never forget that final loud moan your stallion from down South let loose followed by 'damn, Maggie, yeah, girl, just like that. Take all of me now.'"

Just the almost green look on the kid's face has me starting to lose it, well, until she looks at me. I almost hit my knees at the daggers she's shooting my way, along with that still disgusted look on her face. I can't help myself when the first snort bursts out, then another, before it just can't be helped. My laughter is loud and comes clear out of my mouth, which has three heads whip my way in total awe and shock.

"What the hell is wrong with you, Auntie Zoey? You find something here funny? Well, I'm sure if you had to listen to it most of the night, you would think differently, but since you never came home last night, it's a moot point. And knowing the freak you are, I'm thanking God I wasn't near whatever bed you were in because I would sure as shit need to go for intense therapy afterward, just saying. Even though just the thought of you and sex scares the shit out of me, I can't imagine you would be thrilled to fuck in the missionary position."

Something must have landed in her mind's eye because Hannah starts cracking herself up. This right here is something I will treasure with my entire heart forever and never want to give it up, or worse, lose it. Hannah, or as I call her Squirt to piss her off, has burrowed deep into my soul and will probably be the only relationship I am blessed with like the one we are growing and sharing. Feeling eyes on me, I lift my head to see my bestie watching me intently. Doing something so totally out of my normal, I give her a small lift of my lips, tilting my head to the left, never losing her eyes. She returns with her own tiny smile, but her eyes are asking a million and one questions. I shake my head, letting her know now isn't the time. I see when she gets it then I glance at Hannah, whose face is as red as a tomato. It must have finally hit her what she said to me, not only her 'Auntie Zoey' but a club member and the enforcer. Damn, this kid, she's gonna have to learn to hide those feelings if she doesn't want to get in a really bad situation because she's an open book. Something else I'll have to teach her. Well, here we go, grasshopper, let's start with how far to push me.

"Oh, lil' grasshopper, you have a long way to go before I'll even consider sharing with you my preferences when I fuck. Though when that time comes, if you prefer to watch a video, I can provide that so maybe you can learn something. Now back to your utter disrespect. I never let a prospect speak to me like you just did, so besides apologizing you will clean my suite today and wash the bedding since you are so interested in my nonsleeping hours. Oh, and wash my clothes that are all over my room. After that, you will go to Momma Diane's house and offer to clean their entire house, no matter what she says, without telling her it's your punishment. Finally, you will clean their yard and, yeah, that means pick up all the shit from their dogs. Got it, prospect?"

I try not to let my mouth run wild with how hilarious Hannah's face is as her eyes pierce me with a heated glower, then she changes her face completely, giving Goldilocks the look of a child who is being unjustly punished. Noodles turns, trying to hide his laughter, but his shaking shoulders give him away. My bestie just looks at her for a brief moment then slowly shakes her head, lifting her shoulders.

"Prospect told you of all the club sisters the one whose bad side you don't ever want to be on is standing right in front of you. Shadow's a bitch on a good day but when pissed, watch out because the demons of hell are let out to play. So, suck it up, Hannah, and do what she's told you. As far as wanting another bedroom, that's fine, pick between the two that are currently not in use. Both have en suites. And just so you are aware, it never crossed my mind that my headboard was on the same wall as your bed so when Noodles was pounding into me, never gave it a thought. Guess later when I was the one pounding on that same wall when I sat on his face, still didn't register. Guess all I got is, sorry, kid."

Hannah is shocked for about two point five seconds, then all color fades from her face as she fakes puking before turning and going to the coffee station while flipping off her prez. Everyone laughs and things go back to normal, whatever that even is in this house.

My exhaustion starts to settle in but not wanting to leave because I love the feelings I get when around my bestie and Squirt, I settle in while listening to all their bullshit banter back and forth. Sleep is overrated, or that's what I tell myself.

FIVE
"PANTHER"

CHAHÓÓŁHÉÉL NAABAAHII T'ÁÁ SÁHI
DARK WARRIOR WALKING ALONE

I feel the moment Zoey decides to try and sneak out of my bed, get dressed, and then quietly leave my house. Even though I'm sure she pushed her bike down part of the drive, the loud as fuck pipes on her bitchin' bike can be heard from probably half a mile away. Knowing going back to sleep is an impossible dream, I get up, heading to the master bathroom and into my steam shower.

This was one of my self-indulgences I included when I redid this ranch. Fuck, after all I've put my body through, the thought of a steam shower seemed like a fantastic idea, so I went with it. The interior designer Avalanche was fucking at the time wasn't so thrilled with my request. Oh well, since I was her customer she ultimately had to do as I asked. Not to mention, the other steam room is outdoors. We sometimes use it for a sort of a modern-day sweat lodge for spiritual cleansing.

My mind goes full circle to what we are doing today. Fuck, when will it ever end? When will evil this disgusting be wiped and voided from our world? Unfortunately, my brain knows that it's a pipe dream but the dreamer in me can have a vision and goal, even if it might be forever hopeless.

As I start to wash my body, I then run up and down over all my scars from bullets, stab wounds, and torture marks. Let's not forget to mention injuries from the day-to-day ranch work, including the stud portion of the ranch. I've been so hard on this body and continue to push through, no matter what I do to it. I'm beyond lucky to still be alive and breathing, and fuck, don't I know it.

When my hand hits my morning wood, instantly Zoey's eyes come to mind. What a contradiction she is. I know just from what she does for her club that she's probably on the spectrum between genius and a total psychopath. Just looking at her, one would think I'd run in the opposite direction but, for some reason, that skull tattoo draws me to her every single time I see her. It's like she's the other half of my spirit. Many years before I even saw her getting that ink, I had my entire chest done to resemble my skeletal self. So seeing her do her face made me almost follow in her footsteps, but it was Avalanche who talked me off that idea. He reminded me if I did that, no way in hell would I be able to go undercover without being made so listening to his reasoning, I did the second-best thing. It's easier to hide tattoos under my clothing than right there in the open on my face.

I think of all the bullshit Zoey goes through because of it: the ignorant assholes, curious church women, mean ass kids, and downright prejudiced pricks out there. Not to mention the ones who are missing a screw, or twenty, and think because of it they can hurt her because she either wants or deserves it.

Just having her in my thoughts, my cock starts to lengthen and fill out, thickening in my hand. The sensations running through my body tell me that to get my day started, I'll need to release some of the pent-up desires raging in my body. Last night Zoey had terrible nightmares again, so I knew she needed space. All we did was cuddle and fall asleep wrapped up together. Well, after she gave me one of the best hand jobs in my life.

With that thought, I start to move my hand up and down my hard cock, running through images of Zoey. Her long as fuck legs and muscular arms. That long, dark as midnight hair and those goddamn ice-blue eyes that look right through me sometimes, like she can read into my soul and other times like I'm not right there in front of her.

Fuck, feeling the heat move through my entire body, I increase my speed while my fist grasps the mushroom head, I twist slightly increasing the tension. Up…down…up…twist… and back down. When my balls start to tighten and lift into my body, I know my orgasm is coming fast, especially when the tingles and shock come up the cheeks of my ass to my lower back. The muscles in my thighs contract as I feel the heat go right through my balls as stream after stream explodes out of me, hitting the marble tile in the shower. I continue to ride my hand until my body is finished and there's absolutely nothing left in me.

Finishing cleaning myself, I shut off the steam control first then the water. I reach out and grab a warm towel off the heated bar and dry off. Walking to the double sinks, I brush my teeth, shave the stubble off my face, brush through my long as fuck hair, and finish with my morning routine. Exiting the bathroom and entering the walk-in-closet, I grab my usual: briefs, faded and worn jeans, and a T-shirt. Then I go back to my bedroom, grab a piece of leather off my dresser to tie my hair after I braid it down my back, and reach for my boots.

Once completed and ready for my day, I head to the kitchen hoping, yet already knowing I won't find a note from Zoey. Though she started the coffee, so she must have assumed I would have gotten up not long after she left. Grabbing a mug of black coffee, I sit at my table trying to plan the day out. I'm playing the waiting game until I receive that call telling me where and when.

Hearing the tapping of claws on the hardwood floors, I know the two beasts are on their way in. Shifting, I look to the opening of the kitchen just as Ma'iitsoh *wolf* and Zhį́'ii *raven* stroll in like neither have a care in the world. I know differently because each morning it's the same. As soon as the sun rises, they go outside to guard the ranch until I wake up. Then, somehow, they seem to know when that time happens because both of them then come back inside to say good morning to me and wait for their breakfast. Some mornings they hunt for something to eat outside but usually, after so many years, they just wait for me to provide them their meals.

I remember the day Avalanche and I found the wolf pups, abandoned by their mother, who I believe deep in my soul was probably murdered by an asshole bastard ranchers. Wolves are not generally loved in Montana by a shit ton of ranchers. So, when we found the four pups, I took two and Avalanche took the other two. Ma'iitsoh is the biggest of the pack, he weighs in at around one hundred forty pounds, while Zhį́'ii is much smaller coming in around ninety pounds. Avalanche has the same, his male is much larger than his female.

Feeling a tongue against my hand, I look down into the most intense amber eyes I've ever seen. Ma'iitsoh's breath is warm against my hand as he tongues me, letting me know he wants to eat. Zhį́'ii, on the other hand, is sitting patiently, as always.

Every morning it's the same thing, my boy begging me while my girl sits like the princess she is, knowing I'll always feed both of them.

While I'm mixing up the raw meat with some protein, dry food, and powder, the door slams and I hear the heavy footsteps of my best friend and brother, Avalanche. The name suits him because he makes me feel small. His Navajo name nitsaa yikah tsintah, *Big Walking Trees,* describes him as he is probably just over six five, which is tall for our kind, probably gets his height from his white father. He's built like a redwood, tall and just as wide. With as big as he is, his speed is what surprises everyone. He's wild and sudden, just like his name, Avalanche. He comes across as a badass without feeling, but I've seen how gentle he is when we are removing victims or helping injured horses.

"Hey, boss, morning. Where's lil' skull anii'? Did she pull another quick stop before blowing out of here like a thunderstorm? When are you gonna open your eyes and see her for what she is, a fucked-up demon from hell?"

Before I can process, I've jumped up and have my hands around his neck. What makes it twice as bad is Ma'iitsoh's is standing right next to me growling at Avalanche, and Zhį́'ii is on the other side of me just watching. Any other person would be shitting their pants begging for forgiveness. Not my friend, he's smiling like a lunatic.

"Nitsaa yikah tsintah, I'll not tell you again do not speak of her like that. She is not evil nor a demon. Her life, my brother, you would not have been able to live through. No, not a word, you've angered me beyond thought. We have been through so much, Avalanche, but don't make me choose between you or Zoey. I don't want to, but I can't guarantee that I'd pick you over her. If you care at all, think before you run your mouth like a whining coyote."

As I motion for the wolves to heel and relax, I release him and move away. He doesn't move, doesn't even blink, just keeps his eyes on me. I know my words might have hurt him, especially since I know his history, but fuck. Just when I try to figure out how to explain to my best friend why I'm willing to wait around for Zoey, my phone rings. Son of a bitch, now the call comes in. Just what I don't want, as it means I've got to get into my alter character. Grabbing the cell, I glance at Avalanche giving him a nod which he slowly returns then I answer the call.

"Yeah, Panther here."

"You have the time today, countess, to get this deal done? The man in charge is not happy with you at all, so either shit or get off the fucking pot, chief. Is the tatted bitch with you, he wants to know?"

Fuck, now what?

"No, she's not here right now, but I have a call out to her. For Christ's sake, your boss has to have the hots for a member of the Devil's Handmaidens MC.

It's not like she listens to me and I got nothing to keep her in line. She ain't got kids or a man, so we are on her time. I'll put another call in and, hopefully, by the time we get together, she'll be there too. That work?"

"Boss says to have that skull squaw's ass there or don't show at all. I'll call back at noon and I want to hear her voice, otherwise the deal is off."

"Fine."

The phone dies without another word. I look to Avalanche, who lifts his shoulders, shaking his head at the same time. Well, what a way to fuck up my already heavy morning.

"Guess that means we need to pick up Shadow so she's around here. Are you going to call her, or do you want me to?"

Knowing how much that hurt, I shake my head again and reach for my phone. I scroll through the names until I see Zoey's then I push it. It rings and rings, but she doesn't answer. Son of a bitch, now what? I need to think and for that I need another cup of coffee, so I turn to grab it and feel a hand on my shoulder.

"Panther, my senses are on high alert, so we need to be very careful. These assholes are ch'įįdii *demonic spirits*. I don't want you to walk into a trap. So, grab your coffee, let's sit down and talk this through. I put a call in to some of our boys. They're on the way here, should be here within the hour... so around nine. That gives us about three hours to come up with a half-ass kind of a plan. Also informed your handler without letting him know where or what you're doing. I don't trust that coyote boss, he's a viper no doubt."

Glad to know that our disagreement is over with, I just nod, knowing this morning is going to fly by. My only concern is what Zoey is doing and why she's not answering her phone. I need her, not only for this meet but to know that she's okay. Going to keep calling until she picks up since that's my only choice.

SIX
'SHADOW'
ZOEY

If it was my choice, I'd have ended her when I had the chance but, of course, Goldilocks and Glory had to give her a what a... third or fourth chance. For God's sake, how many times does she have to fuck up before we just end her useless addict ass? Now I have to look across the table at her still fucked-up face, eyes downward, refusing to look at me. I'm sure she feels my anger and rage, but shit, she's won because the bitch is still here.

Her one hand looks raw and the three fingers I broke are still wrapped and braced. The other hand the nails are starting to grow back slowly, but that tip of her ear I cut off never will. I can feel a sneer on my face as I remember taking the wire cutters to her ear as she pleaded then screamed, while telling me whatever lies she could think of to get me to stop. Obviously didn't work. She betrayed our club and more importantly our prez. Knowing Hannah was probably at that camp and her not telling a soul, just so she could get drugs, made me sick to my stomach.

Her nose is going to heal crooked but, all in all, she got off the hook pretty easy in my opinion. Hearing the rest of the sisters coming into Chapel, I sit straighter in my chair as the Devil's Handmaidens enforcer can't show any weakness. My personality of Shadow is to square my shoulders and show no emotions on my face. As I look around, I feel something, so I look across and down a few seats. Heartbreaker is peeking my way but when I focus on her, she drops her head immediately.

Knowing that today's meeting is to determine her future, I take a minute to really think about her. I've never liked her, even from the start. She's always been a whiner who doesn't put the work into anything she does. Yeah, she got clean but that was because everyone was there holding her up, especially Goldilocks. And from what I hear, this last time was really rough, and that's saying a lot since she almost died a few times when she first came to us. I dig deep, trying to figure out why I don't like her because technically she's never done a damn thing to me. I think it's because she shows her weaknesses while I hide everything, always have, and it seems to be the road I'll always continue to be on.

Heartbreaker has always tried to befriend me, but I've pushed her away each and every time. She reminds me of that abused puppy who no matter what, continues to go back to their abuser because they don't know any better. Something about her sets my alarms off whenever Heartbreaker is near but have never been able to figure out why. Goldilocks calls the meeting to order, and it starts off like any other one. As Taz goes through the financials, I feel my phone vibrate in my rear pocket but ignore it, knowing that fuck, I was supposed to have left it outside of Chapel. Clearing my throat, I give Goldilocks a look then do the unthinkable. I leave Chapel, walk to the safe, open it with my handprint, reach behind me with my other hand, and without even looking at it, I throw the cell in with everyone else's. Slamming it shut, making sure it caught, I hightail it back to Chapel just as Taz finishes up stating everyone is caught up with dues. That has my head lift, and my eyes meet Heartbreaker's, as this is the first month that she's paid before being told repeatedly. Maybe she's on the rebound. Who the fuck knows anymore? Glory starts off listing all of Heartbreaker's offenses, giving details to all of them. She saves the big one for last. That she had an idea where Hannah was and never told any of us. Now, back in the day, that would have gotten her tortured and killed by my own hands. But even though we're one-percenters, our purpose is larger than that now. We've dedicated our club and lives to helping and saving those in trafficking and violent domestic situations.

Before she fell off the wagon, our girl Heartbreaker was immersed in helping those who were brought to the ranch to heal from their physical and emotional injuries and for intense therapy. She worked very closely with them to make sure they had the best fighting chance to reclaim their lives and survive in today's society.

She did all of this along with her job at the Wooden Spirits, the club-owned bar in town. She's actually one of the most requested waitresses at that business. Townsfolk have waited for her when she worked the diner area because they like her so much. And from what I've been told, her tips when she would work the bar were the highest of all of the waitstaff.

When she wasn't high off her ass, she always gave back too. She used her own money to buy and bring small gifts to the victims living in the dorms. Especially the younger ones, who were having a hard time transitioning into their new lives. Things like bath bombs, hair scrunchies, and smelly lotions. Shit girls like.

Trying to focus, I hear Glory finish and ask everyone for their opinions. No one says shit. This is so not like me but still when I get ready to give my two cents, our shyest member, Peanut, starts off in her hushed voice.

"I know Heartbreaker did wrong and like the rest

of you, I'm very upset with her and hurt. Saying all of that, she has done so much good since the last time she was on the drugs. Remember, none of us are perfect, some are worse than others."

With those words she looks at Heartbreaker's hands then glances my way briefly. Holy shit, what the fuck, now Peanut is calling my ass out? Thought she was our little mouse but now she's showing us her backbone. And pissing me the fuck off.

"No one knows this, but Heartbreaker has always been there for me. I don't make friends easy, and even though I love every one of my sisters here in the Devil's Handmaidens club, I have demons, just like the rest of you. She's the one who's been there and has had my back. Each and every time. I think she deserves a chance to prove that she can come back from this bump in the road. Like when I was a kid, my folks beat into us that verse from the good book. 'Let him who is without sin cast the first stone.'

"Sisters, whoever has never sinned you can cast your vote to take our sister Heartbreaker's kutte and vote to remove her ink. The rest of us should show her some mercy. That's what I think, might not mean a lot, but it does to me. Thanks for listening."

Everyone sits there either with their eyes wide with shock or mouths hanging open. I swear to Christ, this is the most I've ever heard our little mouse talk. I look to Goldilocks, whose head is down, and I know she's thinking that this shit is on her.

Then she leans back, lifts her head, and with eyes on Peanut addresses the table and, more importantly, Peanut.

"Peanut, first, thank you for speaking up. I'm very proud of you, little one. Your words alarm me though, sister, so you and I will have a conversation soon. But hear my words because they come from deep in my soul. You as everyone around this table have had a hand in my life's mission. To find my daughter/sister Hannah, even though it was years from when she was taken. You, Ada, are important. I've had your back since you first started to prospect. Your club's name is Peanut because of you being so petite. I see though the size of your heart, so never doubt your worth in and outside of this club. You are very important, never forget that. And Delilah here, or as we all know her as our Heartbreaker, is very lucky to have you for her friend."

When I hear sniffles, I turn my head to see Heartbreaker wiping the tears off her face as she watches Peanut. The room is filled with such emotion, every sister has to feel it. We came together because we all have horrific pasts and though not everyone knows each other's prior life, Peanut just opened up and shared an internal piece of her nightmares without even knowing it. To help her club sister and friend.

Peanut pushes back and stands, then walks to Heartbreaker, giving her a hug before taking her seat again. Next up is Kiwi, and then each and every member speaks about their relationship with Heartbreaker. When there's a lapse in conversation, I decide it's time.

"I met the bitch when Prez sent Rebel and me to go to Chicago to rescue Heartbreaker from her madam. She fought us tooth and nail the entire time. Not to mention my ass almost got caught and jailed because of the incident with that jagoff going at the underage girl at that brothel we found her ass at."

Rebel outright laughs at that, so I give her the finger, which she returns. Bitch got some ovaries, that's for damn sure.

"By the time we got back here, she was in the darkest withdrawals I've ever seen. I didn't think she was worth the effort, and I shouted my case loudly to anyone who would listen. She died what, Goldilocks… two or three times before she got her head outta her ass? Sorry, rehashing the past I get lost sometimes in memories.

"It just hit me why I've been against Heartbreaker all this time and it's because of what Peanut said. It was a hell of a lot easier to hate her than myself. Our lives have gone down similar paths and she reminded me of all the bullshit I've kept buried deep down. I wanted her to fail so I could feel good about myself and the choices I've made. Fuck, this last shit proved in my sick mind that she's a total messed-up bitch. Even when I was pulling her fingernails out, she continued to be the usual pain in the ass that she always is to me. Listening to Peanut, she sees something in Heartbreaker, and I've always trusted our little sister because I consider her one of the wisest ones amongst us. Yeah, lil' sister, we also will be having a talk, but thanks for letting me see our troubled sister through your eyes.

"My thoughts after listening to all of what you women have said is, no matter how many times we fuck up another chance needs to be given. That's one of the main purposes why Goldilocks and I started this fucking club. To give victims another chance, no matter what. We never look down at the women and children we rescue. They've done whatever they had to do so they could survive. If we can do that for strangers, why would we not give that same opportunity to the women we call sisters? So, against everything I'm feeling and admitting my feelings for Heartbreaker, I think she—oh shit—can't believe I'm gonna say this, but let's give her another chance. Put her on a kind of probation or whatever we want to call it. One of the stipulations is that we keep tabs on her."

From there I know what is going to happen, so I sit back, waiting for the vote to be taken. While our prez gives Heartbreaker her choices, which are leave her kutte on the table, get her ink blacked out, and never show her face again, or as I said, be on a kind of probation—no time restraints—and see how it goes.

She'll lose half of her member's income because, in essence, she ditched the club. Though she'll keep her job, cabin on the ranch and benefits, and all of our support.

Before our prez is finished talking Heartbreaker is sobbing uncontrollably, thanking everyone for giving her a final chance. She promises to be the best sister she can. I think to myself, *I give her a fifty-fifty chance to make it through.*

After the vote, the meeting ends with Goldilocks pounding on the table, we all get up to leave. Duchess opens the doors as Wildcat is the first one out the doors. She comes to an abrupt stop, which has Rebel, Vixen, and Raven plowing into each other. The overbearing silence doesn't hide the ominous feeling in the air.

Pushing my way to the front, I shove Rebel out of the way 'cause she's like a goddamn linebacker and I can't see a fucking thing past her. When my eyes take in what everyone is looking at, I almost shit myself. Panther, Avalanche, and four other men are sitting at the bar while our prospects Kitty and the twins, Dani and Dotty, are holding guns on them. Kitty, God bless her soul, has the Mossberg 590S that we keep behind the bar. Both twins have Glocks in their hands.

When he sees me, Avalanche grins like the fucking maniac he is. Before he can say a word, Panther looks at him, shaking his head. I know how bad Big Bird wants to start some shit in my house, so I'm thankful to Panther for cutting him down quickly.

"What the hell is going on in here? Kitty, who the fuck are these dudes? Who let them in and why are they still here?"

Hearing Wildcat's angry voice, I know my secret is about to burst into my clubhouse like a raging fire. And then it does just like that. Panther stands and starts walking toward the crowd. I hear Kitty pump the Mossberg, so I catch her eyes, vigorously shaking my head. She tilts her head then slowly nods but leaves the gun pointed at Panther's back. Knowing my two worlds are going to collide, I try to maintain some control.

"They're here for me. Give us a minute then I'll explain."

My club sisters all look at me like I've lost my ever-lovin' mind and I totally agree with them. Avalanche is chuckling at my discomfort and before I can even think about my actions I flip him off, which sends him into a fit of laughter. As total chaos breaks loose, I hear Goldilocks's whistle right before I hear his deep raspy voice loudly state for all to hear.

SEVEN
'PANTHER'
CHAHÓÓŁHÉÉL NAABAAHII T'ÁÁ SÁHI
DARK WARRIOR WALKING ALONE

Well, if it walks like a duck and sounds like a duck, then it's a fucking duck, right? From the minute we pounded our way into the clubhouse, every single thought I had before went straight out of my head. Even though Zoey told me they were a one-percenter motorcycle club, I thought she was exaggerating. Yeah, no stretching the truth from my woman. Well, son of a bitch, jokes on me that's for sure. When that little girl pulled the Mossberg 590S from behind the bar, I stood there shocked. Motherfuck, I know I'd almost shit my pants in surprise and by the looks at Avalanche and the guys, they felt the exact same. She looked like a goddamn college kid, but she held that gun like someone who knew exactly how to use it. She had it pointed at Avalanche's head while the other two, I think they are twins, had their Glocks both pointed at me. They assumed right, figuring we were the two bastards in charge. Our boys, though huge don't give off those dominant alpha boss qualities.

Then when the door opened and the women started piling out, the first one was a small, very ripped black woman. Next, I saw a girl I'd not want to meet in a dark alley. Then the three who all stopped and plowed into each other. My girl Zoey was swearing and pushing her way to the front. When she saw us, first shock then total anger rushed across her face before her shoulders fell down and the look of defeat landed on her face. Well, suck me, guess Avalanche was right. Yeah, I'm her dirty little secret.

Now we're all at a standstill. I don't want to embarrass Zoey, that's why I reined in Avalanche. I can see his god-awful prickish look before he even attempts to open his mouth. Now everyone is staring at each other, but no one is saying a word. I don't have time for tea and crumpets, but again, figure I can spare Zoey a few minutes, even though at this point don't owe her anything. Dirty little secret, my ass.

"I was looking for my woman, Zoey."

"Whoa, look at those tall drinks of maleness. Damn, Shadow, where have you been hanging out and which one are you claiming on to? I'll take the front one with that long hair. Holy shit, he's drop-dead gorgeous. And those eyes, sweet mother of God, think I'm going to orgasm just looking at him."

Hearing a growl is my only warning before, in a

flash so fast I didn't see her move, Zoey has the mouthy one by the neck and pounds her face into the wall, knocking her out instantly. That starts holy hell. The tiny one, I believe is her Goldilocks, better known as Tink, runs to Zoey, grabbing her by the arm as the unconscious chick slides down to the floor. I see women moving to an off room and before I can move or warn the men with me, four of the women come back armed. One moves to the door, pushing the latch, while the other three move toward me, motioning for me to move back to the bar area. Mossberg girl shifts as I take my seat so now all of us; Avalanche, George, Dallas, Jersey, and Chicago are now sitting fucking deer waiting to be hunted down. Hearing a very loud whistle, I look to see Tink with her fingers in her mouth. The room is suddenly so quiet, it amazes me someone so tiny can shut it down instantly like that. What I was told seems right, tiny and mighty. I wait to see what happens next.

Zoey stalks toward me and when she reaches me, she leans toward me. In my ear, voice trembling, she gives it to me.

"What the fuck? What is so goddamn important that you are here with these damn idiots? Why didn't you just call me, Panther?"

"I did, Zoey, like over twenty-five times. Check your phone. I filled your voicemail and never got a call back. Silly me, I was fucking worried. You know what we are supposed to do today and the fascination the main guy has with you is topping the scales. When they called this morning, they told me without you there will be no deal. So my hands being tied, I had no choice. Sorry, Nizhoni. Guess it's obvious your girls didn't know about me from their reactions?"

She again growls and glares at me but doesn't leave my side. Actually, Zoey's put herself between my men and her sisters. Right in the middle. Is she fucking crazy? *Well, that's a stupid question,* I think to myself.

"Okay, Zoey, what the hell is going on? And more importantly, who the shit are these men?"

Knowing no one but the prez calls her by her given name, I look around her to see the gorgeous tiny woman, hands on her hips, attitude pouring from her, impatiently waiting for an answer. Wait, is she even tapping her foot? Goddamn, she's a badass to be pushing that kind of attitude at this one. Before Zoey can answer, from behind a swinging door, a younger version of Tink walks in, with earbuds in, bopping and shaking her thing to obviously some of that young people's pop or dance music. I can hear it from where I'm at, won't be surprised if she's half deaf. Her eyes almost fall out of her head when she takes in the scene.

Pulling out her buds, I can see the wheels in her head turning as she looks one way than the other, back and forth 'til she concentrates on Zoey. Then a shit-eating grin appears on her face. Oh shit, I feel something is about to go down, just not sure what it is.

"Aw, Auntie Zoey, now I get it, girlfriend. No wonder you've been in a good mood, not off chopping people up or shooting the town up and wearing those fancy, expensive lace panties. Hot damn, look at that male specimen of perfection. I'm assuming he's Native by those awesome cheekbones and beautiful long black silky hair that's almost down to his fine sculptured ass. Maggie, can I have one of those for my next birthday? Or maybe Christmas? Either one works for me."

Not sure why I'm surprised when the women start laughing, giggling, or chuckling, along with some of my men. Zoey moans but doesn't say a thing. Then, of course, Avalanche has to add kindling to the fire.

"Come on, lil' girl, my man Panther here might be a good romance novel character, you know, fictional, but I'm a real man. Just look at me. So whatcha say? Want to take a ride on the wild side? Nothing like sliding down on an Avalanche."

Hannah takes a quick minute to look Avalanche up and down, her eyes landing on his crotch area and then she smirks huge. Aw shit!

"Well, big man, you might be a tall brute, but it looks like you were behind the door when the important size and girth was being handed out. So guessing you lost out where it counts the most. And after seeing what you called him, oh yeah, Panther, I'll take the one who can stalk me and make me his pantheress. I believe that is what a female panther is called, big man, didn't think you'd know that."

With that my mouth drops open as Zoey snorts. The guys all step away from Avalanche as he stands abruptly, the barstool falling from him, pushing off of it. Tink is already on the move before reaching behind her as one of her girls' hands something off to her.

The Devil's Handmaidens MC prez and Avalanche both reach the young mouthy girl at the exact same time. Before my man can do a thing, Tink pushes the girl behind her as she calmly points a SIG Sauer P320 right up into Avalanche's face. I've rarely seen my brother waver but in her calmness he falters, and they both see it. Tink, being wiser, says not a word, just stays the course but the Tink lookalike giggles.

Shadow turns, eyes full of rage, before she closes them briefly and when she opens them, there's absolutely nothing. No emotion, just dead as fuck ice-blue eyes taking in everything in an instant.

"Goldilocks, give me a few minutes then I'll explain. Squirt, keep your goddamn trap shut, leave these assholes alone. Oh, and you can shove that pipe dream about Panther up your ass. For once I agree with Avalanche, keep his image for when you read your romance books. This real live one here is off-limits. Got it?"

The prez looks at her then seeing whatever she needs, nods, and tells the other women to get gone. She pushes, I'm guessing, Hannah back, whispering in her ear. Whatever is said has the younger woman drop her head, not looking at anyone, and quickly push her way out of the room down the hallway. So now, except for the three at the bar with guns, the other Devil's Handmaidens are gone. Besides Tink, who stays too, though she does lower her Sig, which allows Avalanche to move back and stand with our men. Zoey grabs my arm and pulls me, I'm guessing, toward the kitchen.

Once we are behind closed doors, she pulls her hand back, immediately going to swing at my face. I'm way too quick though and grab her hand, swinging it behind her back, pulling her back to my front. Leaning down, I whisper to her to calm the hell down. She takes a couple of deep breaths then nods. I step back and wait.

"What's going on? I'm assuming you left a ton of messages. We were in Chapel and that means no phones, so I'm sorry about that. Did the assholes call and give you a time and location?"

"Not yet, they are due to call in less than thirty minutes, but their one demand is that you be there when they call so the man in charge can hear your voice. He wants you there badly, and that right there, Zoey, worries—no, scares me to death. Why are they fixated on you? We managed, as you can see, to get a few of our guys here in time but definitely at a disadvantage again with this asshole. Zoey, look at me. If I had any other choice, you know I'd never show up here unannounced. I respect you too much. You know what and why I'm asking is with the endgame in my view. I'm sorry, Nizhoni, truly I am."

Watching her slowly nod, I let my anxious breath out. Maybe I didn't think it through enough, but damn, I'm on a tight as fuck time frame and didn't have a lot of choices. Maybe we can still pull this off. Well, that was my thought before the door swings open and Tink walks straight in. She takes in the two of us; Shadow right in front of me, my arms wrapped under her breast area and around her waist, and her eyes bug out of her head. *Hum, that's interesting*, I think to myself.

With my attention on her, I missed the tall man behind her. Oh, fuck, this must be Noodles and from the look of rage on his face, he's claimed Zoey too. I figure he looks at her as a younger sister, but I'm more concerned with how the hell he got in if the doors were all locked. Then it dawns on me, Tink released the rest of the club members so I could have some privacy with Zoey and my urgent matter.

"Hey, this is crazy times, dude. I'm Ellington or L and Maggie's mine, and so that means so is Shadow. Well, kind of. It all depends on how you look at it."

I feel Zoey tense for a quick second before she relaxes and leans back into me.

"Noodles, back the fuck up, you big dorky soldier boy. I'm not yours or anyone else's, and my girl Goldilocks doesn't like to share, do you?"

Shaking her head, Tink looks between Zoey then her man. A smile appears then she looks at, fuck, which name is really his, Ellington, L, or Noodles's hand still in the air toward me. Fuck, where are my manners?

"Hi, I'm chahóółhéél naabaahii t'áá sáhi."

I watch both of their faces scrunch up before Ellington, huge kudos to him, looks at me.

"'Kay, can you break that down for me, so I don't fuck it to hell and back. I'm from down South so might add my Southern drawl, which won't sound right, but I'm game if you are."

Smiling because I instantly like him, immediately, I give in.

"Ellington, I'm gonna give you a break. Just call me Panther, that's what my brothers and friends call me."

"Cool, and to make it easy on you because that one in front of you calls me Noodles most of the time, when she's not calling me nasty shit, call me that."

We shake hands and when I release his, Tink's is right there taking his place. Thinking she's tiny, even fragile, I go to give her a slight handshake when she squeezes my hand 'til it hurts. Holy fuck.

"Told you, Panther, tiny but mighty my girl is."

Tink is smiling at Zoey with love in her eyes and

just that shows me the relationship they share. For that I'm happy, because Zoey doesn't seem to have many in her corner. Just then I feel my phone vibrating and the room goes still. Somehow Tink and Noodles know this is something major so they both nod and back out.

Our game is back on. I give Zoey a quick squeeze before reaching for my phone, just as Avalanche and my guys come through the door quietly. Guess Tink gave them a heads-up, letting them know a call was coming in. *It's now or never*, I think to myself.

"Yeah, ya got Panther."

"Hey, chief asshole, is our little skull pussy around? Boss wants to talk to her."

Hating this, but knowing I have no choice, I hand the phone to Zoey but leave it on speaker. The voice that comes on the line immediately tells her to remove it from speaker.

"Listen here, jagbag, I don't know you from a pile of horseshit in my pastures and you don't know me either. No one tells me what to do, so just tell me why you think I'm involved so I can get on with my day, mister."

The sarcasm in her voice has me grinning until he replies back.

"My dear, one day I'll punish you justly for that mouth of yours, but for now I just wanted to hear your voice. I'm working on a deal with our mutual friend, Panther, and would like you to accompany him to our little gathering later today. Tell me one thing you want and to thank you for your time, I'll have it there. So, what's your poison, Zoey Jeffries?"

The way her body tenses and her breath stops, I know he hit a huge nerve. How in the fuck does he know her last name? I didn't even know that. I look to Avalanche, who nods, then pulls Chicago back whispering to him. Zoey is trying to maintain her control, but I can see the crack in it.

"Zoey, are you still there? Come on, Nizhoni, that's what Panther calls you, right? Whisper to me what you desire, beautiful."

Now I'm freaking out and I see so is Avalanche. His voice is weird but also something isn't sitting right, but I can't figure it out for the life of me. Leave it to Zoey to pull back the puppet strings.

"Okay, I'll play your game, though don't get any ideas that you have any power over me, because you don't. Never will you have that over me, hear me, mister? What I want is a copy of your original, legal, and real driver's license and passport, and show me either another form of identification: bank account, house deed, or something like that in the time we have before we meet, or you can forget it. Oh, and a hundred and fifty grand for my time."

He chuckles for a brief second.

"Well, I see you're going to be a handful. Again. Should be very interesting going forward. Oh, Zoey, I'd have paid you a quarter of a million, all you had to do was ask. We'll save you begging me for a bit later. I'll see you soon, give me back to Panther. "

And with that I know she just got us back on track. Just like that. She read the situation and played him like a fine instrument. This whole situation is getting crazier by the minute.

EIGHT
'TINK'
MAGGIE/GOLDILOCKS

Not sure what the ever-lovin' fuck is going on but know one thing is for sure. My bestie has been keeping major shit from me, and it hurts a fuck of a lot. Why would she feel like there was anything she'd have to hide from, or she couldn't tell me. I'd never not listen or try to help her. We've been in this together since the start. And who the hell was that walking-talking orgasm, who had eyes only for Zoey? My God, just seeing him watch her, anyone with eyes can see he's in love with her. A miracle in itself and now I do believe in God because he not only heard my prayers but answered them for my bestie.

Yeah, I know my bestie is all that and a bag of chips but, usually, when men are around our club sisters; she isn't the one who gets all the attention. Well, unless they are looking at her for being a freak with that tattooed face. He was not only looking but his eyes were devouring every inch of her. Damn, I get hot and wet just thinking of that look. Can never let Noodles know. He's a jealous son of a bitch himself.

Now, besides being hurt, I'm getting really angry and even a bit pissed off. I've shared how my relationship with Noodles moved forward with her, every step of the way. Fuck, I asked her to be my maid of honor, for God's sake. Even before Noodles, she's always been at my side since that night we met in the field on one of my first rescues. Little did I know that Dad, Mom, and I would be rescuing a very damaged girl by the name of Zoey Jeffries. To this day, I don't know everything my bestie has been through but can honestly say that whatever it is, don't think many others would have been able not only to survive but figure out a way to live life.

We've been her only family, besides this club, ever since. She's a hard-ass bitch but once she lets you in, you're there for life unless you fuck up and that is one huge mistake on your part. Because I know from personal experiences, to have Zoey at your back is everything. I know deep down in my soul that she would die for me without even thinking, and I feel the same. Though I'm a bit more human, so I probably would have a brief mini second of hesitation when I've seen she's had none in the past.

So far in my thoughts, I don't hear the big mountain of a man who is standing right next to me, his eyebrows up in the air. Fuck, how did I not hear him? He's got to be at least a foot taller than me and weigh well over two hundred and what... forty.

"Nope, babe, I'm two hundred and fifty-two pounds, good guess though."

My head whips up at his husky as fuck sex voice and wonder, did I say that out loud.

"Tink, you didn't say anything out loud but, well, I'll let you figure it out. Just a warning, be careful around me and Panther. Obviously, we have Native blood, but we are Navajo and like I said, you seem pretty smart, I'll give it just a bit before I'm guessing you'll figure it out."

Not thinking like usual, I just blurt shit out.

"Are you a shaman? Do you have visions? Are you a shape-shifter, or do you see bad spirits? I've read about Native people and the different tribes. Each tribe is unique unto itself, but they all have tribe members with special powers, right?"

He chuckles just when I feel heat at my back as Noodles leans over me again, hand out.

"Hey, I'm Ellington or L. This inquisitive one is mine so don't get no ideas otherwise big man. It'd be a bitch taking you down, but she's worth it. And, yeah, I'd take ya down. Let's not start pissing everywhere to mark our territory. Seems like y'all might need some help with whatever is going on? Can call for backup if necessary. Oh, forgot to mention I'm ex-military, specifically a Navy SEAL.

And all my friends that I'd call are also all ex-military."

I watch as Noodles shakes the guy's hand and I wait impatiently for him to tell us who he is.

"Hey, Ellington, I'm Avalanche. Panther and I grew up together on the reservation in New Mexico then both signed up for the service too. When we split, both going our separate ways, Panther ended up here in Bumfuck, Montana and started his stud farm, along with breaking mustangs. We found each other again and here we are."

For a brief second, the words stud farm and with the way all these guys look, my mind envisions them having all kinds of hot guys on this ranch. But then as they go back and forth, getting to know each other like men tend to do, I pull away from my man and start pacing, waiting for my bestie to get her ass out here and explain what the motherfucking hell is going on. Before she makes her way back into the main room, the door flies open and in walks my dad, Tank, the president of the Intruders, with Enforcer following close behind.

I see a disaster happening before my eyes as Avalanche and his men reach behind them to pull out their weapons, as Enforcer pushes my dad behind him, pulling his Glock out. My girl, Kiwi, still has the Mossberg close by, so she swings it up then realizes she's not sure who the threat is, so the gun is swinging between my dad and Avalanche.

"Goddamn it, Kiwi, put that beast down before you accidentally kill someone. Leave that kind of shit to Zoey, okay? Dad, calm the fuck down and, hey douchebag, yeah you, Enforcer, put the weapon down before you do something I'll regret. Everyone, calm the ever-lovin' fuck down. And more importantly, remember where you are, in MY goddamn motherfucking clubhouse."

At that moment, Zoey and Panther walk out. Enforcer swings in that direction at the exact same time Panther grabs Zoey, mimicking what happened to my dad. Unfortunately for him, she's not a wilting flower and manages to twist out of his grasp and swing around the other side of him, placing herself in front of him.

The gasps throughout the room shock just about everyone, me especially. Never have I seen our enforcer and my best friend ever put herself between anyone but me and my family. Yeah, she'd protect another Devil's Handmaiden but not sure she would be willing to die. And that is what she's saying right now. Dad starts to laugh then bends over, struggling to get air in as he's losing it so much. When he finally lifts his head, his eyes are on Zoey.

"It's about time, Z. Told you when you least expect it and see, since no one knows about that Indian behind you, this must be on the newer side. Enforcer, for Christ's sake, drop the gun, shit for brains. Maggie, what the hell are you into now and who are these brutes? Fuck, could use a few for my club, at least they all look like they could handle themselves in a fight. Any one of you boys interested in prospecting for the Intruders motorcycle club?"

Leave it to my dad to defuse the situation. Zoey turns, squeezes Panther's hand, then walks directly to me. She knows how pissed I am, so she approaches slowly and methodically.

"Goldilocks, give me a chance to explain. I know, but come on, hear me out."

Knowing I should still be feeling hurt, I push past her and move toward my dad, arms out wide. He pulls me in, and we walk back to my office, leaving the bullshit behind me. My dad can always read me and, no matter what, tries to give me what I need. And right now I have to get away from Zoey before I say something I'll forever regret.

"So, daughter of my loins, what's going on between you and Zoey? The freeze you just gave her could be felt all the way to goddamn Alaska. She do something, or does it have to do with those men out there?"

Trying to explain the situation is going to make me sound childish and petty but this is my daddy, so I break it down to him—and I give him kudos—he listens, never saying a word. Until he does.

"Maggie, listen up. I don't have a fuckin' clue to what we walked into but something I've known from the second I met that lost little girl to the woman she's become, Zoey/Shadow or whatever name she goes by, will always love you and have your back. No matter what, and not one living soul will be able to take your place in her damaged goddamn blackened heart. You, my girl, have been the constant in her life and, literally, it was you who was able to breathe some life into her fuckin' soul when we found her. She fought tooth and nail, but you never gave up on her, so don't do it now.

"Did she cut ya loose when your soldier boy showed up or when he won your heart? Nope, she kinda adopted him and his people because that's what would make you happy. Now it's your turn, Maggie. Don't let her down 'cause we both know that's all she's known most of her life. We're the only ones who've had her back."

Listening to the love in his voice when he mentions Zoey, it hits me how blessed I am with the parents I have. My bestie is a handful, to say the least, and they never once treated her badly. In fact, it was Mom and Dad who adopted her into our family and since then have treated her like their own daughter. Crazy daughter, just saying, but still they did it.

Smiling I give my dad a hug, holding on tightly as his big arms crush me to him. His words make sense and if I'd get out of my head, I would have recognized how nervous Zoey was. She wasn't doing anything wrong, but she almost looked like she got caught with her hand in the cookie jar. Maybe she was struggling, trying to find a way to tell me what's been going on, but it explains all the times she's disappeared without a trace, even her phone's been turned off so Raven couldn't trace it. Yeah, I'm that friend. Damn it, need to fix this shit.

Taking a moment to try and gather my thoughts, I head back into the main area to find everyone settled down. Some at the bar, others at the sectional and couches, while others are even shooting pool. Except Zoey, she is sitting at one of the tables, head in her hands, while Panther rubs her shoulders. That tells me everything. Time for the olive branch, Dad's right.

"Hey, bestie, want to have that talk now, do you have time? I'll be in my office. Dad is leaving shortly so come on back or if not now, just let me know. And, Panther, nice to meet you. I know shit is going down, not sure what, but if you need the Devil's Handmaidens sisters help, just ask. We don't judge anyone and would do our best to be allies not enemies."

Turning, I start to walk to my office when I hear a chair scraping the hardwood floors and smile to myself. Yeah, she's ready and so am I. Friends to the end, no matter what.

NINE
'SHADOW'

ZOEY

Fuck, how do I get myself in these situations? Goddamn Panther for showing up and pushing my hand. I was trying to find a way to bring up what's been going on and where I've been disappearing to, but shit, now every single Devil's Handmaiden will be up my ass wanting to know details about my personal life. And I hate that shit, ya know, chatting and gossiping, never been one to talk to my club sisters about that kind of stuff. Well, guess until now.

Following Goldilocks my stomach clenches, knowing she won't push me for anything but deciding to tell her everything, well, as much as she can stomach. I even told Panther to give me a bit, then come on back. Only going to go through this once and having my bestie with me is the coward's way out, but if I want whatever is happening between Panther and me to move forward, he has to know.

Goldilocks motions for me to sit so I grab a corner of the leather couch, pulling my legs under me, trying to get comfortable. She takes the oversized chair, which makes her look even smaller. We just stare at each other, neither saying a word. Then at the same exact time we start to talk. She gives me the floor.

"Goldilocks, I never wanted to hide any shit from you. It just kind of happened and the longer it went on, the harder it was for me to even bring the subject up. Then Noodles showed up and the two of you hit it off. When we found out Buck had Hannah, I spent all my time and effort to find her, so Panther went to the back burner.

"We ran into each other at the animal auction when Taz asked me to go with her. She was off doing her usual ranch shit, so I was wandering around while people pointed their fingers and talked shit about me. When a bunch of school kids started being little assholes, Panther and Avalanche showed up, saving me from either killing the little fuckers or from a jail cell and a call to you for bail."

As I continue on with how we met up again after the first time we put eyes on each other years ago in that tattoo shop, she sits patiently, never interrupting me at all. Not once. I explain how we have a lot in common, how he has been undercover for a few government agencies and on his own trying to break up different circuits. Panther doesn't just concentrate on human trafficking. He doesn't have the resources we do, but he has the knowledge of how this sick world operates and he goes after the nastiest of them. Those who sell and peddle human flesh for everything and anything.

"Fuck, I know you're hurt, Goldilocks, and that kills me. I've never wanted to hurt you. You're one of the few humans on this earth who matter to me. You, Pops, Momma Diane, and now for me, unfortunately, Hannah. I've never been good at this kind of shit, no one ever taught me 'til you tried to save me. Don't give up on me, please. Especially not now, I need you to help me with whatever this shit is."

Her eyes widen for a second then she flies at me, arms wide. She actually lands on my lap, hugging me while crying like a baby.

"You idiot, I'm never letting you go, so don't ever say that shit again. I'm pissed because I share everything including the, you know, private stuff, along the way that happened with Noodles, and you didn't with Panther. That hurts, Zoey."

"Hasn't been much to share, bestie. I actually told him to join us, if you don't mind. Only doing this once and both of you need to hear it, so I'll explain in a bit. 'Kay?"

She nods then, to her credit, she changes the subject to our meeting in Chapel. She thanked me for what I said in regard to Heartbreaker and even asked me to keep a close eye on our club sister. She's struggling right now, we all know that, and some of the others are giving her more leeway, but Goldilocks knows that I don't give a fuck. She's gonna have to work harder than ever to get back the trust she once had earned.

A knock at the door has both of our heads turn. I look to her briefly until she gives me a soft "okay" and I stand, go to the door, open it, and see Panther and Pops. Fuck, I don't want him to hear this garbage that is my life. But the determined look on his face tells me I'm not going to have a choice. Son of a fucking bitch.

"Damn, it's a small-ass world, almost passed out when I saw Panther here earlier. I've known him for a while. I was heading back to talk to you both when he told me that's where he was heading, so that's why we're here. So, what the fuck is going on? I'm assuming, since my girl Maggie is getting her shit together, this must be about you, Zoey, and this one here. So let's hear it. Give it all to your pops."

Pops gets comfortable on the love seat, leaving the other side of the couch for Panther to sit down. Right next to me. His thigh is touching mine and he reaches behind me, putting his arm on the back of the furniture. He looks like he doesn't have a care in the world, or that later today we aren't going to meet one of the largest scumbags in our area. When his fingers barely touch my hair, it hits me. This is his way to give me support without making a big deal out of it. When I peek at him, he must feel my glance because he gives me a small wink. What the fuck?

"I thought it would be easier for me to get this shit out there with the two of you, or now the three of you, so I only have to go through it one time. I'd appreciate it if ya respect my privacy and keep this bullshit to yourselves. Well yeah, Pops, I get you'll tell Momma Diane but besides her, none of your brothers, especially Enforcer or Wrench, please, Pops. And, Goldilocks, try to keep this from Squirt. She's been through enough bullshit already she don't need mine on top of it."

Watching Pops' face, I know he won't tell a soul, that's who he is, and I trust him with my life, always have.

"When I was little, before I could actually think clearly, the man who was my father disappeared. Or that's what my mother told me. She was a huge drug addict, who had no qualms of selling whatever she had at hand to get money for her next fix. I'm not going to go into details, you're all pretty smart folks, so imagine it and then multiply it by a thousand. She liked to also beat and torture me regularly, either by herself or with whatever dick she was using and was hanging around at the time."

I feel Panther's hand on the back of my neck, massaging the tension there.

"I ended up in the emergency room or urgent care weekly. Sometimes just for an X-ray, other times for broken bones, or needing to be stitched up. One time, the cut on my back was so deep they were thinking about surgery until the old whore told them to stitch or glue me up, or she'd take me home and do it herself. So, they did, but the nurse also called the Department of Child Services. They interviewed me and decided she needed some serious help, so they pulled me out of the trailer we were living in at the time and put me into the foster care system. What a fucking joke, but at least I was getting meals and kinda had a roof over my head.

"My mom followed the courts recommendations and after about nine months, I was sent back to her. And that's when the real fun started. I was barely nine or ten. First, was the constant emotional abuse. The things she called me not only broke my heart but made the voices in my head tell me that she was right. When I turned eleven or so, I'll never forget it, she had a john come to the trailer with a friend. Guess they were looking for a threesome, but Mom wasn't up to it. She was still recovering from a beatdown and could barely take on one. An argument started and she offered them me instead. One look at me and they agreed. She made two hundred and fifty dollars, and those two motherfuckers raped me and took my virginity. That was the beginning of the end.

"About three months later, her dealer came looking for the money she owed him and when she didn't have it, she told him to take me, do whatever he wanted for a month, then return what was left. He did and I will tell you, never in my young life did I know evil until that month. He put me in a dog cage, threw scraps at me if he thought about it, and made me do things that were beyond inhuman. When I fought him in the beginning, he took out a huge Bowie hunting knife and started carving my body up. Not deep enough for stitches but definitely left some very noticeable scars. He hooked me on drugs and gave me to his friends, just because he could. As he always reminded me, he had the power to do whatever the fuck he wanted.

"By the time I made it back 'home' I was barely alive. When I opened the trailer door, the sight before my eyes, I think I either had an immediate nervous breakdown or my mind just split. There were three guys taking turns at my mom while beating her senseless. And she was barely conscious. I slammed the door, grabbed the bat she kept next to it, and that was when I totally came into the voices which eventually morphed into Shadow, truly then my rage, anger, and plain old crazy self-came to the surface.

"I had no clue what I was doing, just needed them to feel the pain I had. It took seven cops to pull me off what was left of the last guy. The first two were beaten to a pulp, nothing left of their heads and faces. Number three survived in a coma for two weeks before he too died. Mom overdosed but they pulled her through and put her in jail and in a program. The problem was me. No one knew what to do with me, so a judge decided that I probably needed to go to prison but had a heart, so he sent me to juvie instead.

"The next six in a half years I learned the hard way to grow up fast, keep my mouth shut, and stay out of everyone's way. I became the freak who lived in the shadows. Those who needed a problem taken care of; they came to me. Since money was a no-no in there, they paid me in other ways. I learned how to hone my skills, like torturing someone without killing them or play mind-fucking games just to drive them bat-ass crazy. That night in my mom's trailer, the feeling of blood and brains in my hands changed me. Felt like I finally knew who I was and what I needed, and even today, the longing to feel blood on my skin every once in a while helps keep me sane or as close to it as I can come, I guess."

I take a break and take a few breaths. Goldilocks has tears on her cheeks but isn't sobbing or anything like that, her eyes on me tell me how much she loves and accepts me through those emerald-green orbs. Pops is staring at the wall and Panther just keeps his hands on me softly. That little connection is what is keeping me sane and in the moment. I've never shared this shit with anyone and hope to never do this again ever, for fuck's sake.

"When you ran into me that night, Goldilocks, I was there because the guy running that party was a man who was Satan reincarnated. I had every intention of going in there, torturing that sadist motherfucker like he did to me, but worse, including his asshole minions at that house. When I was done peeling his skin off and ripping his limbs off, I'd finish him by strangling whatever life was left out of him. Then I'd let the kids there go. Finally, I was done, had enough, couldn't do it anymore, so was gonna end it. Kill myself. But instead I meet lil' Miss Good Doer, who was there to save everyone. And when I told you about what I knew instead of running away and hiding, you called your daddy, who just happened to be the president of a goddamn motorcycle club. That was the beginning of one of the most fucked-up relationships I've been blessed with in my entire life."

Tink gets up and kneels in front of me, grabbing both hands in hers, holding on tightly. I give her a squeeze but neither of us say a word. None are needed. We understand each other without any verbal communication getting in our way.

"Goldilocks, I'm sorry but since I don't even know what I'm doing with Panther, trying to explain it to you was overwhelming me. Look at me, for God's sake, and then really look at him. He's beyond what you see, a gorgeous alpha from one of those books our Squirt always seems to be reading. Me, I'm a total messy fucking lunatic. And all these tattoos, if you guys didn't figure it out, are to hide all my hundreds of scars. I took away one secret and now wear my past every day, right in everyone's face. The tattoo on my face let me build that wall up so no one could get through. Well, until I met a small fairy trying to throw her fucking fairy dust at everyone and make everything in our world better."

With that, Pops and Goldilocks laugh while Panther leans forward, pulling me close, kissing the top of my head, and then standing up, guiding Goldilocks to take his seat. He moves to the one she abandoned. For once, I needed to feel her arms around me, so I instigate the hug, which shocks her for a brief second, then she grabs on and holds me like she'll never let go. I pray to Christ she doesn't.

In the background, I can hear Pops and Panther talking but can't make out what is being said. All I know is that three of the most important people in my life know most of my secrets and it doesn't seem to bother them at all. If anything, by the way Goldilocks is hanging on to me, maybe they love me even more. What the fuck is wrong with these people? I smile to myself. Thank my lucky stars that on the night I had planned to take my life, instead I found Goldilocks who gave me a purpose to live.

TEN
'PANTHER'

CHAHÓÓŁHÉÉL NAABAAHII T'ÁÁ SÁHI
DARK WARRIOR WALKING ALONE

While talking with Tank, my mind is all over the fucking place. Of all times, Zoey decides to drop this huge atomic bomb in my life on the same day we are meeting with one of the largest psychopaths and deranged assholes I've ever tried to take down. Watching Zoey and Tink holding hands talking, I can see the relief in their bodies. Whatever it was that drew them together will never be broken. That truth is right in front of my eyes.

"Panther, our girl is gonna be fine, no need to worry. So tell me what are your intentions with her? Don't laugh, you bastard, she's the closest thing to Maggie and now Hannah, not to mention I think of her as my own daughter. Both Diane and I care deeply for that damaged woman. We watched and tried to help Zoey heal over the years. If I find out this is some kind of fucked-up mind game, no matter how much I like you, no one—not even Avalanche—will find you when I'm done with you. Do you understand me, boy?"

I don't take offense to the boy comment or Tank getting in my business because that means my Zoey has some real people who love her in her life.

"Tank, as you heard Zoey say, neither of us knows where this is going, and for me personally, I've been taking it slow. Not going to lie, I want her. And I mean all of her: body, soul, and mind. We both have demons and seem to be dealing somewhat with them by trying to keep this world we live in a safer place by getting rid of the motherfuckers and their garbage. Not sure that answers your question but, no, this isn't a one and done or a fill-in."

Tank looks at me then nods and gives my shoulder a squeeze. I actually feel a ton of pressure come off me. Almost like a teenager at his girlfriend's parents' house while Dad is cleaning his gun. Looking at Tank, wouldn't want to be the one facing him with a gun in his hand, that's for sure.

Hearing some soft laughter, my eyes go to Zoey and Tink who are whispering to each other, glancing back and forth to me. Great, just what I need, the dreaded friends comparing of the guys in their lives. Just when I'm about to walk over to them, my phone vibrates and rings. Both women's heads jerk my way and I see Tank get up, taking a guess, to go get Avalanche.

"Yo."

"Yeah, chief, we got a time and place. Tonight, at ten, at the old mill outside of Timber-Ghost. You know it? I'm sure your skull face cunt can show you, that's her town, right? Boss said she better be there and don't get any ideas 'cause he won't think twice to kill the things you want to buy. Any questions? Good, see you tonight, Indian."

Hearing the call drop, I feel my blood pressure getting higher and higher. What a prick, trying to get a rise out of me by trying to belittle me with my heritage. Asshole, it won't work I'm honored to be Navajo and wear it proudly.

"Boss, you okay? Take a couple of breaths, will ya, before you pass the fuck out. Come on, you got this, we're taking this motherfuckin' prick down, no matter what."

When Zoey and Tink stand, my friend must have caught their movement because I hear under his breath, "Oh goddamn it, shit, motherfucker." I watch Zoey walk right to Avalanche and put her hand on his back for a brief second.

"Hey, we got no problem, promise, Avalanche. First, I'll be there with Panther, and second, no one I'd rather have at my back than Goldilocks and Pops over there. Yeah, I see you standing right outside the door. With your size, can't really hide. Not to mention your stomach is growling like you've not eaten in a few days. We don't need you to go hypoglycemic on us, Pops."

Hearing Zoey try to ease the tension by joking with Tank has me let out a shocked laugh. Every time we're together, she shows me another side of her.

"Thanks, brother, I appreciate you. Zoey, get your ass over here and, Tank, please come in and shut the door, if that's all right? Tink, can I use your office for a minute or two? We might need the Devil's Handmaidens and Intruders to have our backs tonight, if at all possible. All we have right now are my four guys sitting at the bar, and I've got a very bad feeling something is about to go down, and not in a good way."

I watch as Tank ambles in, falling into one of the chairs. Avalanche walks in and leans on the wall, crossing his one ankle over the other, arms across his chest, waiting. Zoey's arms are wrapped around my waist as Tink walks to her dad and leans into him.

"The short explanation is that Avalanche and I have been working this jagoff and his organization for over year and a half. When we seem to get close, he retreats like he's being warned or something. These were the assholes who snuck onto that reservation in rural South Dakota, beating and leaving the parents for dead, and stealing their kids who were there. To this day, they've not been found. Personally, I think they've been sold to deviants around the world. Not sure we'll ever find them all, but we aren't just forgetting them either."

Tank looks first at his daughter then Zoey, saying something without words. When they both nod, he grabs his phone, telling whoever is on the other end to get their ass here immediately.

"Panther, I just put a call into my IT specialist, Freak. If there is any digital footprint, he'll be able to find it. And if he can't, we can call in Raven from Maggie's club or I can reach out to my brother Brick with the Grimm Wolves MC. His IT guy, Karma, has ridiculous mad skills. Reason I'm mentioning this shit is that no matter how invisible someone thinks they are, if they are doing what you think they are, the only way is on the internet. It's immediate contact with buyers and money can also be transferred over the web."

Tank is making a shit ton of sense and since we don't have a specialist in the technology area, I'll take whatever help he's willing to provide. I look to Tink, who's staring at her dad like he's got two heads, and when I look down at Zoey so is she. He must sense something because he takes a deep breath.

"All right, knock it off, you little smart asses. I might not like all that social media bullshit, but I also run a motorcycle club in 2023, gotta have some knowledge about how all that junk works. Freak's given me some lessons and has even let me sit with him when he's working, so now, I can at least talk the talk, even though I'll never walk the walk. Now, Panther, whatcha think, want the help? Oh, and you let us know where the meet is, we'll be there no ifs or ands about it. My girl is involved so the Intruders are too."

As we wait for the geek guy to show up, we start to talk about where and how each club can give us a hand. Avalanche, who's usually such a bastard, is playing nice in the sandbox, which I appreciate right now.

"I'm gonna need to get outta here soon, gotta hit the bank, need some cash for the supposed buy. If I wait any longer the bank won't have time to gather all that green."

"How much do you need, Panther?" both Tink and Tank ask at the same time.

"It's a shit ton of cash, guys. I'm trying to purchase a few *special orders,* and this is the first time one of these types of orders is being filled. I know something is goddamn up. That's why I'm like a dog with a bone, don't want to let this opportunity get fucked up."

Tink goes to her desk, picks up a phone, and tells someone named Taz to come to her office. After she hangs up, she looks my way.

"Panther, Taz is our club treasurer and my personal banker. Not sure if Zoey explained my situation, but I inherited a shit ton of money from my granny. So instead of rushing around like a chicken with its head cut off, give us a number and we'll get the money for you. I'm not worried about it, swear to God. I know Zoey can vouch for me that I use the money for what truly matters. And this is one of those times."

There's a knock on the door, right before it swings open and in walks a woman with long rainbow-colored hair. She's got a gun at her waist and another under her vest, no Zoey calls it a kutte, I think. She goes right to Tink's left side, arms crossed, looking around the room, definitely on alert.

"Yeah, Prez, you wanted me?"

"Taz, step down, we're good. Panther, can I share?"

Shocked but grateful that Tink would even ask, I just nod.

"Panther and Avalanche have a situation that is time sensitive and he's going to give you a number. I'm approving it now, so make it happen. Don't care if it's club or personal. Probably better and will be less questions if it comes from one of my accounts, so go that route. Or take it out of my own petty cash safe, depending on how much. Any questions?"

"You trust him? Yeah, Shadow, don't get all pissy. I don't know either of them from Jack shit, so it's a question I have to ask, sister."

Tink and Taz continue talking, but my eyes are on Zoey as her eyes are spitting flames at Taz for asking that question. She must feel me looking at her because her eyes go to the floor for a brief second before she looks at me, eyebrows raised up. I grin at her then tell Avalanche to let the men know to stick around so all of us can figure out a plan that will work and not leave anyone injured or dead. Now the part I fucking hate. The waiting game.

When I share the amount of cash I need, Taz slightly raises her eyebrows then tells Tink she'll get it out of the one safe in Zoey's room. *What the fuck,* I think until I hear a chuckle.

"No, Panther, it's not my bedroom in the clubhouse. It's called a wet room and it's downstairs, which you need a fingerprint, an eye scan, and the digital number code. The safe Taz is talking about is Tink's personal one and even though you think that's a lot of money, it's not. Tell him, Goldilocks."

"Like I said, Panther, my granny was extremely wealthy, and we didn't have a clue to how much she was worth. Between the ears in this room and I'm trusting you because you come with Zoey, I have five safes hidden in this clubhouse for my personal use, so we always have available cash. You and your boys would never find one so as my parents taught me, just say *'thank you.'* We have much more important things to deal with."

* * *

Sitting in the back of the armored SUV Tank provided, I'm beyond shocked at the resources both father and daughter have in the middle of nowhere fucking Montana.

Not only this specialized vehicle, but everyone is packing the newest and best firepower. The driver is one of Tank's brothers, while Zoey, Avalanche, and I are in the back section. Tank sent around eight or ten of his men to check out the area earlier, and they were to find lookout points and get comfortable.

Tink had two of her sisters go with the Intruders because they are the best snipers she has. Even better than her dad's boys. He shocked the shit outta me when he agreed with her. The two were Kiwi, the chick who held us down with a Mossberg earlier. The other Devil's Handmaiden was Wildcat. They both had sniper weapons and enough ammo to take down a small village.

Avalanche has been extremely and oddly very quiet, which is not like him. I've tried to talk to him but all I'm getting is one-word answers to my questions, so I think, *fuck it, let him pout.*

As we pull behind the old mill, I suddenly get an ominous feeling that goes through my entire body as Avalanche's head jerks up. It's pitch dark, except for the headlights along with the stars scattered through the sky. I see Zoey lean back against the leather, taking in a few deep breaths. A loud noise has all of our attention as the SUV shakes violently, veering to first the left then the right. Our driver is trying his best, but I feel actual fear when he screams back to us.

"Motherfuckers ain't playing, they tried to hit us with a missile. Goddamn it, think the front wheel took most of it. It's probably barely hanging on. We don't got many choices, people, so brace, it's gonna be a hard stop. Son of a bitch, got no control."

With that I say a quick prayer to the Great Spirit for guidance and safe passage for all of us. It's game time, no it's way beyond that. It's war, motherfuckers.

ELEVEN
'SHADOW'
ZOEY

Feeling the panic rolling off of Panther, I reach down and squeeze his hand. On his other side, Avalanche is giving Omen orders, which isn't going over too well. Not how we planned it but most shit don't go according to what we want. Pop's brother, Omen, is busting his ass trying to keep the vehicle upright and moving, but looks like he's about to lose control, damn it.

Bracing after tightening my seat belt, I bend over, hands over my head, preparing for a massive collision. I'm shocked when a body literally covers me completely. Panther's warmth is comforting until more pressure hits my back and I assume Avalanche is doing the same thing to Panther. Problem is neither of them are small men. That thought vanishes when I hear Omen scream, "Mother of Christ, hang the fuck on." Then all I feel is impact from all sides. *God, what the hell did he hit*? I think to myself as the vibrations of the crash flow through my body. The feeling of Panther and Avalanche seems heavier than before but I'm not complaining yet. The SUV has finally come to a halting stop, but nothing is coming from the front seat, or from more importantly, our driver Omen.

I'm starting to feel that dread I always get right before shit goes south. I try to shimmy both men off of me but neither move. Fuck, they're both out. Seems like I'm on my own, as usual. Trying to reach my back pocket to grab my phone, can't do it because of the way Panther's body is lying directly on top of me. Taking a minute to just listen and see if I hear anything is exactly when the loud sound makes its way to me.

Son of a bitch, it seems someone is trying to either help us out or, on the other hand, working to get in to us. Hearing some moaning above me, I shift trying to wake Panther up.

"Holy shit, what the fuck happened? Omen, status. Status, dude. Fuck, Zoey, Avalanche, you both good? Please be okay, talk to me."

"Yeah, Panther, besides your weight crushing me, don't think I'm hurt, probably going to have some bruises, but that's it. The million-dollar question is, are you hurt?"

I feel him try to move but for some reason can't. I hear him cussing and shifting, first back then toward me, changing and shifting left then right. At the same time he's talking to Avalanche, but I'm not hearing a response. Panther's frustration is starting to fill the SUV until he stops suddenly, and we both hear multiple machines operating, I'm assuming to open the vehicle up. This is one of Pop's bulletproof reinforced vehicles, almost a tank. *No pun intended*, I think to myself with Pops's club name being Tank because now I'm beyond thankful to him for letting us use it. Otherwise, we might all be dead or seriously injured and not have protection from whatever is happening now. And this 'tank' will keep those on the outside from coming in and getting to us.

Avalanche calls out hoarsely and Panther answers him. They seem to be talking but I can't make out anything they are actually saying. There is also some fussing toward the front so cross my fingers that Omen is alive. Taking a minute to assess myself, I realize my back is tightening up and when I try to move my legs, they feel weird. Like they are there but not. Not sure if it's all the weight I'm supporting or if during impact an injury happened.

"Panther, hey, need you and Big Bird to try and get off of me. I'm getting some really strange feelings in my back and my legs, seems like they are numb as fuck like when they fall asleep. No, don't try to touch them, just get the fuck off of me now. Please?"

Avalanche tells Panther to hang on and nothing happens at first, until I hear his painful swearing then a decrease in the load on top of me. Damn, that man weighs a ton. Panther tells Avalanche not to move too much until they can give each other the once-over. Panther tells me to hang on as he moves up my body and to the left. Once he's off of me, I feel like I can breathe a bit easier but not by much.

"Zoey, talk to me. What are you feeling? Hang on, Nizhoni, for one second. Avalanche, you got your phone handy? Great, put a shout-out to Tank, Tink, and our men. Tell them we're in serious trouble, most of us hurt in one way or another. We need their goddamn help fucking NOW. Do it, brother, whoever is trying to get in isn't gonna give up from the sounds of it. Now, Nizhoni, you need to tell me what you're feeling. Anything out of the normal, like any pain or numbness."

Just when I'm about to do what he's asked, the vehicle shifts and is bounced on its side. I hit the door hard with my head. Something wet is running down my face so I go to wipe it, knowing already it's blood. Fuck, my forehead split open. Goddamn great, head wounds bleed like a gutted pig and forever.

"Panther just busted my head open on the doorframe. Back pressure let up, but legs are tingly and kind of like they are sleeping. My left arm feels sprained, and my ears are ringing. Besides that, I feel fucking great."

Hearing both him and Avalanche chuckle seems to momentarily take some of the unknown fear radiating throughout my body. It's always been the not knowing what comes next that fucks with me more than anything. Bodily pain I can generally manage and suck it up, but not being in the loop to what is going to happen next freaks the ever-lovin' fuck outta me.

"Panther left a text message for Tink, she's not picking up. I need Tank's number, don't have it. I spoke to Jersey, and they are close since they were part of our backup. He said that he'd let whoever he saw on the way down know, but gonna take a while, there's an accident on that road we turned off on, go figure. Assholes must have planned that too. Thinkin' we're on our own until the cavalry arrives. What's the plan, boss? I believe we drove right into a setup and if we make it out in one piece, I'll personally give Tank a big smooch on his cheek for letting us borrow this kick-ass SUV. If you both think about it, we'd be dead otherwise."

"Can you motherfuckers keep it down back there? I've got a splitting goddamn headache and think my one leg is fucked up. Think I see a bone or something, who knows what the hell it is. And I'm covered in blood and think the headache is from a moderate concussion. Besides that, like Shadow said, I'm feeling fucking fantastic. So glad Tank picked me for this goddamn job. Hope I live to talk about it."

After listening to Omen rant and as we try to get some kind of plan going, my mind is running around in circles. Why did they stop trying to get us out?

What's going on outside? Who the fuck is doing this shit? Is it the 'guy' Panther's trying to take down? Too many questions with not one damn answer.

While I'm daydreaming and feeling my aches and pains somehow Avalanche, or as I like to piss him off with Big Bird, has manipulated his huge body so now he is actually right-side up shimmying to the front to check out Omen. I hear him gasp softly but he doesn't say a word. If it's bad news for Pops's brother, I'll wait to hear from Big Bird before screaming and shouting for status.

"All right, Panther, and skull anii', as they say... *Montana, we have a situation.* I'm looking out of one of the side windows at a... oh shit, a huge loader with a bucket on it coming right our way. Think someone is sick of fucking with this vehicle and knows we have a fuck ton of help coming, so they came up with a new plan. Pick up the entire SUV and bring it with them. Any fucking ideas?"

Omen whispers something to Avalanche, who laughs hysterically.

"Well, brother, your idea, you get to break that news to them."

"It's like this, Tank had this vehicle tricked out and up front is something like a control center. The problem is, with the damage done, not sure if everything is in working order and will have the effect we hope or need. There is a Sterling MK4 SMG under the back of your seat, Panther. Tank loves that gun 'cause it's not heavy and fires like a crazy-ass bitch. His words not mine. I've got a bag of grenades in the center console. And built under the frame is a missile launcher, locked and loaded. We are on our side, so aiming would be a total bitch, but and—we all have to agree—I'd rather go out my own way than with whatever they have planned. Either the missile works and knocks that loader and bucket on its ass and pray to whomever you can that our help arrives in time. Or the missile is damaged and blows all of us up, because even though this is a solid mass of iron that's bulletproof, the vehicle won't withstand the aftershock of that particular missile. So what's your thoughts, people, our window of time is running out."

Just as I'm about to give my opinion, a phone rings and I hear Avalanche's, "Yeah, what the fuck ya want? Oh, hang on, beautiful."

"Hey, bitch, it's for you. Panther, can you reach this?"

Hearing him growl as he puts his hand out to grab the phone, I put it in my mind's book that I owe Big Bird one for calling me a bitch. A phone is pressed into my face, so with one hand I take it, putting it up to my ear.

"Yeah?"

"Goddamn motherfucker, Zoey, you hang on, we're on the way. Don't you idiots do anything stupid, especially since Omen is with you. Don't listen to anything that jackass says, we're only a few minutes away. Dad is also coming but from a different angle. Noodles put a call into Ollie, but they are going to be awhile, too far away. Thank God Panther listened to us explaining why we all had to be within a certain perimeter to the meet. You okay? Anyone hurt? How's Dad's SUV? Not that it matters as long as you're good. I asked are you okay, Zoey? Talk to me, bitch, don't play your usual games with me, not today."

"Fuck, Goldilocks, if you'd take a goddamn breath and let me talk, I'd tell you. I'm sore, head busted open. Panther seems okay, banged around. Avalanche, unfortunately, seems fine while Omen took a fucking beating and will need medical. Might need to have someone alert Doc Carol at the ranch."

"Okay, will do. Come on, Noodles, damn, you drive worse than my gramma did when she was alive. The big pedal makes the truck move, you dumbass. He wants to know what happened?"

"Not sure. Something hit the vehicle, might have been a shoulder missile or some kind of grenade launcher. Blew us clear up then down as we skidded to our side. At first, I thought Omen hit something, but he was avoiding shit they put in the road. Now they are approaching with a front loader to pick up your dad's SUV and take it God knows where because they tried cutting us out but can't get through. All I know right now, Goldilocks."

Hearing Omen swearing, she starts screaming at Noodles before I hear a sniffle.

"Goddamn it, Zoey, you better hang on, you crazy as fuck bitch. I'm not ready to let you go yet so fight, no matter what. Remember what Chains said when he was taken; he knew his club would come for him and eventually find him alive or, worst case, find his body. I promise you that I'll be there, no matter what, and you will be breathing. We're off-roading it because the dirt road is blocked with debris. Must be the assholes you were going to meet. Please, sister, hang the fuck on. I can't live without you, Zoey."

Knowing she's a second or two from losing it, I try to think up a joke, but nothing comes to mind.

"Goldilocks, I'll do my best but just in case shit takes a bad turn, I want—oh goddamn it—you need to know and tell Pops, Momma Diane, and even that little pain in the ass Hannah, thanks for being my family."

The sound of metal hitting metal is overwhelming as all three men start screaming and swearing as Panther reaches behind us for the MK4, while Avalanche is crawling to the front seat trying to fit in next to Omen. As he's trying to make room for Big Bird, I hear beeping and shit being turned on, so guessing he's trying to activate the missile. Then in my ears the screeching starts.

"Zoey, please we need maybe two minutes if that. Fight, pull up that goddamn lunatic Shadow. Think bad thoughts or all the bullshit you've done over the years to those who torture women and children. Get angry, no, make it furious. Let that boil your blood. What I don't want you to do is give up."

When the loader picks the SUV up, lifting us higher in the air, I take a deep breath, let it out, and do what I have to do.

"You got it, Prez. Maggie don't do anything stupid yourself. Bye, Goldilocks, luv ya, sistah."

Before disconnecting, I hear her screaming my name and the word noooooo. The little part of my heart she owns breaks in two.

TWELVE
'TINK'
MAGGIE/GOLDILOCKS

Hearing my voice screaming her name over and over, I have no idea what, where, or how until Noodles violently and suddenly pulls his truck over, unlocks my seat belt, and pulls me onto his lap and into his arms.

"Maggie, calm down, Sweet Pea, breathe. Please, just listen to my voice because we ain't moving until you calm the fuck down, and that isn't going to help Zoey at all."

Noodles saying my bestie's name brings me out of my fog. I instantly stop screaming and, even though the tears are flowing freely down my cheeks, not a word comes out of my mouth. I need to pull my shit together and fast. Zoey is in some deep shit, and she needs me. Shaking my head, I look out the window to see trucks and even some bikes surrounding our truck and sitting in the middle of the road. Fuck, I'm such an idiot.

"Noodles, please start the truck and move, drive like the devil's on your ass because technically he is. They're in some serious trouble and we need to get there like yesterday. Everyone is waiting on my sissy ass. Please do it and thank you for caring. She's my best friend I can't lose her. Not again."

I watch him intently looking at me like he's reading my soul, which if that is what it takes for him to get this beast of a goddamn truck moving, so be it. After what seems like hours but is no longer than a couple of minutes, he puts me back in my seat and then starts up the truck and hits the pedal. As the truck flies forward, all the vehicles around us also start moving quickly to keep up.

My mind is running in all directions and none of them are good. That lack of emotion in her voice scares me to death. When Zoey doesn't have control of a situation, she actually just gives up, figuring if she can take it all, that it will then save her club sisters from harm. I'm worried today might be the one time I've been uneasy about. I'm so anxious about what we will find at the meeting area. Worse though is what or who we won't.

With my dark thoughts running away from me, I almost miss the bodies at the turnoff and the vehicles burning on either side. Goddamn, looks like a couple of flamethrowers came through here not too long ago. Noodles's phone rings once before he picks it up, disengaging the Bluetooth option. That in itself tells me he knows or thinks he knows something about what we are about to find.

I hear his one-word replies until he hangs up, throws the phone in his console, and grabs my hand. Oh, fuck no, I'm not going to be able to handle life if Zoey is not in it. Son of a bitch, we've been together since I was a teenager/young adult.

"Sweet Pea, regardless of what we find or see, you hang on tight to me no matter what. I got you, Maggie, you hear me? Now, from what Freak just told me he found out someone has been searching everything they can get their hands on about a certain Zoey Jeffries. No, don't go there, he's still trying to trace down who it is. But we now know this isn't about Panther as much as it is about your best friend. Or fuck, maybe both of them, I don't have a goddamn clue at this moment. Oh, Freak also did a satellite view. I ain't got an idea how he did that but from what he saw, which was three minutes ago, the SUV from your dad was still there and the front loader was trying to pick the motherfucking vehicle up."

Not that I do it very often, actually only when my life is about to implode, I throw up a prayer to God to keep my bestie safe and to let us get there in time. Also, to protect all of them, Panther, Avalanche, and

Omen. I want them to get out of this fucked-up situation walking and talking.

"Motherfucker, Maggie, look. Grab my phone, call Enforcer, tell him that these bastards almost have the SUV in the loader. We need some muscle right the fuck now."

Just as I send the call, I hear the roar of a shit ton of motorcycles and then I see them fly by me, some being my Devil's Handmaidens sisters and some of my dad's Intruders brothers. What the hell are they thinking? They won't stand a chance against that huge piece of machinery and all that goddamn gunfire. They'll be sitting ducks.

I hear a raspy "Hey" on the phone.

"Enforcer, Noodles said we need help, they almost have Zoey, Panther, Avalanche, and your brother Omen in the front loader. Whatever you can do, please do it now."

Noodles slams on the brakes and, without saying a word, jumps out and runs to the back of his truck, reaching into one of his boxes back there. After unlocking it, he pulls out a—holy mother of God— how the hell did he get his hands on a CS70 rocket launcher? My eyes never leave him as he prepares the weapon, then lifts it to his shoulder, aiming at what looks like the beast of a front loader machine. Dear Lord, please don't let him miss and hit the vehicle they are in.

The noise shocks me but I watch in total awe as

the missile looks to be straight on. When it makes contact with the farthest side of the loader that is away from my dad's vehicle, I let out a breath. Keeping my eyes in that general direction, I almost miss it but see one of the windows go down, right before first one then another leg comes out, then a long lean body. When I finally make out that it's Panther, I feel my breath stop halfway through my bronchial tubes and start a coughing gag, which unfortunately isn't totally quiet. That is until all hell breaks loose along with Satan's demon dogs.

First, Noodles lets another missile go that hits the loader, just as gunfire starts from behind my dad's SUV. When I look in that direction, I see some of my club sisters providing cover fire for Panther, Zoey, and Avalanche with Omen over his shoulders being held in a fireman's hold. All four are covered in blood so can't tell who or how badly they are injured. Just as I get ready to jump down from the truck, Noodles is in front of me, shaking his head. Then he points up for some ridiculous reason. Then I hear it...a goddamn motherfucking helicopter.

It starts to make sense as I see Enforcer hanging off the landing skid holding a Sig Sauer XM250. Just as he starts to fire, bodies come jumping out of the front loader as a bunch of huge trucks come barreling down from the back road with guns out the windows firing.

"Noodles, we have to do something."

"Sweet Pea, we are staying out of the line of fire. When they need our help, we will know. Trust me."

He pulls me close and as I put my head on his chest. I have that weird feeling I get sometimes when one of our trafficking missions is close to ending. It's a troubled emotion because of the unknown factor as to how it will end. Some I can read, while others seem to be one problem after another. That is the feeling I'm getting now.

Seeing Panther and Zoey almost to the line of cover, I cross my fingers, never taking my eyes off my bestie and her man. Avalanche, even with Omen over his shoulder, has my dad's brother's automatic rifle in his hand, firing behind him, trying to give the two people in front of him cover. That is until a bullet hits him high in the thigh and both he and Omen go down hard. We both hold our breath as first Panther then Zoey turn. Panther points to where our club sisters are holding the line then he runs back to his best friend. I watch Zoey look first to the line then her eyes seem to be searching the area, that is until they lock on me. I know before she even moves what she plans to do, and I scream her name, telling her not to do it.

She turns and follows Panther back to where the two men are struggling to get back on their feet. I know Zoey, or at the moment she is totally in the mindset of Shadow, will never leave those men to die. She slides next to Avalanche, takes one look at his leg, then whips her belt off, wrapping it around his thigh, tightening it until he roars. She looks up to Panther while grabbing the automatic rifle from Omen's hand. I look to Noodles in horror as it dawns on me what they are planning on doing. No fucking way.

With my man's attention on the scene in front of us, I slowly shift until his arm falls from my shoulders then I take off running, both of my Glocks in my hands firing at will. When my club sisters see me, they also stand and start to run into the gunfire. From Taz's rainbow hair to Heartbreaker's flaming red locks, every Devil's Handmaiden there is on the move to protect their sister Shadow. Then there are the twins holding back, one holding on to the Mossberg and the other with our MK16 with the grenade launcher attached. Peanut stayed behind too and seems to be the one responsible for keeping them in ammunition, even though she's hanging on to her Desert Eagle, firing when she can.

Watching, not believing my eyes, as Panther lifts Avalanche over his shoulders, one arm around his neck, the other around his knees as he struggles to keep his balance. I see him lift his head, eyes closed, and it takes a moment until I hear the chanting coming from both men. *Oh fuck, ignore it,* I tell myself. Got to get to Zoey, no matter what, even though I hear Noodles losing his ever-lovin' mind behind me.

Zoey and Omen are back-to-back, each with guns in their hands. She has the automatic and Omen leaning his weight against Zoey to probably stay on his feet has something I can't make out. He looks like he's in and out of it, probably a head injury with the blood pouring down his face. Just as I come around the curve, Taz, Wildcat, and Glory are at my flank. My VP pulls me by the collar, handing me something my mind can't make out until she pulls my hair, jerking me back. Motherfucker, that hurt.

Looking down I see it's a bulletproof vest, so I reach for it as I try to pick up speed, but she continues to hang on to me until I'm vested up. Taz and Wildcat, along with Rebel and Raven, have a head start so Glory and I take a quick second, looking around when I see a handful of men sneaking around the perimeter.

Before I can scream an alarm, I hear the chopper blades as Enforcer's hanging off, firing right at the group of men who don't stand a chance at all. By the time they look up, half of them are literally shot in two, with the others close to their last breaths. Turning, I take off running, not paying one motherfucking lick of attention to anything around me, my eyes glued to my bestie. I hear men screaming, some cussing, others—especially Noodles—and now my dad calling my name. I don't give a shit. Zoey has all my focus. She is all I have on my mind at this moment.

Hearing the whoosh before the grenade launcher releases one, the sound feels like it blows out my ear drums, for Christ's sake. Hearing Glory

"Motherfucking, cocksucking" our club twin sisters, I almost grin. I see that my sisters have reached Zoey and Omen. Raven pulls her backpack off, which I know is her medic bag.

Feeling like I'm about to have a frigging heart attack, I'm not even two feet away from Zoey when I slide toward her like I'm trying to steal a base at a softball game. Smashing into her side, she lets out a scream until she sees that it's me, then she shockingly pulls me close, hanging on for dear life. Every Devil's Handmaidens sister is firing their weapons as they form a circle around both Zoey and Omen, waiting for our reinforcements to arrive. No one turns or looks at our club enforcer as she holds on tightly, and only I feel the violent shakes racking through her body. And that will go to the grave with me because she's my bestie and that's what besties do for each other.

That is until I feel two pairs of hands grabbing each of my arms. One man is Noodles and the other is Panther. My man actually lifts me high in the air before crushing me to him, his mouth all over mine. Looking down, I see Panther handling Zoey very gently, whispering to her in his Navajo language while wiping her tears as she glares at him. Yeah, he's going to have to learn the two sides of her fast.

Again, I feel hands on me and before I can look, my dad's deep hoarse voice says, "Maggie" and that tells me everything he is feeling.

Looking up into the sky, I send up a thank-you prayer to whomever: God, Great Spirit, Mother Earth, Budda, or just the Universe. Oh, as much as I hate to admit it, to that bastard Enforcer too.

Today the good women and men won.

THIRTEEN
'PANTHER'

CHAHÓÓŁHÉÉL NAABAAHII T'ÁÁ SÁHI
DARK WARRIOR WALKING ALONE

Never being one who has a lot of patience when someone in my life is hurt, I'm pacing back and forth outside the waiting room and it's killing me. Didn't want to bring Avalanche or Omen to a hospital, but both Raven and Tank explained that my best friend might lose his leg, or even worse, not make it at all due to the amount of blood he's lost. After hearing that shit, Enforcer put both of them on the helicopter, no, Tank told me it was an Airbus EC145. Had no idea how two motorcycle clubs in the middle of Bumfuck, Montana were able to get their hands on a medical transport helicopter with all the bells and whistles, but I'm forever grateful. I think it has something to do with Tank's connections and the money Maggie got from her grandmother but not my business.

Hearing footsteps, I look up to see both Zoey and

Maggie making their way toward me. Behind them are a slew of men starting with Noodles and Tank, who are followed by Enforcer and like six or eight of the Intruders, all wearing their kuttes. Already sitting in the waiting area are all of the Devil's Handmaidens sisters, also wearing their colors. The women are here for our protection. Mine, Avalanche's, and Omen's, or that was what I have been told by Enforcer. Every one of the bikers is packing heat and not one doctor or nurse seems bothered by it. But again, this is Montana, their home ground.

When Zoey is next to me, she hesitantly grabs my hand, squeezing gently. Fuck that, I need to feel her closer, so I pull her tightly to my side, which has her wrapping her arms around my waist. We're both wearing scrubs though she's got her bloody kutte on top, along with the bracelet I gave her on her wrist, also with blood spattered on it. The blood on her kutte looks ridiculous, but I doubt a soul will say that directly to her.

As everyone gets comfortable, time seems to pass fucking slower than pouring molasses on a bowl of oatmeal. The only thing saving me from losing my goddamn mind is that Zoey is snuggled next to me in front of her club, not giving one fuck who sees. I take a second to soak that feeling in. We've been playing this game for a while now and this to me, even though this is a very sensitive time, feels good to have gotten this far with her. Yeah, selfish of me with my brother fighting for his life.

Just when I shut my eyes, I hear a door close and then chairs and bodies standing, when I open my eyes, I see two doctors hesitantly approaching our group of people.

"Okay, who's here for, well, he told me his name, but I can't remember it for the life of me. He goes by Avalanche? Before we put him out, he told me his brother is Panther, so which one of you is him?"

"His name is nitsaa yikah tsintah. I'm Panther and these are our family, so please what's going on and how's he doing? You didn't take his leg, did you? Talk, white coat."

I know that I sound like the ignorant Indian most accuse me of, but fuck, the guy is looking at me like a deer with the headlights in its face. A soft body presses next to me and I know who it is by the feel of her, and the way the doctor's face shows immediate shock.

"Doctor, how is Avalanche doing? You said you had to knock Big Bird out, so can you break it down for us and give us your best and worst diagnosis for not only him, but the other man we brought in. Name is Omen."

"I can only talk about Avalanche as I performed surgery on him. Dr. Davis behind me took care of Omen. The damage done was mainly to the upper thigh and it nicked his femoral artery. Thank God someone had the good sense to use their belt as a tourniquet. I'm thinking that might have been the reason he will keep his leg. Whoever has the medical background, you did good not keeping it on so tightly and slowly loosening and moving it. I had to do some internal and external stitching, and he's going to have a huge gouge in his thigh but should make a full recovery, if he listens to what he can and can't do. I'll turn it over to Dr. Davis."

Before he leaves, he walks closer, leans in, and says something to Zoey. She jerks back then looks to me before actually smiling at the good doctor. What the fuck?

"Zoey, what the hell was that about?"

"Seems like Avalanche's doctor loves tattoos and is covered from the neck down under his clothes. He just wanted to let me know that he wasn't being rude, just that what I did to my face he has always wanted to do to his. That's all, Panther, swear. Now let's find out how Omen is doing because once we see both, I need a shower bad and a handful of something for this horrific headache that's pounding the fuck outta my brain."

Zoey's VP must have overheard her as she tells us how Omen is and that he had a brain bleed, but they were able to take care of it. She tells the both of us that there is a car waiting to take us wherever we want to go, but to be prepared that we can't go anywhere going forward without our own bodyguards. That, I know is going to piss off Zoey, which it does, and the two women start to have words.

Well, until Tank comes by, grabbing Zoey by the upper arms, crushing her to him, and whispering in her ear. I see her shoulders slump then her head falls onto his huge as fuck chest. I almost don't believe my eyes when he turns and walks her away from everyone, but not before I see the shaking of her shoulders. Zoey showing emotion. Holy shit, that's a rare thing.

"Panther, thanks for having her back. I know she thinks she's a badass and all, but without you and the others she might not have made it back to us, and that would have killed me."

Looking down, I see Maggie's watery eyes and red cheeks. Yeah, this has been hard, I'm guessing, on the president of the Devil's Handmaidens. Hearing a commotion coming from the elevator, I see that young girl who could be Maggie's twin come running down the hall followed by a middle-aged woman also in a hurry.

"Auntie Zoey, fuck where's she at? Motherfuckers, where's my auntie at?"

Hearing Maggie softly chuckle, I know the kid is trying to raise Zoey's hackles. Hearing the shuffling of Tank, I turn to see him and my girl making their way back to our group. Hearing the noise, she's got her eyes on the older woman, who actually pushes the younger woman out of the way and pulls Zoey to her, swaying with her arms around her. Figuring this is a moment that should be private, most of us turn around and start to make our way to the seats in the waiting room. That is, except the young woman, arms at her hips, face turning pink.

"Momma Diane, okay, you had your time now it's my turn. Need to make sure my Auntie Zoey is okay."

Hearing a growl, I know that my woman isn't falling for it.

"Goddamn, prospect, calm the fuck down and remember who and what you are. Now, what is it you need to check out about me? I'm here, breathing, and standing on my own two feet, so what?"

Before Zoey can keep piling the shit on the girl's shoulders, she runs toward her aunt and almost jumps at her arms, around her waist.

"What the hell, Zoey? You told me you never take chances so were you prepared for how this went down today? Obviously not, two men are seriously injured, and your sexy as fuck man looks pissed as hell right now. Hey, that look for me, what'd I do?"

Shaking my head, I feel Maggie at my side with Noodles next to her. We move to one of the tables and sit down. My exhaustion is taking over, so I put my head in my hands, trying to take a moment to figure out what my next move will be. I know the kids I was trying to buy are lost to me now. That hits me hard. All I can do is hope that if they no longer walk this earth their parting was quick and painless.

Hearing some giggling, I glance up to see Hannah leaning into Zoey, a huge smile on her face. And my woman for once looks to be relaxed and even has a tiny grin on her own face. That in itself gives me the solace I need for the moment. Next, I need to see my brother's face to make sure he's okay.

* * *

Sitting at the bedside as Avalanche struggles to wake up from the anesthesia, it hits me that I never mentioned his addiction from years ago. Fuck, I hope this doesn't set him back; he's worked so goddamn hard.

"How long ago was he hooked? What? Don't look so surprised, that's kinda what I do, figure out people's secrets. It explains a lot about Big Bird, Panther. I'm going to go let the nurses' station know so they can try their best not to mess up his recovery. Be right back."

I turn to watch her walk away, confidence pouring off her. That's one of the things that has always attracted me to Zoey.

"Fuck, even now I'm in a hospital bed and all you two horn dogs can concentrate on is the attraction between y'all. Damn, brother, what the hell did they do to my leg? I do still have a leg, right, you didn't let them take my limb? Goddamn, my man, talk cat got your atsoo'?" *tongue*

Shaking my head, I lean over, grabbing his hand, giving it a squeeze before I just hold it and be. I want him to feel me and what is going through me. When he lifts his eyes, I see he's gotten it like I wanted him to.

"They had to take some muscle and shit from your thigh and thank God Zoey put that tourniquet on you, probably saved your leg. You're stitched internally and externally. Brother, sorry they had to use some drugs to put you under and think they have you on something right now for pain management. Totally forgot about your past, so Zoey is at the desk letting them know. And don't get your boxers ruffled because she figured it out herself. I never said a word. Tell me, Avalanche, honestly how are you doing brother? Is there pain and if so, what level? Do you need pain meds, should I call a nurse?"

"Damn, Panther, take a breath and let me grab a few, 'kay? I'm okay and, yeah, I feel the drugs in my system, would appreciate them starting to lower the amount as soon as possible. I can take pain, not a problem, as you well know. Being a prisoner of war, there really isn't much that would hurt me to the extent I'd want to be using drugs, even if they are legal."

As we bullshit back and forth, I take a second to thank the Great Spirit for making sure nitsaa yikah tsintah not only made it through his surgery but will hopefully continue to find his *Hózhó balance and beauty*. This is a prayer I've had for my brother since we were rescued from that POW camp.

Hearing a soft knock at the door, I turn just as Zoey opens it, looking in. Seeing me first then her eyes shift to Avalanche, and she gives him a huge smile, probably the first sincere one ever.

"Thank God, Big Bird, you're awake. Need anything? I can go grab a nurse, just let me know. Oh, told them about you know and they are going to put a call to your doctor."

The room is suddenly really quiet and has a deep feeling to it. Turning, I see Avalanche studying Zoey as she watches him. Then to my utter shock, he goes for it.

"Zoey don't have any words to let you know what you did for me means. I know I give ya a ton of shit, but you saved my life, Nizhoni skull *anii'*. I owe you and if Panther hasn't explained our culture to you, we take it very seriously when someone goes above and beyond to help us. For a biligaana *white* woman, you did good. Aho, Zoey, Aho." *thank you*.

Zoey leans down and first kisses his head then his cheek, whispering in his ear. His eyes open wide with shock then he laughs until he holds his leg up high.

"Enough, skull anii', it hurts my wound to laugh."

With that all between the three of us is yah ta hey *good*.

FOURTEEN
'SHADOW'
ZOEY

Glaring at the doorknob, I can feel my anxiety rising with every breath I take. Goddamn it, why is this happening, especially now? My body has gone through the act of sex so many times I can't even count all of them. Yeah, very few sexual encounters throughout my life were consensual. And this one I truly want, especially since it's with Panther. After visiting with both Avalanche and Omen, we spoke to both Maggie and Pops who agree to a meeting tomorrow afternoon.

When we get back to Panther's house, his men are walking around the house and three of the Devil's Handmaidens sisters joined them, helping with the guarding of his ranch home. Raven is inside of the house for additional protection, with Enforcer and Wrench from the Intruders.

I came upstairs and spent at least thirty minutes in

a hot as fuck shower, trying to wash the day away. By the time my head clears, my entire body's a dark shade of pink. Wrapping myself up in a huge bath towel, I walk to the sink and when my eyes see my reflection in the mirror I am shocked at what I see there. A skeleton-faced woman who looks afraid of her own shadow, no pun intended.

After brushing my teeth and combing and braiding my hair, I drop the towel and rub in some of my Victoria's Secret Bare Vanilla lotion that a few of my club sisters gave me for my last birthday. I reach for my bedtime sleeping shirt, which is actually Panther's. It has a dreamcatcher on the front, which he told me is a symbol to help me sleep better and keep the bad spirits out of my dreams.

Now I'm standing at the door, terrified to reach down and open it. For fuck's sake, it's not like Panther is one of the jagoff men from my past, who took what they wanted, no matter what. Suddenly I'm dizzy, so I lean against the wall while my head fogs up. What the hell is going on? We ate, so that can't be what's bothering me?

Then I hear that voice on the phone when Panther was setting up the meet. My skin gets clammy and it's getting harder to take a breath. How did I not recognize it? There is no way they found me after all of this time. Panther said he's been working with them for some time, how could they have put two and two together and come up with us being a couple, even though we aren't together like a regular one.

Not even giving it a thought, I rip the door open, letting it bang against the wall and run right into Panther's chest. His arms automatically wrap around me as my body starts to tremble.

"Zoey, what's wrong, Nizhoni? You're shaking, little one. Talk to me. Come on sit with me."

He leads us to the sofa off to the side of the room, pulling me down, right onto his lap. Feeling his body's warmth surround me, it keeps my demons held at length for the time being. I need to let him know what I just figured out.

"Panther, something came to me just now. You have to listen to everything and try not to get angry or judge me."

He pulls me closer, breathing in my hair and then my neck.

"God, you always smell like a new morning filled with some vanilla. You smell like a warm, sweet powder with a bit of wood and soft cacao. I love your scent, Zoey. I know what you do for the Devil's Handmaidens club, and I've never judged you, why would I start now? Nothing, hey, look at me. There is nothing you can share with me, Zoey, that will change how I feel about you. So, come on, get it off your chest so we can deal with whatever it is and move forward."

"Something's been bothering me since you

received that first call from those assholes who are your associates. I didn't even put two and two together until I was having an anxiety attack, trying to open the bathroom door. The voices on the phone of the contact and then the boss I've heard before. Why it didn't penetrate immediately I've no clue, but something finally opened the locked memories in my head. Hang on, Panther, this is not a good fairy story about my childhood."

I take a few deep breaths then lean back into him, my back to his front. His hands wrap under my breasts, holding me tightly to him as his legs separate so they are on either side of me. *He's such a protector*, I think to myself.

"As I kind of hinted at, my childhood was beyond a living hell. My parents were demons from hell. Both were hooked on drugs and booze. They both were prostitutes, from what I found out later in life. One day, my dad just disappeared for a while until the police came to tell my mother, who was pregnant yet again, that they found his body tortured and left in an abandoned building. Looked like he was living there for a while. When she gave birth, one day she had the baby with her and the next it was gone, and she was strung out big time. As I got older, and I mean, when I got back from child services after my mom fooled them, she started having men to the dump trailer we lived in. When that would happen, or she'd have her parties, I made a place under the trailer behind the skirting, I think they call it. Over time had it set up real nice, took some wood people threw out and put it up so no one would find me. Then I had blankets, pillows, and my favorite two stuffed animals with me. Even was able to have some packaged food I stole from the store kept in an old Tupperware of my mother's.

"Not sure how but think one of my mom's johns must have saw me crawling under one time and told the bitch. She threatened me, said she'd take all my stuff, throw it away, and leave me to sleep outside with nothing. Or I get with the program and let her friends visit with me. Even as a kid I knew this wasn't right, but what could I do? It started slow and all they did was make me dance around or sit on their laps. But that changed one night when they were all drunk and high as fucking kites. All I remember was the pain then being dumped outside. The old lady next door called the cops, who then called an ambulance. I was in the hospital for over, I think, ten days. After I was released, never went back to my mom's but to every hellhole there was in foster care."

I can feel Panther's intense rage coursing through his body, but he doesn't take it out on me. He kisses my neck and tells me to keep going, so I do.

"When I was like, don't really know, maybe twelve or thirteen, got pregnant. My foster parents actually wanted me to have the baby so they could sell it on the black market, but there was no way I was bringing a baby into the dark as fuck world I was living in. Since I had no money or anyone to turn to at school, I went to the library and looked up how to lose a baby. I tried starving myself and drinking alcohol. When that didn't work; I shoved a hanger up there and though it worked, the baby was lost, so was a part of my heart. I lost something I could have loved and would have loved me back.

"My foster parents were beyond pissed and beat me to an inch of my life so when I could, I ran away. Eventually the cops found me hiding out and brought me back to foster care. Went from home to home, being used and abused in ways you can't even imagine. That is until, shit, I was maybe fifteen. The couple who had me also had like ten other kids. They threw parties that we worked, and their friends were animals. One of the guys was trying to rape one of the little girls and when I saw him, lost my mind. I went right after him and I was covered in blood, and he was beyond fucking dead which was too good for his ass. It wasn't too much after that I was sold to an older man, who lived in the country in a huge house.

"I was kept in a dog cage with a bowl of water and some mush with bugs in it once a day to eat. I shat myself and pissed on puppy pads. My muscles started to atrophy because they didn't let me out and smelled like death. One day, this older man was walking by running his fingers over the top of the cages, and there were a ton of them, and stopped at mine. For some reason he was beyond pissed and told one of the assholes to get me out, clean me up, and put me in a girl's bedroom. From that moment on, I was treated like a princess. Well, until I wasn't. He was a sadistic pedophile. There wasn't anything he didn't do to me and if he didn't do it; he watched as his bodyguards did. One night, they forgot to handcuff me to the bed, and I jumped out of the second story bedroom window. Even with a sprained ankle, I ran and ran until the morning sun started to come up. I managed to live in the woods in a run-down cabin for a few weeks, living off berries and some fish I managed to catch from the stream.

"I was going back to get the rest of the kids out and kill those motherfuckers when I met Goldilocks, and the rest is history. I'm trusting you, Panther, with my past. I've not even shared the entire gruesome tale with my bestie. Please keep it between us for now."

I feel him nodding so I continue.

"The voice who called you was his number one guy/bodyguard who manages everything for him. His name is Dino and, somehow, he's part of the bloodline. The boss's voice in the background is a man named or who goes by Dario, I believe. He had two teenage sons he was grooming also to take over his enterprise. Well, from what my memory can recall. Like I told you, being starved and dehydrated, not to mention the physical and mental abuse, I was out of it most of the time. On other instances when they wanted to offer me up to someone of importance, they would drug the fuck outta me. This way whatever pervert or freak who bought time with me got to do exactly what they wanted."

Panther is now pacing back and forth, his shoulders tense. I know my words are putting him in a dark mindset, but fuck, I've lived in that world forever, my whole goddamn life. That is until Goldilocks entered and shined her sunshine on my darkness. She makes me want the things I never would ever let enter my consciousness before. I don't blame her actually, sometimes I get a bit envious of her.

Not that her life is perfect, far the fuck from it, but she always seems to find something good in every goddamn situation. Even when the worst happens when we are breaking up a trafficking circuit, and there are no survivors, she makes sure to find a positive in a room of darkness. That's why I'm still here because my bestie brings sunshine into my life every time she walks into it.

"Zoey, how many times am I going to have to tell you not to be embarrassed. We are just talking. Nothing, especially from back then, is happening right now. Come on, please try and relax, beautiful. I don't want to cause you any more pain than you already are in, so lie on the bed, I'll rub your back. Hey now, don't give me that look, Zoey. I said just your back, remember I know how you like to have a good back rub. Maybe you can relax enough to doze off for a bit."

Intently watching his face, I can see his sincerity. How in the hell did someone like me, a fucked-up mess, get a guy who is stable and emotionally strong? No matter what I tell him, he never falters and stays right by my side. I remember the first time I thought we could have sex. As soon as his fingers moved past the band of my panties, I broke out in a cold sweat and before I could help myself, my hands formed fists and then I attacked him, and not in a good way. He ended up with a black eye and a bruise on his cheek. Knowing I owed him an explanation, I gave him as little as possible, just to move forward. Fuck, since I've told him as much as I have tonight, might as well finish it up.

"Panther, instead of that back rub, even though it sounds like the shit, do you have a few more minutes? There are a few things I'd like to share with you. Think you're up to it?"

"Zoey, for you I'll always have time or if not, I'll make some. Come on, let's lie down and get comfortable. Then you can tell me whatever you think you have to but, Zoey, not sure how many more times I've got to tell ya, there's nothing you can say that is going to push me away. That I can promise."

As we make our way to the bed, I cross my fingers behind my back, hoping he's telling the truth.

FIFTEEN
'RAVEN'

Fuck, I'm exhausted but when one of us gets an order from our prez, Tink, we make sure to do whatever it takes for her. She doesn't ask for anything usually, so I'm dead set on getting her as much information as I possibly can get my hands on.

Hearing a knock right before my door opens, I turn to see Heartbreaker coming in with a tray of food and a coffee carafe, along with a sugar and cream set. Her eyes are on the floor as she approaches my desk but is smart enough to put it on the small table in the corner.

"Um, Raven, I thought you might want something to eat. From what the twins said, you've been going at it all day so thought this was a way I could contribute and help. I'll come back later to pick it up and if you need more coffee or your usual energy drinks, just text me, I'll be up, probably in the hall."

I watch her the entire time and she never raises her eyes, just keeps them down with her head tilted to one side. She's finally almost all healed from the beatdown she received from Shadow. She's lucky to be breathing actually, from what I heard. If Glory wasn't right outside the door, this club sister might be six feet under right now.

"Hey, Heartbreaker, look at me, sister."

She shakes her head, so I lean over, grabbing her left hand, which is still bandaged but not as bad as her right one. Her head shoots up and her eyes are glassy, not from any drugs but from emotions.

"Sister, we all make mistakes. Don't let that one thing be what everyone remembers you by. You are more than your addiction and weakness. Now is the time to suck it up, sister, and step up to the plate. Our club is so stretched and with all this shit going on with Shadow, we're vulnerable without her strength. You're smart, Heartbreaker, figure out how to be indispensable. I've been told since you can't waitress you've been doing a lot of the bussing and clean up with Peanut. Well, you're working for her now that she got the promotion and from what I'm hearing, you're doing a great job."

Wiping the tears from her eyes, she shakes her head at me.

"Nothing I do, Raven, will ever change the fact I betrayed our club and more importantly, my president. I'm beyond shocked that Tink even talks to me. And Hannah acts like nothing has happened and she of all people knows how weak I am. I left that poor child there. Fuck, I'm a goddamn loser. All of you and our club would be better without me, I should just put my gun in my mouth and pull the trigger."

Shooting out of my chair, I push her toward the wall until her back hits it. Getting in her face, I try to catch my breath.

"Never say that again. Delilah, yeah, that's right, your given name, sister. This is serious as fuck stuff. Maybe you'll hear me now. D, life is about doing good and bad. They balance each other out. Think about it, if you hadn't fucked shit up Tink might never have found Hannah at all. So quit eating your humble pie and move your ass. Never let an opportunity pass. Heard that from Momma Diane when I first came and prospected."

Grabbing and pulling her close, I pat her back and try to let her know she's important to me and our club. Yeah, she majorly fucked up but it's not the end of the world. Most of her fear is from Shadow and what she did. I get both sides but anyone who fucks with Tink will always get our enforcer in their face, no doubt. Heartbreaker is lucky to be alive and breathing because usually when Shadow gets you in her grip, you are carried out and dumped into a hole six feet deep. That is after a hurt of pain.

"Now, sister, want to thank you for thinking about

me. I'm starved, and yeah, that was my stomach growling. I can't wait to dig in and the coffee will also help. If you're bored later, come back with some coffee. I'll take a break and we can talk more. I'm always here for you. Never forget that. We are part of the Devil's Handmaidens MC, Heartbreaker. We made it through the prospecting and all that bullshit. Never forget that you're a member. A sister. Now get, got work to do."

She gives me a small smile then walks out, closing the door behind her. Back to work for me.

* * *

Son of a bitch, my back is cramping up like crazy. I know the fuck better but when I get involved in trying to find shit out, time escapes me. Trying to stand up is painful as fuck but need to get my circulation back to working order. Leaning over, I save the document I've been working on. Don't want to lose all that work because of my own stupidity. I grab the open water bottle on my desk and start walking back and forth in the room to get the blood flowing through my lower limbs. Not sure how Tink knew to have me research the little information she had, but damn, she hit a gold mine. Doubt either Shadow or Panther knows what they've gotten involved with.

Hearing an alarm go off on my computer, all thoughts of my pain immediately disappear as I quickly sit my ass down, just as boxes start opening up all over my computer screen. There is no goddamn, motherfucking way someone would be able to hack my system. I'm not conceited at all, but I'm that good. Realizing someone is putting up a smokescreen to try while doing their damnedest to get in, I smirk to myself then start pounding on one of the three keyboards in front of the three thirty-two-inch monitors. As I rotate between each keyboard and monitor, I feel the thrill of the hunt take over.

Ever since I became a full-fledged member of the Devil's Handmaidens MC and their IT person, I've always taken extra care to protect what is ours. The stuff I store here, and off site is PHI, better known as protected health information. We dismantle trafficking circuits and rescue victims, so yeah, we keep records for documentation and court cases to make sure those motherfuckers stay in jail for a long time. Or until they have a planned or unplanned accident.

Getting the asshole's IP address, I immediately try to find the location they are programing from. It pings off of a couple towers which is normal up here in Buttfuck, Montana. As I wait for that information, I pick up my phone, find the name, and hit it.

"Hello."

Hearing Heartbreaker's hoarse sleepy voice, for a brief second I feel bad, then realize this is serious shit that's heading our way.

"Hey, sister, it's me. I need a huge favor. You're good to drive, right? Need you to ride out to Tink's with information I'm going to give you. Take one or two other Devil's Handmaidens prospects with. Got a feeling we have eyes on us now. Ya got to get moving now though. Yeah, I'll get it ready, no worries. Thanks, Heartbreaker, don't want to use a phone, text, or email, not sure who's watching or listening externally."

Hearing the sound I use when the search is over, I turn to look at it, shocked at what I see. No goddamn way, that's not even possible. How in the ever-lovin' fuck is someone transmitting from our survivors' bunkhouse, trying to worm their way into my system.

Throwing in a flash drive, my fingers fly over the keyboard as I try to get myself together. Reaching into my desk, I pull out two automatics with their cases. One goes on my belt the other is a shoulder holster. Next in the closet I feel around for my bulletproof vest, which I put on then cover it with my kutte. My gut is telling me we need to go in silent and fast, so that's what we will do.

The knock at the door comes right when I'm finishing up, so I shout a, "Come in."

Heartbreaker, Kitty, and Peanut walk in. I see

Dotty, Dani, and Kiwi waiting in the hallway. Damn, thank God Heartbreaker read between the lines.

"Fuck, we got trouble, sisters. Someone put a shoutout to Shadow, think she's at Panther's ranch. Son of a bitch, what is that, like forty or fifty minutes from Tink's? Well, it is what it is. Someone has been trying to hack into our club system and I caught them. That's the good news, the bad news is I've pinned them down to our ranch in the survivors' building. Which is a hop, skip, and jump from where Tink and Noodles are."

Hearing the three in the hallway move in closer, I look up to see them all waiting. And they are prepared with their own bulletproof vests on, locked and loaded.

"Sisters, we're gonna have to go in quiet but fast as hell. Kitty put a call in to my brother, Ollie, see if he can get some of his ex-military folks over there to meet us before we go in. Dani, you call Enforcer, let him get word to Tank. Just make sure they know this is going to be on the down-low. No noise, so no loud ass pipes, don't care, tell them to ride in a cage. And use a club landline. Those I've checked, not sure if they can hack into the cell phones.

"Peanut, go get the box truck started and warm it up, will ya? Make sure it is loaded with our usual weapons, please. Kiwi, grab some extra vests and night goggles, along with a few extra boxes of ammunition and clips. We meet out back in five minutes, don't be late or we'll leave your ass here."

Hearing boots hitting the floor, I grab the drive, stuffing it in the inside pocket of my jeans. Then I push another one in and repeat what I just did. When that finishes, I pull that out, secure my system, arm it with every single wall I have, then shut everything down, and move out to the main area of the clubhouse.

With us between our missions, we all ended up here tonight after the situation with Shadow. Some to chill, others looking for the camaraderie that comes after a bloodbath. Thank God our injuries were minor. Tank had a few of his brothers who had blood drawn, but nothing too serious. Well except poor Omen. But when your adrenaline starts to drop, you need to do what works best for you and most of the club sisters needed to be here together.

When I hit the bar, Heartbreaker is fixing a few to-go mugs so when I sit, she slides one to me. I grab her hand and shove the flash drive between her fingers, making a fist.

"No matter what happens, you make sure that Tink gets either the one you're carrying or grab the one off me if I'm down. It's in my inside jeans pocket in front. I'm trusting you, sister, so don't let me down, got it?"

She stares at me, mouth slightly open, like she's in shock then nods vigorously.

"Um, thanks, Raven, this means the world. I won't let you down, swear to Christ, sister."

"I know that Heartbreaker, that's why that drive is in your fist and no one else's. I have total faith in you, never forget that. We better move our asses before all shit breaks loose at the ranch. I pray to God we aren't too late."

SIXTEEN
'SHADOW'
ZOEY

Lying next to Panther, for once I'm not ready to jump outta my own skin. He has that effect on me, always has. He's holding me close, and I have a hand on his chest. Even that first time in the tattoo shop, I can almost swear he walked in with a light surrounding him. And fuck, I wasn't drunk or high at the time. Thought it was the sun or the way the hippie bitch decorated the shop.

Since then, we'd bump into each other mainly there at the shop. Probably didn't even have a full conversation, just a few words dropped during our tats. My eyes could see how drop-dead gorgeous he was, but he was never gonna be mine. Where he was actually beautiful; I was the devil's daughter and the two would never blend.

That night when I was out riding and needed a minute, I pulled over. Never did I expect anyone to stop, let alone Panther. But he did make sure I was okay. And since I'd connected with him when Taz and I went to that large animal auction, for some reason that night we started to talk and, as they say, one thing led to another. I didn't want him to know how much he was affecting me, so my badass bitch came out. Panther never let any of my anxiety, panic attacks, or just me being plain downright rude get in his way of burrowing into my heart. Not sure I'll ever tell him how much of me he owns.

So, me wanting to make sure he has the story of all that is me, I finally feel like I can share the rest. Taking a deep breath, I let it out and start.

"I told you the part where I was sold by my fucking mother to her drug dealer. That asshole was a total dick, and I'll never regret making him one of my first kills when I was older and wiser. When he trafficked me at first, thought that I'd been saved by the old fucker but then I realized I just switched one hell for another. His boys were demons, as was the old man. When they started selling me to whoever had the cash, there were no rules, Panther. The buyers did whatever, whenever, however. And they didn't care if it was one or ten, as long as they paid the asking price."

I take a minute because the next part is the hardest to get out. I've never talked about this to anyone close to me, only the doctors and a few therapists over the years. Well, that was when I still thought I could be whatever is considered 'normal.' Now I know differently.

"One night, a group of men bought me for a party they were having, along with a few other of the girls and two boys. It started out like all those strange as fuck parties. We were serving appetizers in barely any clothes as the men started drinking and doing drugs. By this time in the game, I'd learned when the party took a turn to make sure that my ass was somewhere else. Bathroom, kitchen, outside, wherever it I could be safe. Didn't work this time because these bastards had a plan in place.

"First up was one of the guys. Not sure what they gave him, but he was pretty out of it. When they all surrounded him on the coffee table, I felt the change in the room. They became predators and he was the prey. At first, I had no idea what they were doing to him to make that boy scream so loud. When I took a chance and got closer, holy fuck, I couldn't believe my eyes. They were circumcising him right there. Blood was squirting everywhere but that wasn't the worst. They were raping him at the same time. My brain took a quick second but when it hit me what was going to happen to all of us, I turned quickly and started to make my way out of the room. That is until the doors closed and were locked from the outside. Trapped inside with a bunch of sadistic motherfucking deviant maniacs. One night that changed the course of my life. Yeah, before this happened, I thought my life was fucked up. After what they did, I realize that evil was very real, and money made people think they could do whatever they wanted to whomever they could buy.

"Out of the seven of us who went there only four came out alive. Well barely. One of the guys and two of the women died that night, and no one gave a rat's ass. They actually just threw them in an open hole in the ground with some acid on top of the bodies. I prayed like never before that they were actually dead. We were thrown away like garbage. But the damage was done. To be honest, Panther, I've never enjoyed sex, as you well know. I mean really enjoyed it like most people do. I know you're probably thinking *what the fuck*, right?"

Glancing up, I see how confused he is looking down at me, I give it to him.

"Panther, have you ever wondered why we've never fucked? Yeah, you've gone down on me just like I've blown you. Also, you've used your fingers on me a couple of times and I've given you plenty of hand jobs. But never penetration, well, not vaginally. I've been surprised that you never asked me why I offer anal. Not many women do, if the talk around the clubhouse tells me anything. And the Devil's Handmaidens sisters aren't wilting little flowers. They've all got a story that follows them around. Well, here it is. That night not only did they sexually abuse us, but they took it a step further by physically hurting us. I mean by cutting, burning, branding, just to name a few. They wanted to see how much a human being could take before either passing out or, I guess, dropping dead. For me, I never made a sound through all their depraved torture. Until the one jagoff came at me first with a large knife. At first, I had no clue what he was going to do 'til they held me down. When he penetrated me with it, the pain is something I've never experienced since. But, and for some reason don't know why, I never screamed. Not once. I guess when the bleeding was too much, he then took a warmed-up curling iron and performed a sort of sick cauterizing to stop the bleeding."

When Panther pulls me on top of him, I tense up until I look into his eyes. I've never seen them so dark and with so much emotion.

"Nizhoni, my God, woman, that you survived is a miracle. I didn't ask or pressure you, Zoey, because I knew one day we would be right where we are now. If we can't or you never want to have me penetrate you, we will find other ways to satisfy each other. I'm looking for a life partner, beautiful. Someone to share my good and bad days with while claiming their nights to sleep next too. A woman who is able to take care of herself but strong enough to let me, because she owns every beat of my heart. Will understand that, even though I love this ranch, my life's mission is to rid the world of predators who prey on the young and weak. Someone who will have my back and never have to question where they stand in my life because they will be beside me until my last breath comes from my lips and I make my last journey to the Great Spirit. As a Navajo, we believe that there are four classifications within men and women. There is in each gender a masculine and a feminine. With you my beautiful, Zoey, you are an enigma. I say that with my heart because you are both a masculine and feminine female, equally split down the middle. Neither is stronger than the other. In our culture, we also believe there are three genders. A woman begins the first gender, a man second, and the last is what we call a nádleehí, who is born as a male person but functions in the role of a girl in early childhood and in the role of a woman in adulthood. I share this because I believe my culture is way more open-minded than yours will ever be."

Listening to Panther as he speaks his words in that deep soothing voice of his, it feels like my shattered heart and soul are slowly coming back together. It scares the living crap out of me because that means things are changing. And I don't do well with change, fuck, Goldilocks is always saying that. My head is beyond fucked up because Panther didn't react the way I thought he would. Like a normal man would.

"So, what you're telling me is that nothing I've said bothered you and you're good maybe never having normal regular sex? I mean, I've done the deed before but usually after way too many drinks.

The doctors have told me that I'm healed but from what I recall every time I've tried, it's been way too painful. Oh, and you're also able to live with what I do, which is kinda freaking me out, Panther. I'm an evil, bad person, for Christ's sake. The Devil's Handmaidens MC is a one-percent club and even though we try to balance our biker lives with our rescuing of the survivors, sometimes it's not nearly even ground. And just so you know, I'll never leave Goldilocks or the club. They're my life and even though they piss me the fuck off, the thought of not being part of them, you might as well put a bullet in my skull right now."

"Beautiful, if you haven't learned by now, I'll take you any way I can get you, then you're not the smart as fuck woman I thought you to be. I'm not all good either, Zoey. We both walk the path of light and dark. Maybe together we can balance each other, or at least prevent the other from falling into the pits of hell some of the time."

Not sure what to say or do, I just gaze into his eyes, which show me everything he's feeling. One thing about Panther, he's never hidden his emotions from me. I, on the other hand, have given him nothing. Or what I thought I could give him without committing. Just that word makes me want to puke. He must see something in my eyes because he leans down and very gently presses his lips to first one eye then the other. Down my cheek, across to the other, and then rubs his nose next to mine. Hearing him hum softly brings a smile to my face.

When he feels that, he opens his eyes, penetrating my soul with a stare I feel throughout my body down to my toes. When his lips touch mine, I immediately open and he devours everything I give him. He tastes like a warm smoky night. Also, a slight minty flavor, probably from one of those sprigs of green he's always chewing on. And his natural scent is musky, which has always drawn me to him. I don't think Panther even wears cologne, maybe it's his shower gel or shampoo plus his deodorant. I do know most of what he uses is generally leaning toward the natural as much as possible.

His tongue is taking a leisure tour of my mouth and lips. He's kissing, sucking, licking, and nibbling. The more he kisses my mouth the more he hums, which is relaxing me. His hands are around me, not holding me tightly but kind of like a whisper that I know is there but isn't overbearing, grabby, or invasive.

I take my hands, putting them on his head, reaching for his braid. I prefer his hair free and wild. Carefully, so as not to tangle it, I unbraid his hair spreading it out all around him. Raising my head so I can memorize this moment in my mind, my breath stops. He's beyond gorgeous and those forest-green eyes are looking into my soul. Feeling desire flow through my blood, I'm shocked as I feel between my legs getting wet. *Holy fuck, no way,* I think to myself.

"No way what, Zoey? You okay?"

Shit, I said that out loud, for Christ's sake. I lower my head for just a second but when I raise my head, his eyes are twinkling. Oh, son of a bitch, somehow he knows the effect he's having on me.

"Nizhoni, don't be embarrassed but I can smell your desire and it's making my mouth water. Just the thought that you want me as much as I want you has my cock harder than ever before. See for yourself. Touch me, Zoey."

Between his words and the look he is giving me, for once I'm all in. As I push my hand between us, I reach down and feel the bulge in his pants. Just when I go to pop open the top button of his jeans, both phones start ringing.

What the fuck?

SEVENTEEN
'TINK'
MAGGIE/GOLDILOCKS

Feeling the tingling starting to subside, I sigh and snuggle closer to Noodles. We're both covered in a sheen as he worked me over good tonight. Probably because he knows my mind wasn't going to shut off, even after we talked to both Zoey and Panther. I'm worried sick about my bestie, especially since it seems she's been keeping quite a lot of secrets from me. What the fuck, Zoey? Since that night in the woods, after she got over herself, neither of us have kept anything from the other. For Christ's sake, I shared everything when Noodles and I first started and all the shit that came up with that situation.

"Sweet Pea, you good? Need anything? I'm going to go grab some water, you want one?"

"Yeah, Noodles, bring me up one of my flavored Propels. Need to replenish my electrolytes because you plum wore me out. I'll need more than a minute,

Noodles, if you're even thinking of a second go. Just a friendly warning."

I watch as he leans in, kissing the top of my head, then gets out of bed, making sure the blankets stay on me. He goes as far as to tuck me in. What a sweetie. Then the best part of the Noodles show. My man has an ass. Firm, high, round, and thick. Watching him walk naked as the day he was born to where he dropped his jeans, my mouth waters as he grabs and pulls them up, going commando. Fuck, everything he does makes me hot. Something has to be wrong with me.

"Like the show, Maggie? Next time should I dance a little, what do you and Shadow always say, something about your moneymaker? Think this could be my moneymaker?"

With that he slightly turns, cracking his own ass cheek. I can't help but laugh as he's always goofing around and making me feel good and so alive. I've not giggled or laughed this much in forever. Now it's all the time. Even after a day like we just had.

"Be back in a few. Don't move from that bed, Maggie, if you want to clean up, I'll help you. Just relax and enjoy the afterglow."

Chuckling, he opens our door then quickly closes it. Even though this is my ranch, other Devil's Handmaidens members and prospects stay here or in the cabins surrounding the main house. You never know who you might bump into when you leave your private sanctuary. Like the time I walked right into Glory and two of my dad's brothers coming out of one of the guest rooms. Talk about embarrassed. Not the asshole Intruders but Glory and me.

Snuggling into the soft blanket, I close my eyes, replaying the last hour or so in my mind's eye. Damn, I can almost feel my body getting excited and wet, but fuck I'm too tired. He did wear me out. All I can think about is getting a good night's sleep now that Zoey is okay.

Just when I'm about to fall into a deep sleep, something jerks me awake. I look around, no one's in the room but I feel something, not sure what. I'm just about to get out of bed when the door opens and Noodles instantly puts his fingers to his lips, shaking his head. Oh, son of a bitch, now what?

I watch as he pulls a small black box from his back pocket and starts running it up and down the walls, around the furniture. I know what he's doing because Raven does it every time we meet for Chapel. It's to make sure there are no listening devices in the room. But, and that's a huge but, how the fuck would someone get into our bedroom to put one in? Since all that shit that went down here on the ranch, because of Buck, everything has been upgraded. That was Zoey and Raven's demand, so as a club we did it. The main house, each and every cabin, and even the survivor building. Though in their area, cameras are only in the common rooms, each bedroom suite is never recorded.

When Noodles is satisfied, he moves to me, pulling me close.

"Goddamn, I hate to be the one to say this again but, Sweet Pea, we have a problem. Just had one of your dad's brothers here, who was ordered to come speak to me personally. Raven being Raven kept at it and found something, so she went and traced the IP address, and you'll never guess where it's coming from."

I raise my eyebrows, anger flowing through my body.

"Do not say the location is anywhere on this ranch, Noodles. I'll lose what's left of my fucked-up mind. Jesus Christ, if I had any luck besides bad, I'd shit myself. What do you know? Where are they? What's the plan?"

As I'm demanding answers, I'm already out of bed, his T-shirt thrown back on the mattress. Grabbing my jeans, I pull them over my boy briefs then reach for my bra, well, until two huge arms wrap me up from behind.

"No, Maggie, ain't happening again. This time you listen first before you run headlong into a situation you can't control. Your club is on the way and from what I've been told, locked and loaded. Shadow has been called back, along with Panther and his crew. Guess your dad called Ollie and the bunch over there.

In about twenty or so minutes, this ranch is going to be crawling with so many badasses it's going to be comical to watch. They'll be bumping into each other scratching their asses, not sure what to do. And we both know the men won't want to listen to any of the Devil's Handmaidens sisters because, yeah duh, they're women. I'm sure a fight or two will break out. Whoever is on this property will probably and most likely have a stroke or heart attack from laughing before any of us can reach them. Is that how you see this going? I mean, our luck has sucked so why change now, right?"

I'm giggling before he even finishes with the images in my head of two motorcycle club members, ex-military from Ollie's sanctuary, and whatever the fuck Panther, Avalanche, and his guys are from. When Noodles starts explaining what Dad said might work, I just listened for a change. This has something to do with Zoey and Panther, I can feel it deep down. My gut says it's particularly about Zoey because they are on this ranch, which is her home. What the hell they're looking for I have no goddamn idea, but whatever it is they are not getting my bestie, no matter what. Tiny and mighty is what they call me, and for Zoey I'd fight the fucking goddamn devil, so bring it.

As Noodles waits for me, I grab my guns, knives, and Kevlar before covering everything with my kutte. Goddamn, all we ever wanted to do, Zoey and I, is help victims become survivors. Seems each day is getting more and more complicated. And it's not even with the trafficking circuits we are busting up and the assholes who, if they are left breathing, are thrown in jail for life, usually that's how bad their crimes against society are. Nope, all this shit is personal and it's from our members' baggage that we are carrying.

I'm going to need to have a serious fucking sit-down with Zoey, which I know she's going to hate as I've been asking her for years, but I need to get all the details on her horrific past because I have a feeling it's back to bite her right in the ass.

* * *

Driving in Noodles's truck with the lights off, I'm fucking shocked at all the vehicles we are passing by. Not to mention all the trucks and SUVs that are following behind us. Every time we pass a group of vehicles, one flashes its light at us. Not sure how this is going to go, but I'm guessing Dad and Noodles know what they are doing.

When we approach the building in question, I see the Devil's Handmaidens box truck and passenger van. Most of my club sisters are either sitting inside of the back of the truck or the van seats with the doors open.

"Sweet Pea, no matter what, you keep that fine ass right behind me, you hear me? If by some chance I go down, either you go down too or get to Tank or Enforcer. Got me, Maggie?"

"Noodles, who the fuck do you think you're talking to? I'm not a stay-at-home mom who drives her kids to soccer in a minivan, but a badass one-percenter of a motorcycle club. And to top it off, I'm the fucking president of said club. I get you're worried but I've survived this long, soldier boy, with the help of my club sisters, so knock it off, asswipe. I don't need the macho shit, okay?"

He chuckles, which pisses me off more, but before I can say a word a huge black beast of a truck blows past us, dust and gravel hitting the windshield as whoever is driving slams on the brakes, making the entire back end full of glowing lights. As the gleam of our lights highlight the truck, the passenger door flies open, and fuck me to death if my bestie doesn't look like the daughter of Satan as she jumps out. Zoey's face tattoo in the light glows and looks ethereal, while her ice-blue eyes are gleaming from the fires of hell. Her hair is loose and flying all around her as she stalks toward Noodles's truck. Fuck me, she's got her two handguns at her sides, along with her Bowie hunting knife. Hanging from a shoulder strap is the type of gun I told her never to use again after that incident in South Dakota a few years ago. Looks to be, and can't be sure, a .22LR machine gun, which I'm assuming is Panther's. I'm going to have to have a conversation with the horse rancher aka Zoey's man and soon. They must have been one of the first calls that Raven made when she discovered what's going on here at the ranch.

My door flies open, and I'm pulled from the truck violently. I hear Noodles swearing like a sailor, but all my eyes can see is Zoey. The crazy in her eyes tells me she's probably unaware of what she's doing right now. When she gets like this, she goes into full survival mode and for her that's always making sure I'm safe. Since back in the day, when she accepted me, I've had a demon guardian angel and I know how insane that sounds.

"Goldilocks, for fuck's sake, thank God, when we got the call, I had flashbacks of last year. Can't go through that shit again and how in the fuck did someone get on this ranch without any of us knowing? Something ain't clicking. So are we going in now or what's the holdup? Don't want to give this person or people a chance to run because tonight I feel the need to shower in blood. The voices are in my head again, Goldilocks, and I finally open up to someone about my past and we get interrupted. Can't I ever catch a goddamn break?"

She must have seen the look on my face as it hits me she shared her entire past with Panther before me. I lower my head so maybe she won't see how much it burns, but leave it to my best friend.

"Aw shit, Goldilocks, it ain't like that. I swear to Christ. He and I have been playing this cat and mouse game for a while, and I felt that he needed to know why I'm so fucked up in the head. Promise you and me are gonna have a sit-down and there will be nothing off-limits for you. But, and I mean this, just the two of us and only this one time. It's hard enough to get up every day and not blow my brains out, so bringing this shit to the forefront won't be helping my crazy and damn mental health."

Not knowing what to do and expecting her to knock me on my ass, I rush her, arms around her waist, hugging her tightly. To my utter shock, she slowly raises her arms and hugs back. That does it and before I can control them, the tears start. Even though I hear our club sisters coming close, then surrounding us, I hang on tight to my bestie because again I don't have a good feeling.

EIGHTEEN
'SHADOW'
ZOEY

Listening to Tank and Noodles going at it while Enforcer stands next to his prez, a huge smirk on his face, as he watches my every move. First thing Pops told him was to not let me out of his sight. And he's one person I'd never disrespect, so here I am waiting for the 'men' to make up their minds on how we can go from talking like a bunch of hens to some serious action.

Panther also hasn't left my side. Not everyone knows him in this group, so some of the looks from some of the Intruders, and even Ollie's folks, are starting to royally piss me off. They better not be assholes about it because he's Navajo 'cause I'll skin the motherfuckers alive. So stuck in my head, I almost jump outta my skin when I hear the deep raspy voice of Ollie, Raven's brother.

"Hey, don't think we met and since the two

roosters have their feathers up, thought I'd come over and introduce myself. I'm Ollie, live down the road and all those assholes trying not to stare at ya are my people. They're generally good folks, just don't have an ounce of couth. And are nosy as fuck and gossip like the two hens going at it right now."

Then, just like that, Ollie extends his hand toward Panther, who looks down at it. I hold my breath because Panther can be as big of a motherfucker as me, and he's told me about the racism and prejudiced assholes he's met over his life. As I wait, he finally reaches down and grabs Ollie's hand shaking it.

"Hi, Ollie, I go by Panther. Much easier than my Navajo name, chahóółhééł naabaahii t'áá sáhi, which means Dark Warrior Walking Alone. I'm a friend of Zoey's, if that's what you're asking. And, yeah, might want to tell your people to quit giving my boys those dirty looks, not sure how much longer some of them are going to be held back. They're also military so they can read what's going on. Too many fucked-up folks with PTSD and guns to be glaring at each other when we got more important things to deal with, don't ya think?"

Ollie just nods then puts his fingers in his mouth and makes a weird noise. Not sure how but he communicates something to his sanctuary folks and, one by one, they come and introduce themselves to Panther until Goldilocks's man comes up to us, serious as fuck.

"All right, sorry, Shadow, Tank is a stubborn motherfucker at times. Tried to explain to him that you won't sit back and let this happen. After I broke it down for him on how it will go if you don't get to bust through the door, he gave in. So, Panther, you, Enforcer, and Rebel are the first in. The back doors and all windows will be covered. All we ask is don't kill whoever is in there until we can question the motherfucker. Wrench is waiting, but again, Tank has been warned this is your party. We go in four minutes."

I watch as he looks at his watch then at both Panther and Ollie. Oh, these fucking military men, *let's coordinate our watches*, for Christ's sake. See, us Devil's Handmaidens sisters have our own way of doing things, but since none of us know what's waiting for us, I'll play nice… for now.

With Rebel and Enforcer at point and Panther right beside me, the door is busted open thanks to Rebel's sidekick. The main room is dark but there is a pungent smell I can't place. As I try to adjust my eyes, I hear voices off to the right and back, so very quickly the four of us make our way down the corridor. As we get closer, the smell is worse, but it's the terror and crying that is fucking with me. Currently, we don't have anyone living here since we are in the process of researching our next rescue. That's probably how they got in here, because no one's been keeping this building in their sights.

When we're outside the door, the sounds from inside have my mind already imagining what we are going to find. I've been on the other side of a door just like this and the smell and noises now make sense. Someone is in the process of torturing a person or two, can't tell. Leaning over, I tap Rebel on the shoulder and give her a chin lift. She gets it and again busts the door open. And that's when, for the first time in my entire life, I almost lose my dinner at what I see.

I hear Panther like he's far way but the noises coming from him sound like a wild animal. Fuck! Enforcer is holding him back as Rebel walks into the room, checking both left and right, making sure the room is okay to enter. When she gives me a look, I push past the guys and walk to the left side, staying close to the walls that are dripping with blood, shit, and God only knows what else. My eyes can't believe the scene, so I take a few deep breaths as the two motherfuckers step away from their victims and glare at me, hatred in their eyes.

"Aw, look, we got the whore's attention. Dad was right yet again, and it's going to suck to admit it to him. So, long time no see, Zoey Jeffries. See you've been busy working at being the biggest goddamn loser you could be. Oh, by the way, love the face. No, Dad's not happy with that either. He's already, well, I'll leave that for him to explain."

My head is screaming at me that I should know

these two who obviously know me, but nothing. Then Panther pushes past me, walking right into the mix, not even sure what he hopes to achieve. When the taller asshole pulls a gun and puts it to the little girl's head, he stops immediately. There are four girls in the room, all in the process of being tortured. They all look to be like Panther, Native, but I'm not sure. Son of a bitch, are these the kids he was trying to buy? Please don't let them be those kids.

"So, Zoey, you have two options. And we need your answer immediately. First, I'm going to grab my phone, motherfuckers, so no one get any ideas of shooting me because the consequences won't be in your favor. Hold that thought, bitch."

I watch him push some numbers and turn the phone our way after putting it on speaker. When the line connects, and his voice fills the room, I know my nightmare is about to begin.

"Zoey, Zoey, Zoey, tsk-tsk-tsk. What did I tell you a very long time ago? You may run and even get away, but I'll always find you. The boys have grown, haven't they? Both of them work with me fully now to make my dreams come true. You know what that is, so I'm surprised you'd lower yourself to be involved with that animal at your side. Looking at that fucking pig I get sick to my stomach. That someone of his kind would even think to put his hands on you. I'm sure he's thinking of trying to keep his bloodline going through you. I've been trying for years to rid our country of people who are not like us, but they fuck so fast and have so many kids it's almost impossible. I've combined my efforts with a couple of right-winged assholes, but at least they get the job done, though messy at times."

I listen as Dario rants and raves about bloodlines and shit like that. He's always been crazy about the strongest people are his race, but fuck, why me? I'm a mix of who the fuck knows what. When the room gets quiet, I look up, realizing I've drifted.

"Zoey, pay attention, you little whore. Goddamn, nothing changes. The way this is going to work is you will leave with the boys, or before you or your friends can do anything, the rest of my men will kill as many people as they can before the explosions start going off. You didn't learn a thing living in my fortress, did you? This would never happen to me because I've told you time and time again, trust no one, especially family. If you don't come willingly, those four girls, you are signing their death warrants, and Panther will start to receive packages of different body parts of some of the children we have living with us currently."

Standing here I feel like I'm watching from above my own body as I listen to the insanity of a mad man. Why me? I'm no one and when I was bought by Dario, he never touched or fucked me. No, not his hands but many, many others. He made a small fortune off my body, the jagoff. But he somehow has been able to get in my head because if there was one reason I'd go with them, it is the kids. Since Goldilocks and I started the Devil's Handmaidens MC, we always had a pact that we do whatever necessary to save children. Fuck!!!!!

"What's your decision, Zoey? Time is ticking and we have a lot of catching up and games to play, my little cunt. Are you coming or am I calling my men in? Tick-tock, tick-tock?"

He laughs into the phone as I turn to Panther. The agony on his face must reflect my own. Each of our life's mission is to rescue and help victims become survivors, so he already knows what I'm going to do. Hearing a ruckus behind us, I know it's a matter of seconds before Goldilocks starts a scene. Need to keep her out of here, no matter what.

"Rebel, go keep her the fuck outta here 'til I'm gone. Sister, make sure the club protects her, no matter what. Don't let her do anything stupid. I got this. Go, get the fuck outta here."

Being the badass she is, no expression is on her face but the look in her eyes tears my heart out. She's been one of the few sisters I could just hang with who didn't ask me stupid questions or pry. We'd work out together and she's a badass to the full extent. I know she thinks that between the three in this room with me, her along with Enforcer and Panther, they could handle the situation. What she doesn't know, and I do, is that Dario is one crazy psychopathic maniac. I watched him back in the day torture all types of people. Adults, teenagers, children, and even babies. This motherfucker isn't human. I know this because he's the one who taught me to be who and how I am today. As the fear of the unknown starts to penetrate throughout my body, I have no choice.

Rebel walks out, following my orders, as Panther pulls me close, leaning down so I can hear his whisper.

"Nizhoni, don't do this. We'll figure something else out but if you leave with these assholes, I get the feeling I'll never see you again. Zoey, without you I might as well be dead. That bracelet I gave you, if at all possible, keep it on you. There's a tracer in it, as there are in the earrings and in the jewelry in your piercing. As long as you keep one with you no matter how long it takes or where they take you, I'll find you, beautiful, or I'll die trying."

Hearing Goldilocks screaming and swearing, I know got to get this party started. Grabbing Panther around the middle, I put my head on his chest, trying to memorize the feel of him and his smell. Without a word, I push him away and start to walk to the two jagoffs who are smirking at me.

"Um, forgot to tell you, bitch, he comes with too. That's not a request. Dad said it's the only way he'll be able to control you. It's him or that crazy as fuck bitch out there howling like a lunatic. You pick but again, do it fast we gotta move now."

"You'll take me with, Zoey. Lead the way, gentlemen."

My head jerks back at how Panther addressed them. Is he crazy? They hate anyone who's not white. What they are going to do to him I can't let happen, but they can't take Tink either. This has to be God's punishment to me for the shit I've done over my life and for who I am. But I wasn't born this way, it's assholes like these three who made me what I am today. Their abuse split my brain in half. Why do I have to continue to pay for the damage that was done to me?

Before I can give it any thought behind us we hear gunfire, then three men come in, guns pointed at us. One walks up to Panther and me while pulling two syringes out of his coat pocket. Oh shit, no, not like this. I start to fight, which means Panther and Enforcer join in, but it's a losing battle. Especially when one of the men aims and fires a bullet into Enforcer's knee. He goes down but struggles to get back up. That same jagoff walks up to him and puts the gun to his head. I instantly put my hands up as I watch the man I once had a crush on and dreamed of being with get his ass beaten. Right before I feel the needle, one of the brothers raises his gun to the worst of the girls and pulls the trigger.

When the darkness takes me under, I do something I never do. I thank God for the darkness of this drug abyss.

NINETEEN
'PANTHER'
CHAHÓÓŁHÉÉL NAABAAHII T'ÁÁ SÁHI
DARK WARRIOR WALKING ALONE

The intense pounding in my head is what brings me out of my unconsciousness. My mouth is dry and every muscle in my body seems to be contracted. Must be whatever drug they used to put me under.

We are in some type of large vehicle going down a motherfucking messed-up road. I know Zoey is right beside me as each time we hit a bump, our bodies collide and bounce all over. We must be in a back end of a huge SUV with the seats down. I'm in the dark as a blindfold is covering my eyes. Not wanting to let our captors know I'm awake, I control my breathing and take a moment to find chahóółhéél naabaahii t'áá sáhi. I need that Dark Warrior right now, so I wait until I hear and feel the beating of drums and my heart slows down. Using my senses, my ears are picking up some of their conversation.

These two can't be Dario's sons. They are stupid

as fuck. They are arguing about where to grab a bite to eat, like they didn't just drug and kidnap two people after killing at least one of the girls. I can't believe, right before my eyes, they ended her life. Yeah, she was in a horrific way from their torture but no one, especially a child, deserves no say in if they live or die.

Feeling Zoey start to wake, I move closer as we are also tied up. Hands behind our backs but legs free. Dumbasses, don't they know the damage a person can do with their legs and feet? Trying to pass on to her to be careful, I feel her reach her fingers out and tap my side. Yeah, she got it.

While she works through the drugs, I continue to try and get an idea of what our choices are and if there is a way to get these assholes in hand and get away. I'm thinking someone other than Dumb and Dumber is controlling this abduction. Probably someone who is following us. I can hear the steady engine directly back there.

"Okay, motherfucker, I'm not afraid of Dad like you. We've got a goddamn long-ass drive ahead of us, so we are stopping at that truck stop so I can take a piss and grab some food. If you feel the need to ask for permission, go for it, but I'm a grown-ass man. So whatcha gonna do, Donny?"

I can almost smell the wood burning as 'Donny' takes his time trying to decide. When he agrees with his brother, I let out a small breath. We'll have to utilize every opportunity, even if it's to leave a clue or something for those who will be looking for us. I move my ass and am relieved that my phone is still in my back pocket. That means we can be tracked by it, not to mention all the jewelry we both have on. Avalanche might be down, but he'll let someone know, and they can pull the software up and see where we are at. That is until someone smarter than these two takes it off and discards the items. I pray we have some time left for the others to trace us.

When the vehicle starts to slow down, I lean close to Zoey and whisper, telling her to act like she's still out. She nods once. When the back opens up, I squint to see what the fuck they are planning. Son of a bitch, they both have a syringe ready. Without thought, I pull my legs back and kick with all my might. My right foot hits one brother in the chin and my left low in the gut. He goes down as Zoey handles the other asshole brother. Before we can even move to get out or something two more men run up, kicking the two assholes out of the way before leaning down and coming up with the needles.

When the needle hits my thigh, instantly I can feel it traveling through my body as the heat hits my stomach and I feel nauseous. Right before my mind goes blank, I feel Zoey's finger reach out and touch my side. That is my last thought.

* * *

Slowly coming to, I'm having a hard time breathing. Did those bastards break some ribs or did a lung collapse from being beat on repeatedly? My hands and legs are free, so when I reach up not even a full arm's length above me, I hit wood. *Wait a motherfucking minute,* I think to myself as I reach sideways and again hit wood. Takes a minute before my brain can comprehend what's happened. Those motherfuckers have buried me alive, for Christ's sake.

Feeling my heart try to beat out of my chest, I close my eyes, humming softly. I reach for the warrior deep in my soul. He needs to come forward if I plan on getting out of this alive and in one piece. I don't know how long I stay perfectly still, humming softly. The sound vibrates throughout my body, helping me to stay calm and be one with my being.

When I'm as calm as I can be, I move my hands to get an idea of how big the box is that I'm in. I've got a few inches on both the top and bottom. Also, the sides are pretty wide. The lid is on, not sure how, but it's pure wood so very heavy. My mind starts to play games with me as I remember some of my own past. The worst time had to be in the POW camp with Avalanche. I've never talked about that time with anyone but my brother and that was hard enough.

Listening to Zoey talk about her worst times, it hit so close to home I was shocked. There is evil everywhere in the world, that's for sure. Both Avalanche and I, when being held as prisoners of war, prayed for death numerous times. If there was a way we could have killed ourselves, we would have, but they watched us twenty-four seven. The camera's red light reminded me of a beast's eye. There was that one time I thought Avalanche was going to die. After what… thirty-six hours of them doing atrocious things to him, when they threw him back into our dungeon, he was bleeding from every orifice on his body. I almost didn't recognize him; he was so swollen from the beating they gave him. Somehow, not sure how, I managed to keep him alive, barely. Thank God in less than twenty-four hours from that moment we were found by a group of Navy SEALs and Marines and were removed. We never were told or even asked what happened after we left. Personally, I hope they burned those bastards alive or left them naked, tied to a tree, to die a horrific death. After that close call, I finished my time then decided to go for discharge while Avalanche felt the need to give our country another, shit, was it two or four years, don't remember and never understood why.

He never told me how the hell he found me when he did. I'd been approached by the government, who was seeking a certain type of person to work the circuits of trafficking and help disband them. They reached out to me because I was a Native American and there had been a ton of my people who had disappeared never to be found again. At the time, I was working this jagoff here in Montana so instead of trying to find a rental or something like that, I decided it was time to put down some roots. Bought the property first and put a small modular home on it. With the idea of starting my horse ranch the notion of expanding into the stud service came to me when yet another person reached out to me after seeing my horseflesh.

I was working that fucker's angle when they caught me off guard. Threw me in a dark room and left me there half naked, freezing my ass off. No heat, blankets, or even food or water. Thought I was gonna die right there. When I heard some kind of ruckus going on, I tried to get up and defend myself but was too fucking weak to even lift my head. When the door was busted open, I almost shit my boxers when I saw Avalanche. The shock and surprise on his face quickly turned to anger and fury. I never asked him, and he's never shared, but I think someone from our past had my back and sent him in to save me. The rest is history.

Feeling a bit queasy, I try to breathe deeply and slowly. Not sure how the oxygen is getting in but don't want to panic and pass the fuck out. Going over the years, my best friend and brother has been my savior more times than I can recall. All I know is, without his help, guidance, and experience with horses in general, the ranch would have never succeeded. It saddens me I might die before I get the chance to thank him for all he's done over the years.

Also, for being a phenomenal brother, who I love dearly, and that I'll miss him. Fuck, suddenly I'm feeling woozy. Then I hear the sound of the gas, I'm guessing, they're pushing in. That is my last thought before I go back down hard.

* * *

My head feels really heavy, and my eyes don't want to open. My arms and legs are nonexistent at the moment. It takes a few but then my memory kicks in, and the last thing I remember surfaces. The fucking gas. Panicking, I try to push up or kick my legs but can't. Squinting, I almost scream when I see light and realize I'm outta the box. Thank fucking Christ.

Hearing noises, not sure what, almost like people are whispering and cackling in the background. I'm lying on something hard and cold like a metal table of some sort. The room is extremely chilly, thank God there's some sort of covering on me. Slowly the murkiness starts to leave my head and, struggling, I slowly pry my eyes open just a little bit. What I see sends a shiver right down my spine. Motherfucker, I'm screwed, no way out of this one. I try to control my reaction, don't want to feed into the hunger that's watching my every move.

The room I'm in has windows all around it. There are some people in chairs and others standing observing me. With that thought, it dawns on me that

I'm butt-ass naked like the day I was born. Oh shit, this ain't going to be good at all. *What a messed-up way to go out,* I think to myself. Who the fuck are these insane motherfuckers? The background noise is starting to rise but I refuse to open my eyes. Need to find a place that will help me get through whatever their plan is for me. What I do know from prior experience is that this won't be quick or painless. When the clapping and whistles start, it dawns on me that I'm the show they've paid for and have been waiting for. Son of a bitch.

"Hello again. Thanks for your patience. It's been a long time coming, but I think you'll enjoy our show this evening. After many years of searching, I've found one of my proteges who I was in the process of molding and training back in the day. I'm happy to report she has become more than I could ever imagine. Without further ado, let me introduce you to our own Woman in the Shadows."

I feel the fear going down my spine as the claps, howls, and whistles become erratic and insane. Not knowing what to do, I squint but can't see a fucking thing. No matter what, even if it's Zoey, can't let my guard down. Who knows what the fuck they've already done to her. I've no clue how long I've been drugged and out of it. I'm thinking we're both going through hell at the hands of our captors, just a different version for each.

Before another word is uttered, I feel her hands on

me. Softly, they search my body to make sure I'm okay. Hearing snickering behind her, I know she's not supposed to be showing any empathy, but that's my girl. When her hand touches me, I feel the brief squeeze of her fingers and know immediately that she can tell I'm awake and in wait. Without making it obvious, I give her a squeeze back.

"Sorry, folks, our girl is still trying to come back to herself. You will see an improvement over the next few weeks, I'm sure. She will become more like her old self, which was very emotionless when working. For today, she will be showing you how she's been able to grow in her torture skills. So let's give her a warm welcome, please."

I hear Zoey's intake of breath and know she had not been warned about her upcoming performance. If I can get her darker side of Shadow to surface, we might both make it through this. Well, she will, not too sure about me. Her torture skills have been honed over the years with the Devil's Handmaidens and in her job as their enforcer. Some of the shit she's told me had my skin crawling.

"Now, since each of you graciously donated to our cause, right now, please take a moment to grab some refreshments and use the facilities while we get things in order for your viewing pleasure. The drapes will now fall over the windows until the show is ready to start. You will have approximately fifteen minutes to return to your seat. If you miss that window, you will be shit out of luck, no matter how much of a donation you've provided. Be aware of your time, please. See you soon."

The room seems to go darker for a brief second before I hear the sound of heavy-duty lights switching on. A door opens then slams before the sound of flesh being hit is right to the side of me. Oh no, motherfuckers, do what you want to me, but no way can I lie here and let them abuse Zoey. Not again and definitely not on my watch. My eyes pop open as I roll to my side, landing on unsteady feet. Shocking one of the brothers who has his hands around Zoey's neck, pressing tightly, I can see the struggle as her face is turning colors. This motherfucker is totally crazy. If he kills her, what does he think his old man will do to him. Reaching over, my hand grabs one ear, jerking him back. My other hand, fisted, lands right in his ball sack and he crumbles to the ground unconscious before his head cracks on the concrete floor.

Turning, I see Zoey staring at me in shock. Looking down I see why. I'm covered in bruises and bite marks. Well, someone had fun. I lift my head to see her standing there just staring. Until the anger washes over her.

"Who the fuck put their lips on you, Panther? What whore had the nerve and then to leave marks? I'll tear her limbs from her body, cutting those lips off, and shoving them up her own ass. And fuck, who beat the shit out of you? Didn't you even fight back? What are we going to do? We have like twelve minutes until the curtains raise. Every one of those assholes watching paid at least a half a million to watch this show. From what asshole number two told me, it's being broadcast through the internet also. I can't hurt you. No matter what they do, I refuse to do anything to cause you harm. It'd be like inflicting pain on myself."

Pulling her to me, I hold on tight. If this works, and that's a huge if, I still have no idea how the fuck we'll be able to get out of this messed-up world of evil. Hold on a minute, that voice said she was back. Zoey was here at one time, maybe she remembers the layout.

"Nizhoni, have you been here before? Hey, no judgment, but if you have, we might stand a chance of at least getting out of this monstrosity of a house. I've been kept, I'm thinking, in the basement and this room, though large, doesn't seem to be above ground. Think, Zoey, try to remember. I know you've pushed everything to the back but you need to be strong. Please suck it up, beautiful."

Those last words have her face turning red while her hands become fists. I actually step back a step or two, knowing she's walking a fine line right now. Don't want to give her anything to lose herself. Watching her, I know time is flying by but if I've learned anything, you never rush her. She needs time to think. When that smile crosses her face, I know this will be worth the wait.

"Yeah, Panther, I remember. Everything, and there is a way out of this place, if it's still there and open. Do you trust me? Because if we do this, I'm going to have to hurt you first then try and get the fuck out of Dodge. So again, will you put your trust in me to get you out of this situation?"

"Zoey, there's no one I trust more, not even Avalanche. So do whatever you have to, I'll manage. Just please don't fuck with my dick or castrate me. That's definitely a strong no."

Her smile gets larger as her eyes start to twinkle. The she gives me a very short hug before reaching down for the jagoff on the floor, who is starting to come too. My gut tells me shit is about to hit the fan. My heart informs me that my woman has this under control. I hope and pray, for once, I can follow my heart's direction.

TWENTY
'TINK'
MAGGIE/GOLDILOCKS

I'm beyond pissed and there's nothing anyone can say to bring me out of it. I've already gone off on my dad, Noodles, Glory, and just about every Devil's Handmaidens sister. And if I could, I'd take Rebel's kutte, blacken her ink, and kick her goddamn ass outta my club after I beat her senseless. After all the opportunities not only the club, but me personally have made available to her, this is how she repays everyone. I don't give a rat's ass what Zoey told her, she's the clubs S-a-A. With the title comes the understanding that when we're drowning in shit, our club can depend on our sergeant at arms to protect every member and prospect. Not only are they the head of the club's security, but also to make sure everything is running smoothly. What they do not do is listen to the orders of our enforcer, when in a situation like Zoey's, who shouldn't have been barking orders in the first place.

When Rebel came out and literally picked me up, holding on to me for dear life, I knew deep inside that life as the Devil's Handmaidens knew it was over. When she explained the situation, I did everything I could think of. I kicked her in the stomach, punched her right in the face, pulled her long-ass red hair, spit in her face, clawed her up and down, but to her credit she never let me go. When Noodles came up beside us, she actually held me in one arm while with the other drew her weapon and pointed at Noodles, telling him to step back, she was following her club enforcer's orders.

I screamed and swore in her face, telling her I was higher up than Zoey and she should be listening to me. That we needed to save both our sister and Panther, but she adamantly ignored me. Not until the strange men came in, guns blazing, did Rebel finally drop me, then put her knee on my back as she got involved and shot as many of those motherfuckers as she could. Even in the eye of the storm, she protected me while making sure—as best she could—that those assholes, well not all of them, were stopped before giving aid to whatever was going on in that room.

When we heard the shots and horrific screaming coming out of that room, by that time more of my dad's and Ollie's men were there. But before they could do a thing, we heard the vehicles out front take off like the hounds of hell were chasing them. One of dad's brothers went down the hallway to check it out. When he came back out, his face as white as a ghost, my heart actually stopped beating for a second.

"Damn, Tank, we need medical right now. There is one dead and three others who are close to it. And no, Tink, none are Shadow. Looks to be innocents ranging between, damn, maybe eight to fourteen, all females. I'm gonna go back, need to help."

As he walks away, Rebel leans down toward me, no emotion at all on her face.

"Tink, you know I love you more than my sister. That you would think I just left Shadow to die, fuck, Prez, don't you know me at all? The room was about to erupt with more rage and fury than I've ever seen. When they threatened you, Shadow ordered, no demanded, I keep you the fuck away from the two belligerent assholes, no matter what. That was the order I followed. Because, as you sarcastically reminded me of my place in the club, I'm to protect its members and prospects. But more specifically, its officers. And you, Tink, outrank Shadow so my duty was to make sure you were safe and secure. I'm gonna give a hand to Malice and Half-Pint. And if you're serious and want to take my kutte and blacken my ink, vote me out of our club, I won't fight you. I will say this though. We all have known from the start that you and Zoey would die for each other, no questions asked. We've seen it time and time again.

What kills me, Prez, is that you don't even realize the rest of your club sisters would do the exact same for you. Would you do it for us? That's the million-dollar fucking question."

Then she turns and walks back into whatever hell is waiting in that back room. Then Dad comes to me, pulling me into a hug. When he tells me to really hear what Rebel said, I know right then that I was so fucking wrong. I let my sister down when she was actually doing what she was taught and voted in to do.

"Dad, I'm so fucked up. How can I lead these women when all I can do is panic and worry about Zoey? Is it fair to them, as they all kind of know she's my favorite? Have I lost control over the Devil's Handmaidens; do you think? I'm so tired, Daddy, and beyond worried for my best friend."

He holds me tight and whispers all the right answers in my ears, taking in all my fears and anxiety. Just like he's done my entire life. As time passes, I feel people walking in and it starts with just one hand on my back but when it keeps going, I lift my head to see my club sisters all around us, waiting for the next order of business. Fuck, the relief that flows in my blood almost chokes me, but I manage one sentence to them.

"Everyone, meet at the ranch for Chapel now. We need to find and get our sister Shadow back. Sooner rather than later, don't think she'll survive this one otherwise. Let's go."

When I walk out of that building, I have every single one of my Devil's Handmaidens sisters right behind me, following me up to the house. When I turn, I can't believe my eyes. Rebel is at the end, picking up slack. So as a group we make our way to the room sectioned off in my ranch for emergency meetings. I watch as Raven checks the room out for bugs or listening devices, as the prospects grab more chairs so every single woman will be part of the planning. Even our prospects. My bestie has no idea how much she is loved in this club. About time she figures that shit out. We ain't letting her go without a goddamn fight.

* * *

Son of a bitch, after all these hours we still have no plan in place. It's like Zoey and Panther just fell off the earth. We have every one of the IT nerds available searching for them. Dad's brother, Freak, is right beside our sister, Raven. Dad also reached out to Brick, the president of the Grimm Wolves, and he has Karma working with both Freak and Raven. And, to my utter surprise, Hannah is in the mix, as I was told she has mad skills when it comes to computers and searches. I don't want to know how or why, but I've given them all carte blanche to use whatever resources or to hack whatever is necessary to get a lock on Zoey.

Noodles has been beside me every step of the way. Ollie has some of his ex-military using some of the government's access to see what they can find. And, yeah, that means they are taking a chance hacking into those sites, but none of us care. We have a purpose and that's what we are working toward.

When Avalanche, with the help of his men George, Dallas, Jersey and Chicago make their way through the door, we immediately get the big guy comfortable. How the fuck he got out of the hospital, I'll never know. But by the look on his face, if it was me, I'd have held the door open for him. In the short time I've known him, he's never looked so fucked up.

"Whatcha got so far, Tink? Anything on a location? Do you want me to reach out to our government contact, see if they know anything? What the fuck can we do beside sit here with our fingers up our own asses?"

I get how frustrated he is, plus from what I've heard, he's refusing pain meds due to a prior drug problem he had. His patience is at zero. Before I can even start to explain, Noodles sits next to him and starts up a conversation.

"Avalanche, everything that can be done is being handled. We got some of the best hackers in the country on this and they are all over too. From what Freak just mentioned to Tank, I'd hold off on reaching out to your government contact. There are some interesting things they're finding out. I know Panther had concerns about how this jagoff was always a step ahead of you, right? Well, someone with government clearance has been in contact with that main guy what's his name... Dario, that's right. And that motherfucker has been holding a ton of large parties for his kind, we just haven't found where that is at. It's more than just a circuit party because what Freak and Raven are finding out, the cost to get in a party starts at a quarter of a million and goes up depending on your proclivities. And Karma with the Grimm Wolves, has been able to trace down some names of those who have attended in the past. Hold on, Avalanche, some are government officials, while others are military, both active and ex. Some are movie stars and music artists. We are in the midst of breaking down a circuit of the rich and famous. And I know that don't mean shit to you, but I wanted you to know, even though it don't look like shit's getting done, it is, brother. We'll find both of them."

After listening to Noodles and watching Avalanche's response, I know my man can handle this. I turn and head to the kitchen, needing some coffee. Sitting at the table, head in her hands, is Rebel, coffee untouched in front of her. Time to fix my fuckup.

"Hey, sister, want a fresh cup of coffee, my treat?"

When she raises her head, I see the anguish in her

eyes. Yeah, she's beating herself up about Zoey. Goddamn it, I can be such a bitch at times. We've got some of the best women out there in our club, I just need to see that. When she just stares at me, I shove her over on the bench and sit down facing her.

"I'm just going to say it, Rebel. I was so fucking wrong to get in your face and threaten your patch. That should have never happened, no matter what. Please, you got to believe me. Sister, what you said earlier is both right and wrong. Yeah, Zoey and I have a very close personal relationship. Saying that, I also have individual personal relationships with each of you. Don't try to compare them because each is different and based on my club sisters and my interactions. Just know I trust you with my life and never doubt I'd give mine for you. Love you, Mya."

Reaching over, I grab her hand, giving it a squeeze. When she returns it, I stand, grabbing her mug, and get us both a fresh cup of coffee. At least I was able to fix this shitshow. Now we wait to see what needs to be done to clear up this mess involving our Zoey and her man, Panther.

TWENTY-ONE
'PANTHER'

CHAHÓÓŁHÉÉL NAABAAHII T'ÁÁ SÁHI
DARK WARRIOR WALKING ALONE

By the time backup came for the prick who dared to put his hands on Zoey, the two of us had come up with some sort of plan. Was it perfect? Fuck no, but it would give us a chance, a very small one, but beggars can't be choosers.

Now that the room has been cleaned of all the blood on the floor from the asshole's head that cracked open, I'm back on the table, but this time my hands and legs are bound. When I turn my head, I see the other asshole brother talking to Zoey. Seems like he's trying to get a feel on what she's planning to do with me. I'm kind of thinking about that myself. When I questioned her, she asked me if I trust her. When I said with my life, she said that was a good answer. She just hoped she could maintain that life. I almost choked on that until she started to smile a wicked grin.

Now the drapes are back up and the viewing room is packed. I could swear I recognized some of those faces in the darkened room. If I'm not mistaken, that guy in front was in that blockbuster movie that came out last year. Then I see two men I know for certain are from the military. Goddamn, what lair or nest of inhuman motherfuckers did we just step into? The looks in those animals' eyes are like a pack of wild beasts hunting for their next prey to eat. All I see is evil everywhere.

"All right now, calm the hell down, the show is about to start. Our girl has pulled her shit together, so hopefully, this will be something you remember for a long time. Now today we are priviledged because we have with us a guest of honor. He's a Native American who goes by the code name of Panther. His Navajo name, and I'll probably fuck it up totally, is chahóółhéél naabaahii t'áá sáhi, which in Navajo means Dark Warrior Walking Alone. Now we all have the belief that our world would be a better place if everyone one was of the same race. Saying that, personally I have nothing against Indians. Well, these types from our own country. My house staff is mainly made up of his people, and once properly trained, they do exactly as they are told. Well actually they have no choice but anyway, I drift. He will be the masterpiece that allows Zoey to come back to us. Saying that, let's begin, shall we?"

Not sure what to expect, I almost jump when Zoey

appears before my eyes. Her eyes are dead. I mean they are her usual ice blue, but there is not anything in them. I don't even think she sees me as a person at the moment. That's when it hits me, she's not my Zoey but the Devil's Handmaidens enforcer, Shadow. Only way she can get through this, I'm sure. Closing my eyes, I start to hum very softly. Then I feel her two fingers on my arm, tapping in rhythm with my hum. She gets why I do it. One of the few things that got me through all the day-to-day torture overseas when I was a POW. I go to my safe place and chant.

She pulls a table closer, and out of the corner of my eye I see all the shit on top of it. A collection of surgical and sexual tools that I'm guessing she plans on using on me. Oh well, at least it's at her hands not some degenerate's. I start to slow my breathing but keep my eyes on her, changing my chant to a darker type of hum. Her eyes shoot to my face, and she watches me intently. I see when she gets it, not sure how. What I'm doing is chanting so she can then do whatever is necessary. I'm guiding her into the very dark side of basic human nature. Only time will tell if this crazy as fuck idea of mine will even work.

When she grabs some kind of pliers, I cringe. Fuck, this is gonna be hard. She walks to the foot of the bed, never looking toward the crowd. Her hand holds down my non-dominant left foot, using the pliers to grab my little toenail. It's over before I can even prepare and as much as it stings, it's not too bad.

That is until she reaches for a bottle of alcohol and pours it on my nail bed. Holy fucking shit, it feels like every nerve has gone through a bath of alcohol. How I manage to keep my mouth shut is a miracle in itself. The crowd is laughing and clapping, enjoying the show. After a breath or two, I look up to see Zoey watching me, the pain in her eyes tearing my heart out. I take a chance and give her a quick small wink. That pulls her out of her self-induced misery and melancholy. Dropping the pliers back on the table, I watch my toenail fall to the paper towel. Guess our game is on.

* * *

My God, I'm getting sick of these smelling salts, since I'm passing out so fucking much. Whatever.

Trying to figure out the most recent punishment from Zoey, nothing is penetrating the constant pain I'm in. I've lost all the toenails on my left foot, along with two broken toes. She broke my pinky and thumb on my left hand. A long deep cut is on the forearm of my right hand. It's finally starting to stop as the blood coagulates. I've got a form of road rash on the top of my thighs from the rough as fuck sandpaper she used to take a layer of skin off of them. My chest is burning from where her whip hit a bit too hard. The red lines are becoming more prominent. The needles that were place along my neck and connected to some type of electrical device after about ten minutes had my muscles contracting involuntarily. She finally turned that off a bit ago.

When she held up the plastic tubing, I did almost pass out. I believe it's used as a foley in the medical field, not sure what she was intending to use it for. But that voice came on and told her to save that one for later. When she pulled out the hand drill, I knew where she was going because I've been here before and have the scars on my thighs to show it. Zoey also knows the extensive nerve damage done to my legs has killed some of the nerves, so my pain levels are off. To prove to Avalanche awhile back, I stuck a steak knife in my thigh and didn't feel it, until it was at least three- or four-inches in. To say the least, I won that bet.

Knowing to make this shit work I have to put on a good show, I try to envision what it felt like the first time those freaks overseas shoved those metal things into my legs. Fuck yeah, they're called, fuck, think knitting needles. I watch Zoey attached the battery to the drill and put a bit in. It's not as huge as I anticipated, that is until the voice said no... bigger. Well, fuck me blue. Can't catch a break. When she replaces it with a bigger bit, she walks toward me.

As soon as she turns it on, the look on her face is heart-wrenching. Each time she does something to me I feel like she's leaving pieces of herself here. Nothing she can do, at the moment we're both fucked. When the tip of the bit hits my thigh, it's the heat I feel not the penetration. I see my blood splash all over Zoey but nothing. That is until she must have put some weight behind it because it feels like a pinch or something. After a few up and down motions, she pulls the drill out. Fuck, that's a lot of blood on her. That I didn't expect. Nor did I think I'd feel so dizzy all of a sudden.

"Oh, fuck, need some help here. Might have hit an artery or something. Goddamn it, Dario, get me some medical assistance or that's it, put a bullet in my head, you asshole. Better yet, I'll drill into my own carotid artery and bleed out. You know I'll do it."

The drapes immediately fall down amongst many pissed-off folks screaming. Right before I pass out, Zoey is right beside me, telling me it's going to be all right. Then suddenly bright lights come on, the door flies open, and a bunch of people rush into the room. One is pushing a cart with medical supplies while the other two come to my side, immediately checking my leg. One of the men grabs the drill from Zoey's hand and pushes her to sit down. He's got a mask on which I think is kind of strange, but fuck, my head is messed up. I'm getting cold and my mind is pretty fuzzy. Too much blood loss so quickly.

Zoey tries to stand but the same guy pushes her back down, gently leaning in he says something to her. I watch as her head flips back and her eyes narrow as she stares at him before she looks at me. I can't read the look on her face, so I shrug my shoulders. When someone presses down on my leg, I let out a low moan because that hurt like fucking hell.

Next thing I know, they are wheeling me out of the demonstration room, down a long hallway, and then into a surgical suite. And I mean that to the fullest. It looks better equipped than a hospital. I'm shifted onto a narrow bed as they hook me up to monitors. A woman comes to me, letting me know she's going to start an IV so they can give me fluids and some medication to calm me down and put me in twilight before they knock me out. She asks me all kinds of medical questions, which has me believing in a prior life she had to be in the medical field. I don't ask because I have no idea who she is so I don't trust her. I think she can feel that by the looks she's giving me.

When the IV is in, she leans into me quietly, whispering to me when no one is looking.

"Don't worry, Panther, we got you. Just know you're not alone. We're here. Let's get you fixed up."

That is the last thing I remember, right before a shot goes in the IV. Almost immediately, I feel my body relax as my eyes close. Right before I go under, I hear Zoey telling me she's sorry. Like it was her fault. We are just pawns in this goddamn sick as fuck game.

TWENTY-TWO
'HEARTBREAKER'

I'm making another, God only knows the number, of coffee trips to Raven and Freak. They've been working like two crazy people, going through everything and anything to try and locate where Shadow and Panther are. I also wanted to get away as Avalanche, George, Dallas, Jersey, and Chicago, who are driving all of us fucking crazy. It's like they think we can just snap our fingers and bam… we know where they are. It can take hours, days, weeks, months, or even years. For fuck's sake, look at how long it took for Tink to find Hannah. No thanks to me.

I knock on the door with my elbow but wait to go in. Since I lost my mind and got strung out, trying to be very careful. Let's face it, I'm walking on ice.

"Yeah, come in."

That sounded like someone other than Raven or Freak. When I open the door, I see it's one of Freak's

Intruders brothers. I forget his name, it's really cocky, which he is not. I know he's a newer member just getting through his prospect time. Also heard he has a kid or two, but no ol' lady. That's interesting but at the moment I'm invisible, only speak when spoken to. Need to prove myself to my club sisters before I do anything else.

"Raven brought you guys a fresh pot of coffee and some leftover roast they had at the diner today. I think there's enough if Freak's brother is hungry too. Hey, Freak, you want coffee?"

He looks at me with his weird eyes, not saying a word. With him watching me, I feel like a fly under a microscope. His brother elbows him in the side, which has Freak pulling back and cracking him upside the head.

"Brother, pressing your luck. You don't know the history here so back the fuck up. Do as your told, look through those notes and see if you can find an address out in the country. That's got to be where they're holding Shadow and Panther. Gotta find that location now. Keep looking, dude. That's your job today."

Putting the tray down, I pour three cups of coffee and give each one to the three folks in the room. I wait to see if they tell me what else to do. Thank God Raven takes pity on me.

"Heartbreaker, can you help Stud try and find any addresses that are listed? We are downloading shit faster than the two of us can look at and read. Do you mind or are you in the middle of something else?"

I shake my head, letting her know I'm not doing anything important and start to go through the documents she placed right in front of me. Feeling eyes on me, I see Stud is watching my every move. Well, not sure what his damn problem is but got enough of my own shit, don't need anything else that will piss my club sisters off, so I ignore him. Knowing how important this is not only for our club, but more specifically our prez, Tink. She is losing her fucking mind not knowing where her best friend is.

It seems like time is passing extremely slow, but it doesn't matter to me because my one and only job is to look at these papers and find an address. That way Raven or Freak can research it and see if it's a possibility. Every now and then, I hear Stud asking them if an address he found could be the place. Unfortunately, I've not seen one address, so I just keep going over each page, word by word.

While reading my current page, something stands out. Holy fuck, this can't be true. I go back and look at the pages before it, but yeah, it's true. This is crazy, no one is going to believe it.

"Um, Raven, we might have a problem. I've been reading each word on these pages. Can you look at this? Am I reading this wrong, because if it's true, Shadow is going to lose the little bit of her mind that's left."

Passing her the paper, I watch her face until she gets to the part in question. Her face turns pasty white. I watch as her lips begin moving, she goes back to the beginning starting to read out loud what she's seeing.

"Holy shit, Heartbreaker, go get Tink, Tank, and Avalanche. Now, sister, we don't have time to waste. If this is true, Timber-Ghost is about to implode on itself."

I stand and move quickly. When I hit the great room of the ranch house, I see both Tank and Avalanche, so I tell them to get to where Raven is. Next, I go on a search for Tink. She's not in her room so go to the kitchen and there she is, sitting by herself drinking coffee, I think. I've hated talking to our prez since what I did. She looks up and the devastation on her face pulls at my heartstrings. This woman gave me my first chance and so many after. For some reason she never doubted me. Even when we were looking for Hannah, Tink tried to keep an open mind. When she found out what I had done she was beyond pissed, but again she took a minute, listened, and somehow found a way to have my back after my betrayal. So lost in my thoughts, I jump at the sound of her voice.

"Yeah, sister, need something?"

"Tink, come with me. Raven needs you now. We might have fell into something, we're not sure."

As I watch, she stands, takes a second to get her

balance, then adjusts herself, feeling for her two handguns on her waist, the other behind her back. When she gets close, I clear my throat to get her attention. When she shifts her eyes my way, I almost get lost in the pain in her green eyes. Before I know what I'm doing, she's in my arms and I'm holding on tightly to her. I feel it almost immediately. As her tiny body starts to tremble, my arms tighten around her, giving her the one thing I'm capable of. A shoulder to lean on, though mine is battered and weak as shit. I owe this woman my life, need to remember that more often.

* * *

"Son of a bitch, Raven, I've told you a thousand times this can't be right. No way in hell is our town sheriff involved. I've known George my entire life and, yeah, he's not the most energetic lawman, but for Christ's sake, he's not part of the *'family.'* I think if he was, somewhere along the line someone—maybe Dad, my mom, Ollie's family, or some townsfolk—would have had some questions why all of a sudden all these Italians are hanging at George's place. Dad, want to jump in? You went to school with George. Did he have any siblings, what about his parents? Come on, Dad, please we need to get some answers and quick."

"Damn, all right, Maggie, calm the fuck down, daughter. It's not like I just graduated last week, it's been years. And I've kinda had other shit on my mind in that span of time. Yeah, we went to school together. He started in like the sixth grade. He lived with his mom, grandma, and grandpa if I remember correctly. We weren't close. He was kind of a nerd and always up the teachers' asses asking a million and one questions. Studying all the time while I was, well, interested in other things and leave it at that."

Everyone in the room, including me, chuckles. Tank can be a riot but also a badass too. Fuck with his family and he has no boundaries. He takes a gulp of coffee and continues.

"Something happened later in high school after a summer break. He came back different. Moody, irritated, and became almost an introvert. He started dropping friends left and right, just being by himself. When his grandparents were killed in that fire at their family homestead, it was just his mom and him. Never knew him to have any siblings or a father, as far as I can remember. After we graduated, he hightailed it outta here, went to college. I was actually surprised he came back after and joined the police force. He worked his way up to sheriff and even though I give him a ton of shit, he's done a good job for Timber-Ghost, I think. He walks that line between the law and us. George kinda gives us enough leeway and we repay him by taking care of the town. One hand washes the other."

While Tank is talking, Raven and Freak are

pounding away on their keyboards. I heard Freak let out a 'fuck me' but nothing since. I'm wondering if I should make myself scarce but don't want to do the wrong thing, so I sit quietly and listen. When Freak starts swearing up a storm, I know shit is about to hit the fan, so to speak.

"Bullshit. It's gotta be bullshit, Raven. That jagoff's been pulling the wool over our eyes all these years. Wait, what is this? No fucking way. Holy shit, bet this has something to do with what's been going on recently around town. Starting to make sense, don't you think, girl? Yeah, I know, but suck it up, I'm not disrespecting you at all. Look at this. Wait, no way. Oh, goddamn, if that is true—fuck—Shadow is gonna lose her ever-lovin' mind."

"Goddamn it, Freak, want to fill the rest of us in or is this a private conversation between you and Raven? For Christ's sake."

I know what he saw that has Freak losing it. If it's true, he's right. That long-asked question will finally be answered. But for my club sister and enforcer, it might not be what she wants to hear. While listening to my head, I miss what Raven started with.

"Okay, chill already. While y'all were talking, we did a quick background on our town sheriff, George. He didn't exist before he came here in grade school. Nothing about him, his mother, or grandparents. That made me suspicious, so I hacked into the U.S. Marshals Service to see if any WITSEC were relocated here to Timber-Ghost Montana, back in the day. And go figure, there was one family that is still in the program. Well, the son is, the mother and her parents are now all gone. And yes, again it's our own Sheriff George McDaniels. Though that isn't his real name. That is Giorgio De Luca. And yeah, that's the name of the huge Italian Mafia family in New York. Though that's not the worst. Go ahead, Freak, tell them."

Freak's head jerks up and he glares at Raven for a second or two, then swallows looking right at Tink. Shit, feel a shitstorm about to start.

"Well, it seems like Tank said, shit happened that one year when they were in high school. Seems like Giorgio went back home, which he wasn't supposed to do. At the time they weren't in WITSEC. His mom left the father, Niccolò, because he was cheating so they agreed to live separately but no divorce. The whole Catholic church shit. Anyway, Giorgio's mom, Fiorella, moved out here with him while Niccolò stayed in New York with his brother, Dario, and sister, Palmira. Does one of those names sound familiar? Yeah, same jagoff who fucked up Shadow. Dario De Luca is our good old Sheriff George's brother. And it seems, according to what we found, at one time around say… thirty-four years ago, Sheriff George was hot and heavy with one of the Blackfoot young women. They were pretty close, that is until Quiet Dove became pregnant. She kind of disappeared for a while, then returned with a baby girl many months later. She was not accepted by her tribe because the father of her baby was Áápi, *Blackfoot for white*. Dove struggled and the father of her child tried to help but she was bitter. Life was rough and she made it worse by getting hooked on drugs. And the rest is history, as they say."

I watch both Tink and Tank as they take in the story Freak just told. It hits Tank first, but Tink isn't far behind. Her face gets pink first then bright red. Raven looks at me with big eyes and I shrug my shoulders. Right at this moment, nothing we can do but let this play out. Tink stands and starts to pace.

"Are you trying to tell me that George is Zoey's father? Can that even be? And if he is, why did he let that sick son of a bitch Dario get his hands on her? His brother treated his niece worse than an animal! You know, right? He sold her to whoever would pay with no limits at all. Fuck. No way. I can't believe he would let that happen to his own flesh and blood. He's always helped the underdogs, but he leaves his daughter to struggle on her own. If we find them alive, how do I break it to Zoey that not only was she abused, trafficked, sold into prostitution and slavery, but the person who did it was her own uncle? Oh, and to top that off, bestie, Sheriff George is your father. Yeah, that should go over really well."

Tank stands, moving to Tink, pulling her close as he drops his head onto hers. Watching them, I realize I've never had that from a parent figure in my life. I don't even really remember mine and after I started messing with drugs, I couldn't have cared less about anyone who was in my life. Nothing mattered but my next hit, so I'd steal from anyone I knew. A very small part of me was kind of jealous, no maybe envious, of Tink that she has what she does with Tank and Momma Diane. But then again, my prez went through her own hell too. Tank turns and asks the million-dollar question.

"So, do you know where the fuck they're at or not? We need to get wherever Zoey and Panther are and get their asses out before we lose the opportunity to bring them out alive. Talk to us."

TWENTY-THREE
'SHADOW'
ZOEY

Sitting on my ass in a dark dank room, I feel nothing. After they removed Panther and Dario's two sons, along with the two other men who rushed the room. I was literally within my head. When asshole son number one approached, I had one of the scalpels from my worktable. So when I sliced him from throat to belly button, I knew right then and there I signed my death certificate. Dario will not let this go. His sons have been trained from the beginning to take over their father's sick as fuck empire someday. And I have no idea where Palmira is or if she's still alive.

One of the men struggles to pull the asshole out of the room, screaming something in Italian. In seconds, I hear footsteps running toward the room. When the man comes back in, his eyes watch my every move. When he speaks to asshole son number two, I know he thinks he can read me and my thoughts and has a plan. *Dumb fucking Italian, he don't know nothing*, I think to myself.

When the two men start moving around the room I stay still, waiting. Then they try to get me to go to one side or the other, so they can corner me. Again, a stupid mistake usually done by amateurs. When the one in the dark-blue button-down shirt rushes me, I wait until the last minute then I do a roundhouse kick, my foot landing against his temple. Before he can catch his breath, I'm on him from behind. In less than, say, five seconds I've snapped his goddamn neck, dropping him to the floor. Grabbing the scalpel off the floor I remove part of his scalp, just because. Maybe with Panther and Avalanche being Navajo or maybe my head is fucked. Not the first time I've done it probably not the last.

Son number two is slowly moving, but not in any particular manner. He's screaming in I'm guessing Italian at someone but since I don't speak it; I couldn't care less. When he moves right then fakes left, trying to catch me off guard, I actually growl deep in my throat. He backs off instantly, shock all over his face. What the fuck, you dumb bastard, think I'm going to be your sitting prey? My only thought right now is I'll fight ya tooth and nail to the death if I have too.

Looking to the doorway, I see a bunch of dumb motherfuckers standing there waiting for what's to come next. When Dario's second bastard son, who's still in the room with me, rushes me with his head down like he's about to tackle me while playing in a football game, I literally jump over him, turning around in the air. When I land, I think quickly and kick him right in his balls, which drops him like a duck shot in the sky. As he's moaning, holding onto his sack, I grip his hands holding onto his balls. Bending down, I slice right through the gap in his hands, probably partially castrating him. Blood squirts like it's coming from a dying animal's throat, so instantly I'm covered.

The feel of his blood, as sick as it sounds, relaxes me enough so I can focus and read the situation. I hear that fucking prick's voice coming down the hallway, and this time I growl loudly. Not one man in that hallway comes near the doorway. I know what's going to happen but before they kill me, I'll take as many with me as possible.

When Dario looks in the room, the shock on his face brings a smile to my lips. I'm wondering which he is going to mourn more, his sons or his top two soldiers. I wipe the blood from my eyes into my hair. Looking at my fingers, I see the color of his blood as it drips between my digits to the floor. Watching it land, I move my eyes back to the door to see Dario watching me strangely. His eyes are bloodshot, so maybe he already knows about his one son at least.

"So, my little puttana, *Italian for whore*, I see you've been busy. Guess, again, I don't give you enough credit. Maybe it's time we sit down and break some bread together so we can, how they say, put our cards on the table. Or should I let your Indian die like you killed my sons? You know Occhio per occhio, dente per dente." *Italian for an eye for an eye, tooth for a tooth.*

Shaking my head, blood flying everywhere, I just keep my eyes on the doorway and don't say a goddamn word. If he even thinks to hurt Panther worse, I'll tear his throat out and shove it up his ass.

"What, nothing to say? Well, I have a story to tell you, Zoey Jeffries, that might just blow your fucking mind. So either you come with me on your own or I'll have my men drag you screaming, your choice. But make it quick, this bullshit that's happening right now is costing me a huge amount of fucking money."

Cocksucker don't want to follow this asshole anywhere because I don't trust him. But I also don't want to go against what… six men standing at the doorway and in the hallway. I'd get my licks in for sure but in the end, I'd be the one in the worst pain. Trying to think logically is fucking for the birds. And I blame Goldilocks for making me be this way, the little pain in my ass. I wait a bit longer, just to annoy Dario, before I nod in his direction. He again says something in Italian to his men and they slowly move away from the door and back down the hallway, so when I come out, no one is behind me.

I see this action for what it is. Dario wants me to think he's playing fair and with his men out of the way, no one can jump me. But that won't save me from all the other sons of bitches hiding along the way. I look around the room, the bloody scalp still in my hand. Off to the one side, beside the cabinets is a broom. Dropping what's in my hands I grab it, breaking off the bristles so all I have left is the wooden stick part. As I move to leave the room, I see a syringe under part of a napkin on the medical tray. It has liquid in it, don't have a fucking clue what, but don't care either. If I need a hidden weapon, what more could I want but a needle with shit in it. And if they were going to use it on me, I doubt it's Valium or Xanax, for Christ's sake.

Well, time to face my maker. Slowly and cautiously, I move toward the door. Once there, I look both ways then start to walk in the direction the motherfucker Dario did. The hallway is completely empty, though both sides have closed doors there. *What's behind the doors?* I think to myself. At the very end of the hallway a double door is open, and Dario is leaning against the framing, waiting for me. Just the way he looks at me makes my skin crawl. I hate this son of a bitch and if I do anything today, my main purpose is to end his miserable life any way I can. As he motions me in, I wait, shaking my head. His lips snarl that sarcastic grin of his and he walks in, so I follow the devil that he is into his den.

* * *

I never truly realized how fucking insane and deranged this man was. I've listen to him ranting for the last twenty or thirty minutes, never once mentioning or seeming too upset that one of his boys for certain is dead and the other might be following his brother. And both at my hands.

"Now, Zoey, I've tried to give you time, but you've ruined my plans and with that has to come some kind of punishment. I see it in your eyes, but not sure how you manage to sit there so goddamn calmly, like what I just said didn't bother you in the least. My sons couldn't control one of their emotions. If only they would have taken to you, they could have learned from you and the experiences you've been through. But no, they had to first think with their dicks in regard to you, which made me have to handle a delicate situation. Then as with those imbeciles, the jealousy factor came to the forefront. If only the three of you could have worked together, you'd have had the world at your feet."

Not able to hold my tongue any longer, I let loose.

"You lunatic, what the hell is wrong with you? You bought me then trafficked me to anyone who paid you to do whatever they wanted to with me. I was a child; you sick as fuck dick. You have no fucking soul. And when I broke free, did you let me go? No, you still kept fucking with me and those around me. Why? It makes no sense because the little I knew of your business couldn't hurt you, even if I wanted to, which I didn't. All I ever prayed for was to be able to be free of the insanity that is you, Dario."

His face gets bright red, but he sits still, glaring at me. Time goes on with him doing just that, nothing else. That is until there is a knock on the door, and he tells whomever to enter. I refuse to look at who it is because I know deep in my heart that is what he wants. To get a reaction from me and I refuse to do it. I hear soft, hesitant footsteps walk toward his desk. Out of the corner of my eye, I see that it's a woman, small in stature. Her head is lowered, eyes to the floor. It looks like she's trembling, but I could be wrong.

"Zoey, do you recognize her? Come on, rack that deranged brain of yours. Why would I bring someone in here unless I thought it would affect you in some way? It's been a while I know, but she's not changed that much. Maybe a bit meeker and quieter, but that is a good thing. Her voice used to irritate the fuck out of me. Come on, woman, raise your head. Turn around and say hello to your daughter."

I almost fall off the chair. Is he nuts? My mother? I haven't seen or heard from her in years. I thought she died in an overdose or from a beatdown from some pimp or john. The woman still hasn't turned to face me, but I study her. She's about the right height and I guess body type. When she lifts her head, I get a profile, which has the hair on the back of my neck start to tingle. Oh, goddamn, no way. Please not this.

Don't think I can take it. When she turns and looks me in the eyes, it hits me like a ton of bricks. For the love of all that is sacred, it's her. My motherfucking bitch of a mother.

As I glare at her it hits me, she's not cocky or strung out. Doesn't seem like the same woman from years ago. Don't want to think why she's here, but that thought is running through my mind. Maybe it's for the money, who the fuck cares. She was a junkie all my life, never gave one fuck about me.

"No greeting for your momma, Zoey? Come on, let bygones be bygones. It's been, fuck… how long since the two of you have seen each other, years, right? Woman, don't you want to grab your daughter and give her a hug and kiss? What's wrong with the two of you?"

Suddenly the woman turns and hisses. She sounds like an angry cat.

"You're an asshole dick. Of all the people involved, you know the truth because you played all of us like the puppeteer. Yeah, everyone thought I was this kid's mother but you, George, and I know differently. Why, did you think that little bit of money you gave me would turn me into Doris fucking Day? Obviously, it didn't work. What you've done to her over the years, my God, she's part of your family, Dario. How could you?"

Hearing me gasp, she turns and sees the shocked look on my face, and she whirls back around.

"You didn't even tell her? You weak pussy of a man. The stronger sex, my ass. And you seem to forget, you sick son of a bitch, you aren't white either. All these motherfuckers kissing your ass for this supremacy shit your trying to sell are only doing it because you have more money than God. I'm ashamed to have been a part of this. Got no excuses but drugs will make you sell your soul to the devil and, apparently, I've done that more times than I can count."

When she looks my way, I see a very small smile but anguish in her eyes.

"Zoey, nothing I did was intentional or directed at you. I was high and drunk most of the time and don't remember a lot of it. And I'm not blowing smoke up your ass, it's the truth. This asshole made sure the drugs flowed freely and, as you know, when I was high nothing was off the table. Since he's not telling you, I'll do it. The reason all of this went down the way it has is because he was beyond pissed at his—"

The sound of a gunshot shocks me, but I dive for the floor at the same time I feel blood hit the back of my head and back. The thud next to me has me shift to see the woman who I've considered my mother staring at me, eyes wide open. Son of a bitch, he just killed her in cold blood. Why? After all of these years he's kept her, what doesn't he want me to know?

Feeling my hair being yanked, I'm pulled to my feet just as I think the woman lets out a very small moan. Holy shit, is she playing possum? I don't blame her one bit, especially if Dario has held her prisoner all these years. Getting my head back in the present, Dario is dragging me to the farthest corner of the room. When he gets there, he pushes on a part of the wall and a panel opens. Are you kidding me? What is he… ten years old with a secret room?

"Move, you fucked-up bitch, before I put a bullet in your head too! NOW, you've caused me enough trouble. And from what I'm assuming, we should be having either one guest or many shortly. What a surprise for them when we are gone, and your Indian is left bleeding on a table to die."

Hearing him speak about Panther like that my restraint snaps. I pull forward, leaving a handful of my hair in his hand while I reach behind me, grabbing his junk, twisting back and forth. The noises coming from his mouth sound like two cats mating, but I don't give a fuck or care. He deserves whatever, because all he's done is ruin peoples' lives, just because he can. Pulling my elbow forward, I ram it into his face, feeling his nose break as the whoosh sound comes out with the gush of blood. He's fighting back so the kidney punch takes my breath away, but this is a fight for my own life. I know one of us won't be walking out of here alive.

Pushing him back and away from me, I shake my shoulders, concentrating on him and his next move. Dario rushes me, not too smart. Maybe he thought he was going to be able to take me down, but I shift a bit to the left and when he flies past me, I push his back hard, which has him ending up on his ass on the floor. The look in his eyes reflects the sociopath he is. He fumbles, trying to get to his feet when I kick him in the chin, knocking him back down. I jump back, not wanting to give him a chance to either corner me or get me to the floor. That's where I'm my weakest, and with his size he'd be able to manhandle me and get the upper hand.

Again and again, every time he tries to stand, I kick, punch, roundhouse kick, everything I have in me to keep him down. I'm hearing noises outside the door, but my concentration is on the prick whose blood I'm craving at the moment. Whatever is going on in the hallway will not change the course we are on. Or that was my thought when the door bursts open.

TWENTY-FOUR
'PANTHER'

CHAHÓÓŁHÉÉL NAABAAHII T'ÁÁ SÁHI
DARK WARRIOR WALKING ALONE

What the fuck? My head is splitting, the pain in my leg is killing me, and don't have a goddamn clue where I am. Worse, got no idea where Zoey is and if she's hurt or bleeding out somewhere. Hearing some rustling, I try to pretend to sleep. "Panther, try and stay as still as possible. I've got a few minutes if I'm lucky. My name is Stella and I work with your handler. Avalanche got word to us, and I was placed at the party for the weekend. Me, being a physician's assistant, and that Dario knows this, helped your cause. No, don't move. We almost lost you with the blood loss from the wounds. Before you ask, I have no idea where or what has been going down with Zoey.

"We have other undercovers throughout this compound but, Panther, it's beyond huge. And even though, after you were hurt, all the buyers were ushered out, no one was able to get away. We had a line of state police waiting for each and every car, truck, and limousine and pulled them over as soon as they left this property. These rich motherfuckers are going to have a lot of explaining to do. From what I've been told, the cavalry is on their way. Your girl's club traced down the connection and with that have been able to pinpoint this location.

"I need you to just stick to this room. Actually, when I leave, going to lock it. Don't let anyone in unless you know them. Walking is going to be difficult so if you have to tell them to break the door down, go for it. This section hasn't been updated with better security like the rest of the buildings. I'll try to keep an eye out for your girl. Be safe, friend. Thanks for all you and your friends have been doing. This is a big one, Panther, to get this jagoff removed from the circuits. I can't tell you how many lives of innocents you are saving, though that number is huge brother."

I feel the gun she places in my hand before she puts the sheet and blanket over it. Then she places two clips by my other hand, repeating putting everything under the bedding.

"Be safe."

Then she walks out, never looking back. When the door closes, I hear the lock catch, so I close my eyes, taking a moment trying to send positive thoughts out into the universe for Zoey. God, what a fucking disaster this turned out to be. And here I lie like either a cripple or a newborn baby whichever, either way can't help at all. With nothing to do and my mind still foggy from the surgery, I do the only thing I can. I doze off, which is exactly what the drugs given to us are for, so we can start the healing process.

* * *

'TINK'
Maggie/Goldilocks

Flying down the highway in one of the club's large SUVs, or as Zoey would say—a fucking cage—I'm pissed as all get out. How the fuck did our sheriff get by all of us? No, he didn't do anything to Zoey or our town, but he knew that his crazy as fuck brother was involved. And he knew this because when that ranch went up for sale, he got word to his brother, Dario. He opened up Montana to the Mafia and the De Luca clan. I wonder if Sheriff George knew his brother was involved with the trafficking circuits all around Montana. I feel like such a fool. How did Dario manage to build that entire city-like mansion without anyone knowing? Probably has something to do with the mob, but still. From the satellite view, the property is huge and it's a whole city within itself in Nowhere, Montana.

No one is saying a word and the stress levels are peaking at the very top. Every Devil's Handmaidens sister is in one of the SUVs because this is personal.

Zoey is one of us, so no way in hell was anyone staying behind. Even the prospects are with us, including my Hannah. She threw a hissy fit that no matter what, she was going to bring her Auntie Zoey back home. She's wearing Kevlar and is locked and loaded. It was my dad who told me she was ready.

Speaking about my dad, he and his brothers are behind us on bikes and in cages. Again, from looking behind us, think every one of his brothers is following. Behind his group are Ollie and his sanctuary folks, along with Panther's men, including the ever so fucking stubborn Avalanche. How he's able to get around, no clue. But he put up a man hissy fit when Hannah threw in his face that she was going and did Panther know his best friend was a pussy. Everyone thought Avalanche was going to tear her apart, limb by limb. Personally would never say it out loud but the little mouth deserved whatever he did. Instead, he left the room and not five minutes later came back ready for anything by the firepower he was holding. He also had some kind of brace up his jeans to his groin. As I told everyone, he's a grown man, not going to question his abilities. He came by and thanked me for that.

The property we are almost at is about fifteen to twenty minutes outside of our town of Timber-Ghost. The closer we get, the more traffic and official-looking vehicles are along the road and in open fields. There are some really luxurious cars pulled over with what appear to be very wealthy people losing their ever-fucking minds, most in handcuffs.

My phone starts to ring so I grab it from my back pocket.

"Hello, this is Tink."

"Hello, Tink, you don't know me, but I know of you. My code name is Twilight and you and your convoy need to get here now. Shit is hitting the fan, so to speak. I locked Panther in the surgical room on the west side of the compound. I'm going to look for Zoey for him. Be careful, Dario has this whole place boobytrapped, IEDs everywhere, because he is beyond deranged, leaning toward unhinged and demented. And his men are fucking crazy so be cautious, eyes wide open. Good luck."

"Wait, don't hang up. FUCK!!!"

Dialing my dad's number I wait impatiently as I tell Glory to put the pedal to the floor, which she does.

"Dad, just got an anonymous call from someone named Twilight. She told me we need to move our asses because shit is going down. Also tell everyone to be careful the place apparently has IEDs throughout the inside and outside. Tell Avalanche that Panther is locked down in a room on the west side, so get him and his men to go there first. Dad, no matter what, find Zoey for me, please. I know, but my gut is fighting with my heart. Yeah, okay, yeah, bye."

Every single Devil's Handmaidens sister in this

vehicle heard every word but not one asked or demanded answers because they know I'm barely holding on. We've learned so much about our sister Shadow in the last forty-eight hours, and don't think there's a person who doesn't feel empathy for her. How she's survived everything and found her place with our club is a fucking miracle.

We see a large fleet of what looks to be government vehicles at the entrance with men holding AK-47s or some other kind of assault weapon. When Glory stops where there are four cars blocking the entrance to the driveway, a guard, I'm guessing, approaches us, his eyes following all the vehicles behind me lining up, waiting for us to move. Then a single truck comes forward in the grass and it stops on an angle to the guard. Looking over Glory, I see it's Ollie and his four brothers squashed in the back, and their father next to him. When the man approaches, Ollie holds up some kind of ID and I see the guard's eyes almost pop out of his head, then he quickly nods and yells for the cars to be moved immediately. Thank God for whatever trump card Ollie is carrying.

Driving down the longest entrance driveway I've ever seen, my heart is beating like crazy. I'm going insane with worry about Zoey and Panther. But mainly my bestie Zoey. She's been through so much and it just keeps coming at her. Fucking Dario, why can't he leave her alone? Didn't he do enough damage when he bought her years ago?

Approaching the not even sure what the hell to call the obnoxious monstrosity—house, mansion, or compound—it's that fucking big. I can't believe no one knew this was here. How and who built it... because it's not that old. There are like, I don't know, six or eight huge buildings all connected together like you would expect when dealing with the mob. The last attached building is huge, and I'm guessing from my experience, that's where they have all the parties and auctions. That thought makes me almost vomit in my mouth.

"Glory, be careful. We have no clue if this sick fuck has his own snipers out here just waiting to take us down like carnival ducks."

"Yeah, my thoughts exactly, Tink. Hey, all of you in the back, keep your eyes wide open. Don't trust anyone or anything. This motherfucker Dario is a psychopath, who has honed his skills over the years. He's been hunting our sister Shadow for some reason and now he has her, he won't want to let her go easy. No one goes in alone. Everyone in at least pairs or in groups of three. Make sure you're not only locked and loaded but have extra ammo, and one person carrying grenades or other hand explosives. Also, keep your coms on so we can stay in contact. This goddamn place is bigger than a fucking city, so mark when you go in and where you go. Don't go and get yourselves lost. And be prepared for the worst, don't forget he's one of the lowest assholes out there. No heart or soul, all he cares about is money, power and his own sick sense of supremacy."

As everyone agrees with my VP, I smile to myself. Yeah, she's perfect, always has been. She's the yin to my yang. Now to get busy and find my bestie before she either does something she won't be able to handle, or that bastard of an uncle hurts her badly, or worse, kills her. That last thought has a shiver run down my spine. My God, she won't be able to handle what we have to tell her, but she has to hear that shit and then deal with Dario. No, it's too much. Even for her.

Glory slams on the brakes in front of the main entrance. I look around at my club sisters, knowing this is our most important mission yet.

"We're not only a club but also family. One of our own is in there, most likely in danger and could be injured too. The one who would give her life for all of us if she thought it would save our lives. All I ask is careful, keep your eyes open, and remember that Shadow needs us now. Let's go, Devil's Handmaidens, time to kick some major ass sisters."

One by one we empty from the SUV as my dad and his club arrives, along with Ollie, his brothers, father, and all of the men and women from the Blue Sky Sanctuary. As everyone starts to disperse, I walk to Ollie, who watches me with no expression on his face.

"Okay, Ollie, tell me how we got past that guard and bunch of macho assholes at the beginning of the driveway? That guy looked like he was going to shit himself when you flashed whatever in his face. What was it?"

He flashes a smile that makes me realize why his girlfriend Paisley always seems so happy, because this man is beyond gorgeous. When I look into his eyes, I swear to Christ, I just said that all out loud because his eyes are laughing at me. Whatever, I got shit to do. I put my hand on my hip, tapping my booted foot.

"Sorry, Tink, if I told you, would have to kill ya. Though you're very smart so take a second and put it together. You know I was working in Virginia, that's where I met Paisley before I came back home to Montana. When we made that decision, a few former military folks decided they needed a fresh start. Oh, that's right, you know one of them, right?"

With that we both laugh then get serious. I turn and follow the last of my club sisters into the main house. Walking in the double ten-foot doors, I pray like I've never done before that my bestie is hanging on, waiting for her sisters to come and get her ass.

TWENTY-FIVE
'SHADOW'
ZOEY

Who the fuck is the princess standing in the doorway? I've never seen her before, would have remembered that face. It's one of those faces' men would have fought wars over. When she rushes in, I move quickly to the farthest wall from her and Dario.

Hearing Dario speaking in Italian, I figure this is a family member or one of the bitches he keeps around so when the need arises, he has a plaything. His hand up, he must have assumed she'd help him up. I'm shocked when she grabs his hand, twisting it backward and up against his back, never taking her eyes from me.

"Dario De Luca, you are under arrest for everything from kidnapping to grand larceny, human trafficking, prostitution, and let's not forget murder."

As she reads him his rights, Dario is trying to fight and get away. I walk around them, make a fist, and punch him on the side of his forehead by his temporal area. He's out instantly. The woman is watching me closely as she makes sure his cuffs are on and locked. She drops him to the floor and steps back. I follow her lead, stepping back a few steps.

"You're Zoey, right? Zoey Jeffries? Goddamn, girl, been looking for you forever. All I can say is when you want to, you can disappear and hide, for fuck's sake. We have a lot to go over, but first I'm sure you're worried about Panther, right? When you leave this room, turn right then right again at the end of this hallway. Take that 'til it ends and make a left. Second door on the right is where you'll find Panther. I told him not to open the door for anyone and he's kind of barricaded within. Did the best I could with what was there. He's okay, by the way, we got the leg closed off after we cauterized the wound. Go, we can talk later. And, Zoey, I'm happy for you that this is finally over. At least for you it is."

Before I can even get my questions in order or open my mouth, the princess turns and walks right out of the room, going in the opposite direction she told me to go. Looking down at Dario, he doesn't seem to be breathing and I seriously don't give a fuck. My last punch to his head must have done it. Whatever, not wasting a goddamn minute, I follow her directions to the door she told me was the room Panther was in. I look around to make sure no one followed me and knock on the door. When I don't hear a thing, I lift my hand, pounding on the door at the same time screaming his name.

"PANTHER!! Panther! Panther! PANTHER, it's me Zoey. Open the door. Please, open the door."

As I hear shit that sounds like it is being dragged away, I wait impatiently. When the door cracks a hair then flies open, I'm in his arms before I can even process anything. I grab on to him, even though I know I'm covered in so much De Luca blood. He's humming in my ear, and it is the best sound ever.

"You okay, Nizhoni? Please tell me they didn't hurt you, or worse, put their hands on you and touch you? Let me look at you, Zoey. Come on, let me…. holy fucking shit, is that your blood? Motherfucking son of a bitch. No, don't tell me to hang on, we need to see where you're bleeding from."

Pushing off of his chest, I take a step back, trying to catch my breath while my eyes take in every inch of his body. He looks like hell. He's wearing some kind of scrubs and booties on his bottom half. His top half is bare with his long hair wild as fuck. But it's the look in his eyes that has my legs feel weak as my body shivers in a good way. I have to learn not to react first but think. So that's exactly what I do for a minute or two as we just stare into each other's eyes.

"No, Panther, they didn't touch or hurt me. In fact, as you can see by the way I'm covered in blood, there were a few altercations. I won each one. Did you ever doubt my skills?"

With that I grin my cocky, sarcastic smirk. He sees it and his eyes start to twinkle.

"So long story short, I know for sure one of the De Luca sons is dead, the other it's a fifty-fifty call. Oh, and the old man, Dario De Luca, will not be trafficking women and children ever again from the looks of it, though not sure, didn't get confirmation. There are people crawling all over this place, some being the De Luca loyals. Some chick found me, and she told me where you were. I have no idea who she is, but I'm just happy because she led me to you."

One minute he is standing a few feet away from me the next, in a blink of an eye, I'm back in his trembling arms. Neither of us says a word, we just hang on to the other for dear life. Everything that's happen seems to hit me at once, and if not for Panther's arms that tighten and hold me up, I would land on my ass. I don't know how long we stay just like this until Panther pulls me to one of the beds and lifts me so I'm sitting, and he sits right next to me, once again pulling me close.

"Beautiful, something just doesn't feel right. Why the fuck did Dario have to keep a finger on you after all of these years? Do you have any idea? It's like he was watching you because you know something that you shouldn't. Maybe when you were being held you witnessed a murder or maybe saw people you weren't supposed to. My mind is going a mile a minute because my gut is telling me we are missing something very important."

Trying to rack my brain about a time in my life I've tried since then to forget, nothing comes immediately to the forefront. I slightly remember when Dario bought me, he seemed nice-ish. Then something happened and he became the prick, and that was it. First the dog cage and eating from the bowls of filthy water and maggot infested food, which to this day have no idea what it was. When the first party was in full force and Dario was walking a few men through where he kept all of us, it hit me that after the night was over my life would never be the same. And, fuck, was I right. Money does let people buy their idea of what will fulfill their needs or what they think is their happiness. Dario had no limits for any of us, but especially me. As long as the customer paid, whatever they wanted was what I was told to do. Some of the shit damaged not only my soul but my way of thinking of people in general.

So far into my own head, I don't hear the noise off in the distance until I hear pounding of feet on the floor. Looking at Panther, he's already trying to stand. When he's up, he pulls me behind him, probably for protection, though he's so weak I doubt he can do anything. The feet come to an abrupt halt right in front of the door. Reaching toward the medical cart, Panther grabs a scalpel, keeping it behind his back.

The pounding on the door has both of us jumping,

that is until I hear a voice I was afraid I'd never hear again.

"ZOEY, ZOEY, where are you? Damn it, Zoey, make some kind of noise or cough, sneeze for fuck's sake, fart if you have to. Please just don't shit your pants like that time when you were sick. That was seriously gross."

Hearing Goldilocks going on and on I hang my head down. Hearing Panther chuckling next to me, I clear my throat then let out a huge belch. I wasn't even done when the door flies open, hitting some of the shit that was piled in front of it so when it flings back it hits Goldilocks right in her face, and she goes down like she's been shot. As her ass hits the ground, she is cracking up, which has our club sisters watching her, smiling and softly laughing. That is until I hear Hannah's sniffles.

"Auntie Zoey. Oh my God, is that you? I was so worried that I'd never see you again. Oh, Auntie Zoey."

She's on the go and before I know it, her arms are around my waist, her little body shaking. Feeling wetness soaking my shirt, my arms hold her close. This poor kid has been through so much, I feel like shit that all of this is upsetting her so much. Not sure how she's wiggled her way into the little bit of heart I have left, but she did.

"Come on, Hannah, I'm okay. Look at me, Squirt, I'm still breathing, don't worry. Give me a little bit of time and I'll be as crazy and bitchy as ever. Hannah, come on, breathe, kid. Dry those eyes, prospect. This isn't showing me you've got what it takes to be a Devil's Handmaidens sister. I vouched for you, don't let me down, dry those fucking tears, pull yourself together now."

I feel her go stiff in my arms for a second, then she pushes me away while drying her face off. When her eyes lift to mine, I'm blown away by what I see. Unconditional love. Holy fuck, the only other times I've seen a similar look was on Goldilocks, Pops, and Momma Diane's faces. This kid is going to be the death of me. Turning so I can have a minute or two to get my shit together, I hear Panther ask Hannah if she's okay. My heart fills up with some much emotion because he's giving me the time to adjust myself. Just listening to him making sure she's okay shows how much empathy he has inside of him. Then arms go around my waist from behind.

"Zoey, my God, are you okay? Is this your blood or Panther's? Do you know where Dario is? I don't know if he said anything to you, but I've got some shit to tell you that is going to blow your mind. Not here though. Let's get you both out of here and go home. Right now, between our club sisters and my dad's brothers in the Intruders, along with Ollie and the Blue Sky Sanctuary folks, and law enforcement officers, we are going room by room to see what we can find. Praying there are no victims here, but if they are, we'll help them."

"Goldilocks, I know for sure there are victims here. In that huge building they had both kids and adults in the dog cages next to the fighting dogs. I'm not sure how many. Also, in Dario's office is a woman I thought was my mother but from the way she tells it, Dario paid her to fake that. Oh yeah, speaking of Dario; thinking he's dead—though I didn't check for a pulse—but he looked dead on the floor. Didn't look like he was breathing. Also, one of his sons is gone, not sure about the young one. I'd give him maybe a fifty-fifty chance to live. Don't have a fucking idea what the hell's been going on all my life. I've been racking my brain and memories to try and figure out why I caught Dario's eye and he's always been in my life. For now, if possible, I just want to go home and get Panther some medical help before we both fall asleep for a fucking week. Is that possible, Goldilocks? Bestie, can you make that happen for me—no for us?"

"For you, Zoey I've always told you I'd do anything. So, if you need to get home that's what we're going to do for you. And we are definitely going to have a long talk, but for now, just seeing you breathing and hearing your voice gives me so much comfort and relief, for Christ's sake. Come on, bestie, let's get the fuck out of here. Panther, you need help? Hannah, grab that wheelchair in the corner, give him a hand. Then follow us and push him because there's no way in hell he's going to be able to walk through this mausoleum of a house."

I watch as at first Hannah's temper starts to rise until she takes a real long look at Panther, then she moves toward the medical equipment across the room. My eyes move until they are caught by Panther's gaze. I see what Goldilocks sees, but I also see a man who almost lost his life, not only because of me but because of his promise to always have my back. And that right there has my heart beating faster as I feel something very rare. Panther is definitely a man of his word. And for that I thank God.

Once Panther is comfortable in the chair, his legs lifted up, Goldilocks wraps her arm around me, which is ridiculous since she's so much shorter. I let her though, if it's helping and making her feel better. The worry that I've seen across her face and Hannah's, don't think I can take any more of these emotional reunions. Just as that thought goes through my head, I hear my name being yelled down the hall. I squint and see the rest of my club sisters running, yeah running, our way. And to my utter surprise, the first one to reach and grab me, pulling me tight, is Heartbreaker.

"Thank God, Shadow, fuck, I'm so—um well—I'm so glad you're okay. And once again, I'm sorry for everything."

She goes to let me go, but I pull her closer to me.

With all that's happened, I need to make sure I let those around me know how much they mean to me.

"Delilah, no need to apologize, sister. Just make sure you follow your program and keep your shit clean. I've got your back always, sister."

Her hands grab mine, squeezing tightly, as the tears fill her eyes and flow freely down her cheeks. Then she nods, gives me one more hand squeeze, then lets me go, turning and walking away. Before I can stop her, another club sister is right in front of me showing me her love and support. What a fucking day. Even though this makes me feel good, I can't wait 'til this bullshit is over so we can leave and get back home and to our everyday lives.

TWENTY-SIX
'PANTHER'

CHAHÓÓŁHÉÉL NAABAAHII T'ÁÁ SÁHI
DARK WARRIOR WALKING ALONE

I'm beyond exhausted. By the time we are allowed to leave Dario's compound my leg is pounding, along with my head. I'm starving and stink like a skunk has sprayed me and I got hit by a car and am roadkill. My mood has deteriorated too as we really aren't getting any answers from anyone. The only highlight of my shitty day was when I saw Avalanche staggering around with an assault rifle over his shoulder and a brace on his leg. Fuck, even when we get injured, we're like the Bobbsey twins, for fuck's sake. Guess that pact we made years ago, and the sharing of our blood is truly real. I'm one lucky bastard to have him on my side, for sure.

Now we are on our way back to Tink's ranch. That is another thing that pisses me way the hell off. Why we need to go there, I have a home that I'd like to go to. Not to mention I have my two dogs to take care of and need to check on my horses, mares that are ready to give birth, and just because that's where I want to go. It was a serious pissing match between Tink and Tank verses Avalanche and me. Everyone around us, their heads were like they were watching a tennis match. Finally, it took Zoey putting her hands up, looking first at her family then at the two of us. Shaking her head, she just said quietly to whomever, "I'm going home, you all can go wherever the fuck you want."

Then she stomped out the front door. Everyone followed her, not only out of that house but into vehicles and then currently making our way to Tink's ranch. I'm in the truck with Avalanche, Chicago, George, Dallas, and Jersey. Zoey is with me after another meltdown from Tink, who wanted her to drive with the club. Finally, knowing she'd had enough, I lost my shit.

"What the ever-lovin' fuck? Are we fifteen, in high school, and have to do everything together? Goddamn it, Tink, she just about died in the process of killing only God knows how many people, and on top of it she was worried about me, feeling guilty when she had no choice. Now are we going to put her through a pick me, pick me situation? She's going to your house, let this go, will you for Christ's sake?"

Tink glared at me until Noodles came up behind her, literally picked her up and carried her to the large SUV. I owe that man. Looking around, everyone is very quiet. Zoey is actually leaning on me, asleep. My eyes are heavy, but my mind is running at peak performance. Feeling his eyes, I look up to see Avalanche watching the two of us with a weird look in his eyes. When he sees me returning his look, he shoots me a very small grin before gazing back out the window. Now what the fuck is that all about? Seems to me I'll be having quite a few conversations in the near future.

Zoey seems agitated all of a sudden, so I wrap my arm around her, pulling her tighter to me. She calms down immediately, and her breathing goes back to normal. The last thing I remember is the way her body feels next to mine. It feels like home.

Feeling the truck rolling to a stop, my eyes slowly open up to see we are parked right in front of the ranch. Gently, so as not to disturb her, I lean Zoey away from me, unlock my seat belt, and get out of the vehicle. Just being able to stretch my legs is heaven. I can feel the tightness from the fresh stitches and know I'm going to have to try and take it easy. Looking around, the silence and peacefulness is refreshing after all the chaos of the last few days.

Hearing other vehicles emptying out, my eyes see someone walking toward the group with a few folks behind them. As she gets closer, I recognize Dr. Cora, the club physician. She walks directly to me, puts her hand on my forehead, then tsks under her breath.

"Panther, come on, let's get you inside and off of

that leg. Tank and Noodles filled me in but will need to examine you. May I suggest a shower first, want to keep that area clean and dry as best we can. I see Shadow's out, she's also on my list to see immediately once everyone arrives. Let me go in and set up in Shadow's suite. I'll be waiting on you both but take your time, no rush."

With that she sets off to get her shit together and I guess just wait for us.

I walk to the other side of the vehicle, opening the door to see Zoey is gone to the winds. There is no way I'm going to be able to pick her up and carry her up the stairs to the second floor. Feeling a hand behind me, I look to see Ollie standing there with four other men who look like his brothers and, thinking, maybe his father.

"Panther, let me give you a hand. No, it's no problem. She weighs probably no more than one of our ranch dogs, for Christ's sake. Got your back, brother. Come on, let's get you two settled. After the day you've had, probably just want to lie down, go to sleep, and forget about it all. I know that's what the fuck I'd want. Oh, hey, sorry didn't mean to be rude, this is my family. That's my dad, Benjamin, and those four lugs are my brothers. From left to right that's Orin, Oliver, Bennett, and Brooks. You've already met my sister, Brenna. I mean, Raven, she's in the Devil's Handmaidens MC along with Shadow. One other sister, Onyx, isn't here but I'm sure you'll meet her shortly. Now, let me get your woman up in that house so the two of you can just chill. From what I heard; Momma Diane has been cooking all of Shadow's favorites so there will be a decent spread of chow. Our mom has been here helping, along with a few other town ladies. You lead the way, big man, I'll follow."

When Ollie and his brothers leave, I check on Zoey, who is zonked the hell out. Carefully, as to not reinjure my thigh, I start the water in the shower then push down the scrubs and the dirty T-shirt I'd put back on just for some covering. Next, I throw down the puffy rug right outside the shower, which is what Zoey always does. When I step into the shower it feels like heaven. I stand here for a few minutes just letting the water run down my back. When I'm starting to notice that I'm feeling more like a human being, I grab the soap and washcloth I put in the stall. Every body part I wash feels like new when I'm done. Getting all that off of me is such a relief. Next, I grab Zoey's shampoo and attempt to wash my hair. I usually use a special hair cleanser that's natural, but my hair stunk the worst. After two shampoos, I put some conditioner on the ends then rinse it off.

Just this little bit has me beyond exhausted, so I shut off the shower and squeegee off the walls and glass doors. Then I reach for my towel, drying myself off. Knowing I'm going to have to either go to bed naked or put on dirty clothes, I pick option one, which is my all-time favorite anyway.

I grab a few washcloths and a large bath towel. I carefully remove the bloody clothes off of Zoey, planning on throwing them in the garbage. Next, I use the wet cloths to wipe her down and remove as much blood as I can. Then, when I'm finished, I take time to carefully dry her off. Finally, when I'm done, I reach under her pillow and pull out one of my T-shirts. Holy shit, by the time this woman is done I'll be lucky to have like one or two T-shirts left.

When I crawl into bed, my exhaustion hits me immediately and before I can lean down and give Zoey a kiss, I'm out like a light.

* * *

Waking up to someone's hands around my neck is not what I call a good way to open my eyes. But to see Zoey completely out of it, with her hands trying to strangle me, has me on alert and freaking the fuck out. Yeah, time for us to talk and find out what that psychopath Dario's plans were, especially for Zoey.

"Nizhoni, it's me, Panther. Zoey, take a few breaths and blink. Come on, you can do it. I'm not the enemy. That's it, breathe, feel the air going in and then coming out. Listen to what is happening, especially my voice. You know me, Zoey. Hey, there's no screaming or swearing. No strangers screaming in pain. You can do this, I know it. Look at me, beautiful. See me, I am chahóółhééł naabaahii yikah t'áá sáhi. You own me, Nizhoni, never doubt that. I won't ever put my hands on you in anger. That's my promise to you."

I continue to watch her, though her hands are now resting on my neck, no longer digging in for dear life. As I continue to talk, her muscles seem to relax against me until she's lying on top of me, her hands in my hair. *Fuck,* I think to myself, *how good Zoey feels this close to me.* My hands, I place lightly on her shoulders but don't trap her in. Last thing I want is her to come to and panic. Been there, don't want her to experience it.

Very slowly Zoey starts to come around. First, I feel her shift to get more comfortable. That is until she realizes she's supposedly been sleeping directly on top of me. Her eyes shoot open to see mine twinkling at her.

"Hey, beautiful, how're you feeling? I tried to clean you up before putting you to bed when we got back here. Know you have lots of questions, so do I, Zoey. But first, when you're feeling up to it, let's get you a shower, some clean clothes, and maybe some food in your belly. Then we'll look for Tink because I know she's biting at the bit to talk to you about what they found out. First though, Nizhoni, I want you to relax for a bit right where you are in my arms. Not sure about you but this feels good, nope, even better than that. Phenomenal."

She stretches and I feel her entire body over mine. The heat from her core lying directly over my hardening cock. Oh my God, as much as I want her, don't want to scare her with the intensity of my feelings or my cock. Moving my hands, I caress her face, my thumb running over her cheekbones. Her ice-blue eyes slowly close, enjoying my caresses. As I pull her down for a kiss, a knock on the door makes me swear under my breath.

"What the fuck, how do they know? It's worse than having a bunch of kids running in and catching us in the mood trying to get busy, for Christ's sake."

Her eyes open wide, mouth dropping open to form a perfect 'O.' As her eyes roam my face, taking me in, there's another impatient knock, no a goddamn pound, on the door.

"Who the fuck is it and what do you want? Can't we have a little time after all we've been through? Son of a bitch, we both almost died."

We wait but nothing. No answer or anything. Like someone isn't there now. Jesus, I gently move Zoey off of me, making sure she's covered and comfortable before getting out of bed, reaching for a pair of sweats I laid on the bottom of the bed. Pulling them on, I stomp to the door, turning to look at Zoey all snuggled in the bed watching me.

When I open the door, I feel like such a total

asshole. Hannah is standing there with a huge tray in her arms. Behind her is another woman from the club with a tray in her arms. When they see me, both look alarmed. Yeah, total dick that's me.

"Hey, ladies, I'm sorry, didn't mean to come across like a total asshole. Come on in, please and thank you. Believe me Zoey has to be starving, she went to bed without dinner. And just saying I'm always hungry, so let's see what you brought us."

They move to the little table off to the one side of the room while I walk to the bed to help Zoey. She looks so small in that bed, even with her badass inked face. I see uncertainty on her face, so I reach down and kiss her forehead. She swings her legs over the bed and between the two of us we manage to pull my T-shirt down, making sure she's covered. Fuck, just seeing the bruises and bites makes me want to go back to that fucking place and tear each person apart who put their hands and goddamn their teeth on her.

Helping her to the table, I see both Hannah and Kitty look up. Without thought Hannah comes directly to Zoey, hugging her tightly. When she lets her go, Kitty moves in and even though she gives a hug to her, it's not as tight or long.

"All right you pains in my ass. Enough of that shit. Since when do I allow hugs from my club sisters especially prospects in training? I'll let these ones go, but let's not make a habit of it. What's for breakfast? Holy shit, that's every meal for today at least. Let me guess, Momma Diane has been busy. I see my favorites. Damn, Panther, you better get your ass over here and I hope you're hungry 'cause there's enough food here to feed a small country."

As the women softly laugh, I feel some of the weight lift from my shoulders. I'm amazed at how my woman; wait a minute. Well, yeah, she's my woman for sure, and it makes my heart happy that she's able to bounce back from what happened yesterday. She took lives but she had no choice, it was their lives or hers, no ours. Survival of the fittest.

I just hope that whatever we find out she we'll be able to manage just as well.

TWENTY-SEVEN
'SHADOW'
ZOEY

Man, I'm beyond stuffed. And having both Squirt and Kitty around, they made breakfast a riot. The two of them together, I see trouble in the future for sure. Now I'm sitting in a hot tub soaking. Usually, baths aren't my cup of tea, but Panther insisted, so trying to relax and just enjoy. He put in some bath salts he found under the sink, which are helping to calm my muscles down.

This is the first time since yesterday I've had a moment to think about the last twenty-four hours and again; I know I'm missing something, just don't know what. There is no explanation for why Dario was so fixated on me. Seeing him on that floor not breathing means I eliminated that problem, so not sure why it's still on my mind. Panther has been wonderful, but I know he's been running shit through his head too. Nothing makes sense, especially since Dario seemed to hunt down the one person who was in my personal life. I'm trying to make sense of it, even though I know Dario and his associates were working with Panther and Avalanche way before I even came into the picture.

What has me stumped is how did Dario know about Panther and me? It's not like we acted like normal adults going out to eat or to a movie. Maybe take a weekend away. Neither of us had the time to do that kind of shit. Between my responsibilities to the Devil's Handmaidens and my club sisters, and his dedication to his stud ranch and his Native family, we didn't have a lot of time left. Also, when he explained what he considered his mission in life, I jumped in with both feet because it ran right alongside what Goldilocks and I, along with our club, were fighting also, so it made sense to me even though some of my thought process was selfish.

I trust Panther, obviously, but also have a gut feeling something is about to drop. A bomb of some sort. Leaning back, I let my head rest on the pillow, taking a few deep breaths. Dozing off, it feels good just to be in the moment. I never take time for myself, can't remember the last time. Well, to be truthful, there's never been a time. I try to keep moving so I don't have downtime because then my whole life will go under my mind's microscope. And that thought scares the fuck out of me.

I love my life, but lately with all the bullshit our

club has been through trying to break up the trafficking circuits, and me personally dealing with the scum of the world, it's starting to weigh on me. And that bothers the motherfucking hell out of me. I'm the club's enforcer, there is no alternative for that job. You have to be able to separate all emotions and just do your goddamn job.

A soft knock brings me back into myself.

"Yeah, who is it?"

"Beautiful, it's me. Can I come in? Won't look, just need a minute."

That feeling of dread starts at my toes and works its way into my gut within a second or two.

"Okay, Panther, come on in."

Hearing the door open, I kind of sink farther into the water which is covered in some bubbles and foam. It's not that I'm ashamed of my body but of the unknown. Panther affects me deeply, which makes me unsure of myself and I don't like that feeling at all.

"Hey, Nizhoni, how are you feeling? You look a bit rested, which is something you needed. Sorry to barge in, but I spoke to Noodles and Tank. Want to give you a heads-up before we meet up with Tink in a bit."

With the way he's watching me, and how tense his body is, I already know I'm not going to like whatever he's going to share. Son of a bitch, why does this shit always happen when good stuff comes into my life? It's been like this as far as I can remember. I want Panther in my life and not just as a friend. The feelings I've been having are new to me and scare the fuck out of me too. But as the days go by, I've come to cherish all of our time together. Yeah, me having actual feelings for a person outside of my 'family' is unbelievable. But it's happening and I'm doing my best to process it all. And not fuck it up royally.

"Okay, I'm just going to put it out there, Zoey, just do me a favor. Don't panic, we got this, no matter what it is. I'm not going to let anyone, or anything, hurt you ever again. So, between Raven, Heartbreaker, Freak, and some others they were able to piece together some connections between Dario and someone who's been lying to all of you for years. It's not my tale to tell but just prepare yourself because you won't believe it, I'm sure, 'cause I sure the hell didn't. Now, I'm going to hold a towel. You need to get out of the tub, you're becoming a prune."

Looking down, I raise my hands to see he's right. I'm a prune all right. I let a small laugh out, not sure if it's because of nerves or just a release of my tension. He lifts a towel above his head so he can't see anything, and I stand, reaching for it to wrap around myself. Panther immediately wraps me up in the towel within his arms. His warmth and smell immediately assault my senses. I feel my body react, which always surprises me because that's definitely not normal behavior for me. Usually when someone puts their hands on me, I go crazy trying to break shit, usually a finger, hand, or face.

Feeling his arms tighten, he lifts me out of the tub, gently placing me on my feet on the cushiony mat, not letting me go. My arms are wrapped under the towel so I'm at his mercy. Lifting my head, I see he's already watching me intently with those forest-green eyes of his. Damn, the look in them has goose bumps starting to form all over my body, while I feel my nipples harden. Holy shit, if he can make my body react to him with a look, how am I going to be able to hold it together if and when we take it further?

"Zoey, I want to feel you. Taste you. Hold you, while you tremble in my arms. Let me make you feel good, beautiful. You can always tell me to stop, and you know I will. God, woman, you're driving me crazy. All I ever think about is you. Nothing, not our mission or the ranch, comes before you. Zoey, I need to feel you, especially after yesterday. Is that okay? Promise you'll have all the control, have I ever lied to you? No, I haven't. Trust me."

I watch him the entire time and he never takes his eyes off of me, showing me how much this moment and, more importantly, I mean to him. Knowing that he is aware of my history and still wants to be with me makes me feel warm inside. I've always known this part of my life was going to be hard if not impossible but won't ever know unless I at least try.

And who better than this phenomenal specimen of a man in front of me.

"Panther, I'm not going to lie. I want you. All of you, but at the same time that thought not only shocks me, it terrifies me. You're right, lately all I do is think about you, wanting to know what you're doing and with who. I've not been with anyone in years, and I mean years. It's been easier, if I have the urge, to take care of it myself rather than try to hold back all my fears for a one-night thing. Saying all of that, I'm willing to try, but promise me if I say stop, you will."

Pulling me to him, his mouth crushes onto mine, his tongue already demanding entry as soon as our lips collide. Tentatively, I open slightly, and he forges his way in, taking everything that is me in. He tastes, nibbles, licks, pushes, and pulls his way until I'm breathless and like Silly Putty in his arms.

"Zoey, you never have to worry about me. No matter what, if you say no, then it's no and I won't ask any questions. Thank you, beautiful, for trusting me. I promise to make it good—no, the best for you."

With that he swings me up into his arms, still wrapped in the towel, and strolls into the bedroom, placing me carefully on the bed, his lips returning to my mouth. His hands move to the top of the towel, slowly opening it up like I'm his present. When I'm exposed to him with nothing to hide me, I reach up with my hands to cover myself, but he grabs my hands, holding them down as his eyes take me in. The heat from his gaze warms my skin like I'm outside on a hot sunny day. I feel my nipples start to bead and harden, while my legs are shifting under his intimate gaze. Moving both of my hands to one of his large ones, his free hand starts at my neck, slowly moving down lightly like a whisper, fluttering over my pulse in my neck then moving to the fullness of my breasts. His fingertips tap on my nipples, making me catch my breath. Time stands still as his hand descends down my sternum to my stomach, shifting one way then the other. When he passes by my girly parts to land on my upper thigh, I gasp. His fingers are massaging my muscles as I feel another wave of wetness between my legs.

This feeling is beyond new to me as, I've never had these feelings during the few times I'd had sex. It was usually a slam bam, thank you, ma'am. No, this is definitely a want—no, a very intense need. The more Panther ignores my desire, the more I crave him and his touch. Hearing his chuckle, I growl lightly in my throat. He's teasing me and I like it. Back and forth he touches my breasts, neck, and inner thighs while kissing and eating at my lips. His taste mingles with mine as time stands still. When he sneaks in a fingertip on my core, my entire pelvic area raises up to chase his hand. When he lets my hands go to put that hand on my stomach to hold me down, I start to pant. Panther never rushes or forces his advances.

Slow and steady he works my body like a fine-tuned instrument. I forget everything but the feel and weight of his body on mine. The coarseness of his fingertips on my body, he moves slowly then fast over my nipples, then cupping my breasts, massaging them until I can't take it anymore.

"Please, Panther, I need you. Don't tease me anymore. I can't take it. I don't want to beg but I will. Just do it. Touch me."

"Zoey, no, I won't just do it. And, yeah, I want you to beg me for each and every touch. By the time I give you what you want, you will be mad with your desire and nothing else will be on that beautiful mind of yours but my mouth and hands. If I'm lucky, maybe even my cock too. Nizhoni, I'm going to make your first time one that you will remember forever. And it will be all about desire, want, and love. Now, relax and enjoy."

I don't know how long Panther plays my body. He brings me so close with my breath coming fast then slowing down. His fingers tap, press, but never actually touch me where I want, no, desperately need him to. I try begging, pleading, and bargaining with him… nothing. This is all on him. He is reading my body and only gives me enough to keep me from screaming my brains out. Or knocking his ass out for teasing me.

When one of his long thick fingers separate my labia, and he slowly pressed that one finger into me, I stop breathing. Literally stop breathing for a second or two. Just one finger and my body is already reacting as I can feel my insides clenching to hold him in. He pulls out and when he pushes back in, there are two fingers. The feeling of fullness has me gasping as he nibbles alongside my neck to my ear, whispering dirty little nothings there.

Not sure if I can hold back my orgasm. The rush of desire and emotion running through my body is something I don't know how to handle. Feeling it before it happens, my eyes fill with tears. Panther is so intent on taking care of my body, the wet rolls down my cheeks as I let go of all of my fears. This man owns a part of me and my heart.

When he pulls back his hand and thrusts back in, I scream low in my throat. When he does it again and again, making some changes in his approach, I can't hold it back when a low moan escapes my lips. With his hand still holding me down, I fight to move my hips in rhythm with his thrusts. Feeling something I've never felt before, I need to move or something, so I kick my legs out, never thinking I'd hit Panther. The pain in my toes tells me I must have hit his muscular calf at the same time he swears.

"Damn it, Zoey, that fucking hurt."

With his hand off my stomach, I start to move and ride his hand. Nothing can stop me as I chase my release. The noises coming out of my mouth don't sound human and I don't care one bit, I'm on a mission. All that matters is the feelings flowing freely throughout my body.

"Goddamn, you're beautiful, Zoey. So, Nizhoni, just feel. Let it happen."

Listening to his raspy deep voice while his fingers, now three, push in and out of my core, I can't stop the emotions when I explode. I soak Panther's hand with my release, but he doesn't seem to care as he keeps moving, making sure my orgasm keeps going on and on. One into another as the screams taper to a soft, satisfied mewl. Then he lifts his hand and licks each finger, showing me how much he truly is enjoying himself.

"My God, thank you, Nizhoni, for giving that to me. I'll always treasure that gift. Zoey, it's okay, don't. Please don't cry I'm here for you. This is forever, you know that, right? I'm yours until I no longer have breath left in my body."

With those words everything I've held back for so many years explodes from me. My sobs turn into violent shakes and seem to go on forever. When I'm spent and just whimpering, Panther gently places us under the covers carefully, never letting me go. Throughout my breakdown he never once falters, just keeps me close, never letting me go.

This is what I've always wanted in my life. That one person who could love me for who I am and not for what I could do for them. It hits me in the heart. Panther is my person. I hear Goldilocks's voice in my head, and for once I agree with her. They do exist. Since I met her, my bestie has preached that one day I would meet the one person who would be my soul mate. Feeling Panther's body holding me close, I smile because she was right. And I finally believe it too.

TWENTY-EIGHT
'TINK'
MAGGIE/GOLDILOCKS

Damn, I need Noodles's arms around me right now. What I have to do next is going to break my heart and my bestie's. If there was any other way, I'd do it in a heartbeat, but unfortunately there isn't.

"Sweet Pea, she'll understand and come to appreciate and even be thankful for what you're about to share with her. Everyone needs to know about their family, no matter good or bad. And for your club sister and friend, this coming from you will lessen the blow. Don't sell her short, she's been fighting her whole life to find a way to live. Now you're giving it to her and, along with Panther, she might actually get her deepest wish to come true."

Looking up I see Noodles watching me.

"Soldier boy, what are you rambling on about? Zoey's a badass, she don't need anything, ever."

"Aw, Maggie, you're so blind, Sweet Pea. Yeah,

Zoey or Shadow or whatever you call her she is a badass, no doubt. But that's because of all that has happened in her life. She's learned not to feel or let people in. You and your family got in because at that particular snapshot in time she needed all of you. The fight was killing her, and she needed to feel human and maybe even loved. You gave her that, never doubt it. Now with her emotions all over and her struggling with her feelings for Panther, she's confused and lost. Yeah, she is, and you know it. Has she pulled away from you a little bit, not shared shit with you and disappeared without word? Yeah, I know it hurts to hear but, Maggie, she needs your guidance on what you've found for yourself. Adult love, commitment, sharing and receiving of our hopes and dreams. She saw what you and I have. Zoey wants, no craves it, but didn't know how to go about it. Thank God she and Panther kind of came together by accident. Do you see it, Sweet Pea?"

Letting my head fall forward, I realize that Noodles is right on. Even with me and my parents in her life, Zoey was always lonely. Seeing the two of us come together brought it to the forefront for her. Goddamn, I'm an idiot. I could never be her everything, just like she can't be mine. There has to be a Noodles and Panther for us to be able to live our lives to the fullest. I let that shit sink in for a minute or two, then it hits me. Holy fuck, I can have it all with my bestie. Both of us falling in love, getting married or not, having kids—one or both of us—and growing old while bitching about our ol' men. That thought brings a huge smile to my face. Yeah, the Devil's Handmaidens club is a given and it will never go away as long as I'm alive and victims need to be saved. But as time goes by, we will have to evolve with what comes our way. Grabbing Noodles, I wrap my arms around him and hang on tight to him.

"How the hell did I get so lucky to find you out here in Bumfuck, Montana as you always call Timber-Ghost? Thank you for helping me get my head out of my ass. I need to give her some space, don't I? Like she did when we started our own dance together. My bestie is like you, smart as shit."

Noodles laughs out loud and grabs me close, kissing me hard. When he releases me, I love the feeling that comes with being in his arms. All the emotions and feelings I grew up with watching my parents. To this day, my dad adores my mom and shows her every single day. Not only in what he does but how he treats her. That's what I've always wanted for myself, even when I didn't think so. Putting all my efforts into finding Hannah, I forgot about myself and all my wants, dreams and especially my needs. That's why I've been feeling like I have. And it was Zoey who clocked Noodles first and told me he's better than most, after only meeting and talking to him for like less than five minutes.

"Today is going to be really hard for her, Noodles.

Now that we know most of it and once George puts it all together, not sure how Zoey's going to react. She's spent most of her life hating both of her parents for letting her down. I don't even want to try and think how this is going to affect her. Panther better be the man I think he is and step up to the plate, because she's going to need a strong shoulder to hang on to and cry on. I wish it didn't have to be me, but then again, I'm glad it's me and no one else. Does that even make sense?"

"Yeah, Sweet Pea, it does. You love her and want the very best for her life. Now's your chance to make sure she's going down the right road, that's all. And you're never alone. Now come here, woman, I'm feeling the need to be deep inside you."

Feeling the need as much as he is, I give over the control he craves and demands so we both can experience that unbelievable feeling when we come together. Explosive doesn't even come close.

After coming together with Noodles then a long sensual shower, I'm getting dressed alongside my man. That still takes my breath away. Looking down at my finger, the ring he placed there twinkles right back at me. We're enjoying being engaged and haven't even started the talk about the wedding and dates. Too much shit has been going on all sides with the Devil's Handmaidens, my working ranch, and working on looking, then finding Hannah. I don't remember when I stopped living and was just existing day by day. Glad Noodles woke me up.

Feeling warm arms wrap around me from behind, I lean back into Noodles.

"Sweet Pea, no matter what happens, I'll be right beside you. Today is an important day for your bestie. Zoey and Shadow are going to have to figure out how to blend and live their lives the best way possible. From the little I've spoken to Panther, he's all on board for whatever needs to be done for her. He told me he has no intention of quitting what they've been doing, even though Dario is dead. His exact words were there are many more assholes out there who need to be stopped. You never know, maybe you and your club sisters can find a way to work with Panther and his guys. Gotta keep an open mind, right?"

I cross my fingers and pray he's right and if we all keep an open mind, today will go smoothly and at the end of it, Zoey will better for it.

* * *

I've never been this nervous in my entire life. Noodles and Dad cleared the house of everyone but who needed to be involved. So right now sitting at the kitchen table is my dad, Mom, and Noodles. Also, there are Raven, Heartbreaker, Stud, and Freak. They will actually be the ones explaining what and how they found the information. We are waiting on Sheriff George to show up. He's been so open and honest now that everything is out there. Well, and Dario being dead has to help. Finally, is Hannah, who refused to leave, no matter how many people or times she was told. When I threatened her with taking her prospect kutte she actually took it off and handed it to me, which shocked the shit out of me.

"Maggie, no disrespect, but Auntie Zoey risked everything including her life to find and rescue me. Then she gave me time to adapt to what was about to happen. If you think that lame-ass threat will work on me then I don't deserve to be a Devil's Handmaidens sister. I thought the whole idea of the club was about family and living the best life you possibly can. That's what I want for my auntie. She's got to have someone who's here just for her. Not for any other reason but to support her. No, don't go getting all tiny and mighty with me, I get it. But don't forget you're not only her bestie, but you're also her prez. For me, all I am is the lost kid she found and reunited with her family, which includes her. So, either take this kutte and shut up or let me put it back on and keep your thoughts to yourself. Of course, no disrespect intended, Prez."

I'm lost with what she just said. And how fucking accurate it all is coming from this kid's mouth. Looking around I can see the same look in everyone's eyes, along with their smiles and grins they are all trying unsuccessfully to hide. When I see

Heartbreaker stand and walk over to Hannah, my mouth falls open. Ain't this the kettle calling the pot.

"Hey, Hannah, come on over and sit with Raven, Freak. Stud, and me. We'd be honored, Squirt."

Hannah smiles widely at her future club sister then looks at me, raising that one irritating eyebrow of hers. I look down at the prospect kutte then at my dad, who is watching me. He shrugs his shoulders, letting me know it's my decision. Fuck a duck, this kid is going to be the literal death of me. Between her and Zoey, I don't stand a goddamn chance. Walking to her, I hand her the kutte back.

"Okay, this time you win. If you ever hand this kutte to me again, you won't be getting it back. Don't give a shit why you think it's okay to threaten me with it. Now, I agree, go sit with Heartbreaker and Raven. When they are done and let me be very clear, Hannah, you will not say a word. This is very sensitive and no one in here knows how Zoey is going to react, so keep your trap shut, got it? That's right, nod if you agree. When these four leave, you will go sit with Mom and Dad. You're your auntie's support. Nothing else, so please be respectful of the circumstances of this meeting. Am I clear?"

"Yeah, Prez, you're crystal clear."

Wiping my brow, I think to myself, *another situation that has been made clear*. Walking back toward the parents, Noodles stands and puts his arm around me, pulling me close, kissing my forehead.

"Motherfucker, Sweet Pea, she's your doppelgänger not only in looks but for sure in your personalities. I watched your folks trying not to laugh outright at how mad you were getting. Guessing from that I can assume you were a bit of a handful growing up too? Now don't get pissy at me, Maggie, it was just an observation, that's all. Come on, let's sit with your folks as we wait for George to get here. I'm going to text Panther, let him know that's what's holding us up."

Just as Noodles pulls his phone out, the door swings open and with Rebel is Sheriff George, looking mighty nervous and uncomfortable. His eyes widen in shock when he sees everyone who's waiting. I see him almost turn around, but leave it to Rebel to just bulldoze her way in, not giving him a chance or any opportunity to run. Dad gets up to greet him as Noodles leads me to my mom, who has open arms for me, which is exactly what I need at the moment. A mom hug.

"All right, Panther knows everyone is here. Now we wait for the two of them, probably five or so minutes. Relax, Sweet Pea, it'll be fine. Want some coffee?"

After I tell him yes, he walks to the coffee bar and between fixing me and Mom a cup of coffee he's jawing with Freak, Stud, Dad, and Sheriff George. How can he be so fucking calm, I'm a ball of nerves. When Mom squeezes me, I look at her.

"Maggie, she loves you. And as we all know, she'd also die for you and almost has on a couple of occasions, as she's proven it time and time again. Just let this happen and be there for Zoey. All you can do. If she can't see how many people love her for her, not because of the Shadow persona she made up, then we've already lost her. I love you, daughter."

That right there calms me down. I feel my breathing slow, and my heart rate start to regulate. Yeah, Mom has it going on for sure.

TWENTY-NINE
'SHADOW'
ZOEY

I'm losing the little that's left of my fucking mind. Knowing something huge is about to be revealed, I almost—no definitely—have the urge to just jump on my bike and ride like the devil, never turning back. Unfortunately for my sappy ass, for some reason I can't do it. Not like I used to. My head tells me too many people depend on me, but my traitor heart is screaming there are too many folks I actually care about and don't want to leave. When the hell did this happen, for Christ's sake?

I knew it might eventually take place. Even though I told Goldilocks in the beginning that no matter what she did, I wasn't gonna let her in. That little bitch never gave up on me and time and time again managed to chip away at my emotionless heart, making it start beating, then actually feeling. I can't pinpoint the day it happened, but one day I was able to tell the little pain in my ass no and the next for the life of me I couldn't.

From Goldilocks it spread to Pops and Momma Diane. Then the biggest surprise, that little squirt, Hannah. Goddamn, you'd think I was her mother, for Christ's sake. Something about her had drawn me to her like flies to shit. Which is crazy 'cause she's also a major motherfucking headache. All her bullshit, like those romance books she's hooked on. Always telling me that one day she's going to meet her alpha dominant who can handle her, and they will live happily ever after like whatever heroine she's reading about. Then, let's not forget to mention her inability to respect boundaries. She practically lives with her arms around me. Goddamn, when did I lose control?

The hardest to accept is how I've treated Heartbreaker. Being at Dario's and seeing that woman I thought was my mother my entire life, I can now see how I transferred my hatred for 'mom' to one of my club sisters. All because they both had the same horrible addiction to drugs. The only difference is Heartbreaker has busted her ass to come back yet again.

"Nizhoni, you need to calm down and center yourself. Everyone involved only wants you to have the best life ever, and that includes me too. No, don't say a word, we'll have that conversation later. First, let's get this one out of the way. If you don't want me there, you let me know and I'll leave. Whatever will make this easier for you beautiful. Ayóó'áníínishní." *I love you.*

"Panther, what does that mean? You keep saying it to me."

"One day soon, beautiful, I'll explain to you what Ayóó'áníínishní means. Until then I'll keep showing you in all the ways I can. Now, it is time. Take a minute, breathe, and try to center your emotions. Then we will head down. Noodles texted me they are ready if you are. Come here, I want you to remember how you feel in my arms if you get scared or nervous. Yeah, I know the big badass Shadow of the Devil's Handmaidens MC never feels anything. I was talking to Zoey, who does."

Then he pulls me in for a hug as I take in a few deep breaths. Like always, Panther is right, I feel better and calmer. Hand in hand, we start to make our way downstairs to face whatever it is together.

* * *

As soon as I walk into the kitchen, everyone stops talking. Looking around there are way more people than I thought would be here. I see some of my club sisters, Pops, and Momma Diane, along with Freak and Stud from the Intruders. That's strange in itself as I barely know those two geeks. Oh, great, they let Squirt in here too. Fuck, just what I need. Then I see someone I never even thought about being here.

Sheriff George. He's staring at me intently, eyes never leaving my face. I feel like someone has literally walked over my grave by the way his scrutiny of me continues. Finally, Tink and Noodles are making their way to us.

"Hey, Panther, good to see ya, brother. Can I grab you or happy over here some coffee, water, or a drink? Whatever, just let me know. Come here, Zoey, give ol' Noodles a hug."

I laughingly go, pinching his side when I'm close.

"Who told you it was all right to call me by my name? Just because you're going to marry my best friend don't give you any special rights, soldier boy."

"Ouch, you are such a mean bitch."

Hearing, Panther let out a small growl. I turn to see him glaring at Noodles, who is smirking right back at him. Great time to see who can piss the farthest. Before I can give both men some shit, my bestie is right in front of me, so much worry and concern on her face it's heartbreaking. Then she hugs me tightly, so for her I softly return it with a hug of my own.

"Zoey, no matter what, I'm right here and always will be. We didn't go looking for all of this information, but thanks to Raven, Heartbreaker, Stud, and Freak they found it, which helped us put the pieces together. Let Noodles get you what you want then let's take a seat so we can get this done. And if you need to stop or take a break, just say something or shout out like you usually do, will you please?"

Then she lifts up on her tippy-toes, which has me leaning down 'cause she's so short, for her to whisper for my ears only, something she rarely says 'cause it freaks the fuck out of me.

"I love you, bestie."

So now after saying hello to everyone and getting more loving in the form of hugs from Pops, Momma Diane, and Squirt, I'm finally sitting at the table with my 'family.' Heartbreaker, Raven, Stud, and Freak are doing something with a laptop. Tink stands and clears her throat to get everyone's attention.

"Hey, hoping this goes smoothly, otherwise, the asshole who fucks it up answers to me. Got it? 'Kay turning it over to my sisters, Stud, and Freak. They're going to explain how this kind of fell into their laps. Floor's yours."

Listening to the back-and-forth of Raven and Heartbreaker, I'm so confused. Seems like it was my sister, Heartbreaker, who kind of figured this out with the aid of Stud, Freak, and Raven. As she explains how the pieces started to fall together, I notice Sheriff George is very fidgety sitting next to, holy shit, when did Enforcer sneak in? Damn that man, he's nosier and more of a gossip than anyone I know. But today he looks all business. And his arm is resting on Sheriff George's shoulders, which in itself is strange. Enforcer is like me, he doesn't like contact of any kind.

Hearing something strange, I ask Raven to repeat it and when she does, my eyes shoot to the sheriff. What the ever-lovin' fuck is my club sister talking about? How is that even possible? And who is Giorgio De Luca and why is everyone looking at our sheriff? When Heartbreaker starts to explain, my world seems to explode all at once. Never in my life have I had the feeling of passing out when I'm not being tortured, but right now that is a huge fucking possibility. *They can't be right. My parents abandoned me then one of them sold me into the life I led. And Dario didn't have family, except for the boys and maybe a daughter,* my mind thinks, from what I know. Maybe some illegitimate children, but fuck, he was a monster, doubt he worried about his offspring.

I'm supposed to believe that crazy, insane motherfucker was my uncle. How, why, and what, and not in that particular order. When the quiet hits me, I realize Heartbreaker and Raven have stopped talking. Freak stands now and explains what he's been up to. On the overhead he brings up some documents my eyes can't believe. Birth certificates of Giorgio De Luca and some Native American woman. Then the last one has me gasping loudly. It's for a birth certificate for baby girl born on my birthdate. Her name was Zeona De Luca. Hearing a noise, I look that way to see the sheriff making his way slowly to me. Chairs are pushed back as Tank, Noodles, Enforcer, and finally Panther, all stand at alert. When he's close, Panther moves in front of me so I'm partially hidden. Oh fuck, again with this pissing thing, going to have to talk to him about it. I've been taking care of myself for years and if Panther doesn't think I can handle our sheriff, well fuck, we got bigger issues that's for goddamn sure.

"Zeona, I'm so sorry. I didn't want this to ever come out or to cause you pain. May I sit, please?"

I push past Panther to look into Sheriff George's eyes. All I see is pain. How did I never see how his eyes are just as icy blue as mine? Though at the moment I'm sure mine just look dead from lack of emotion. I'm on overload. Then again how often have I even looked at our sheriff's eyes. When we sit, so does everyone else, except Raven, Heartbreaker, Stud, and Freak, who are grabbing their shit to leave, I guess. Managing to get back up, I walk over to the four of them. When I get close, Heartbreaker steps back a smidge, head down. *Enough of this bullshit*, I think to myself.

Pulling Raven and Heartbreaker to me, I give them my best half-ass hug, whispering my thanks to them. Both are beyond shocked. With Stud and Freak, I extend my hand, which they both look at for what seems like forever before shaking it. When they leave, I make my way back to where I was sitting. Panther helps me sit then plops his fine ass next to me, grabbing my hand, holding onto it for dear life. Then Sheriff George, who I now have come to realize is my dad, starts to tell everyone a thirty-four-year-old story about a man and a woman who fell in love, got married on the sly, and had a beautiful daughter.

From that point on, the love story turns into a dark suspense thriller about how the mob family got involved, and how the family was split apart until nothing was left. Feeling Panther's arms surround me, my heart breaks to hear the story from his lips. He doesn't sugarcoat, lie, or try to hide anything, including his part in this family nightmare.

"Zeona, know this, you were born out of love. Your momma and I were deeply in love with each other and couldn't wait for you to come. The first couple of years after I spilled everything, and we lived in WITSEC, it was a good life. This place, Montana, though cold as a witch's tit in Alaska is also a hidden gem. For your momma, it was harder with leaving her family and coming here to Montana, where it was so very different than where she was from on the reservation. Good things seem to always come to an end, and for us it was when Dario and his men found us. First, he took your momma and to this day I don't know if she is alive, sold to one of his sick friends as punishment, or killed. And now that he is dead, no, figlia, *daughter,* do not worry, I only wished someone would have ended his demented ass long ago. I tried in the beginning, but my brother was a force unto himself and as we both know I failed to rid the world of his evil. But to find out all he put you through, my God, I have no words. Sorry is so useless, but for now it's all I have. I don't expect you to forgive me or even accept what I'm telling you. Just know when I found out that Shadow of the Devil's Handmaidens name was Zoey Jeffries, I almost died. Before I was relocated to Timber-Ghost and disappeared on Dario again, when I was being tortured, he found it hilarious to tell me the name he gave you. Also who he had his whore sell you to for a month. Yeah, that woman was not your mother, never was even a human with a heart. She was a she-devil he put you with. I know she's alive somewhere and that's not going to be for long if I have a say so. Again, not your concern. I know what you do and who you are, Zeona. And a lot of the blame is on me, no, let me finish. I should have done things differently. Hid your momma and you before I told the Feds everything I knew about Dario and his business. The only thing I had going for me is I didn't want into the 'family business' and he did. I literally gave it to him when our parents were killed in the car accident that the Feds later told me Dario planned. He executed our parents so he could gain control. So, daughter of mine, whatever you did to him was not enough pain and suffering for what he's done over the years. I've tried to do my best to protect you and help your club whenever I could. And I will continue to do that, even if after today you never speak to me again. I understand you have total power to make the choice of how we move forward. And I will not fight whatever you decide."

I watch him take a deep breath as his body seems to slightly tremble. When he looks my way, his eyes are wet, but no tears are on his cheeks. I have no idea what to do or say. That is until I hear Goldilocks and Pops tell everyone to give us some privacy. One by one, everyone stands to leave. They come by me first and either give me a shoulder squeeze or, as with Momma Diane and Squirt, huge hugs and words of love and how I'm their family. During this all, I see George never takes his eyes off me. Even after, to my utter surprise, Enforcer comes by, gives me a side shoulder bump, then shakes Panther's hand. When he stops in front of Sheriff George, I hear his words loud and clear like everyone else does.

"Motherfucker, you even think of hurting her again and you'll answer to me. By the time I'm done you'll wish your Mafia family had ended your miserable life years ago. This woman has seen and been through enough. Either be the man you should have been years ago or get the fuck out of Timber-Ghost. Don't make me go psycho on your ass, 'cause I will."

Enforcer then walks out the door, swinging it behind him so hard it slams into the wall. The only people left besides the sheriff, Panther, and me are

Goldilocks, Noodles, and Pops. Looking around, I see something I've been missing for fucking years. My family. Yeah, I've bullshitted around it but these people are my family, not by blood but by their love and acceptance of me. Pops pulls me up, hugging me, telling me no matter what—I'm his daughter like the other two pains in his ass are. Next, Noodles pulls me tight, saying not a word just holding me as my body starts to shake. He gives me to Goldilocks, who's being a smart-ass standing on the bench, so she towers over me. When the tears hit, I'm surrounded by Goldilocks and Panther. Not knowing if it's the right thing to do or not, maybe I'm crazy as fuck, but I reach a hand behind my bestie and my father grabs it, holding on tight. And it feels not only right but good.

THIRTY
'PANTHER'
CHAHÓÓŁHÉÉL NAABAAHII T'ÁÁ SÁHI
DARK WARRIOR WALKING ALONE

Holy fuck, not what I thought would happen today. Confused as hell, it worries me how quiet and calm Zoey seems. I felt her reach out her hand to the sheriff and him grab it. Saw the way he watched her every move during and after his explanation. It's like she's present in body but not in mind and heart. To be honest, I'm not sure anyone could be after hearing her life. I don't know how it's even possible, after that explanation and revelation, she will be able to continue and be who she is. Yeah, anyone can call her murderer or killer, but what about all the good she does within her club and outside of it. When I told her Ayóó'ánííníshní in Navajo, which means I love you, I truly meant it. After what I just heard, there is no way in hell I'll ever let this woman go. I'm shocked as hell she not only lived through all this shit but somehow managed to find a way to survive in this fucked-up world of ours. And on top of it all, try to make it a better place and help victims become survivors.

Hearing her in the shower, I know she's going to need some time. I sure the fuck would. I feel myself get hard just imagining her in there, water running all over that body of hers. The thought makes my already hard dick try to stretch even more. Fuck, but it won't be the first time I've used my hand with Zoey in my mind, won't be the last. I can wait forever, especially now that I know what her life's been like and all she's been through. After last night, watching her explode under my hands, if that's all we do for the rest of our lives, with her fantastic hand jobs thrown in, I'll be a happy man. *Don't get me wrong,* I think to myself, *I'm a hot-blooded man but I would rather go without intercourse than be without my Nizhoni.*

With what we both do, trying to save victims of horrible events, our happiness might look different than others. Hearing my phone ring, I pick it up, seeing it's Avalanche.

"Hey, brother, you okay? How's your injury, is it healing okay? Thanks again for being there and saving our asses. Got lots to tell ya, but not tonight. Need some time to process all this shit."

"Panther, just calling to let you know, thinking about going back home for a bit. No, nothing's wrong, just feeling the pull, ya know? Plus, you and skull anii' are going to need some time alone without a third wheel. Yeah, you can say it but we both know it's true. And we're going to need to figure out what we plan to do next. The guys are sticking around so they'll help around the ranch. We've got a few months before our busy stud season. No worries, brother. I'll stop by tomorrow before I take off to say goodbye to the both of you. All right, you have a good night."

Ending the call, my gut is telling me something is way off with Avalanche. He would never head home without me. Two peas in a pod. What is going on with him? I hope he doesn't feel like I don't want him around because Zoey is here 'cause that is plain thinking like a stupid asshole. I not only want his help, but I also need him for my mental health, and he knows that because he needs me for his.

Hearing the bathroom door open, I lift my head and WOW. Holy shit!!! My already hard as a rock dick starts to leak precum as Zoey walks to me wearing only a towel on her head. The long length of her body almost floats my way. Her eyes are anything but dead as she looks at me, starting at my bare feet, working her way up my worn jeans to where my legs come together. My cock is vibrating from her just staring at me.

"Zoey, what're you up to?"

"Well, I think you have it mistaken. I should be asking you what's up."

Then she laughs almost hysterically. It hits me she's extremely uncomfortable being totally nude.

Grabbing my flannel, I stand and cover her up, which has her shoulders slump while her face falls. Fuck.

"Beautiful, no, don't do that. I'm covering you because I can see how totally uncomfortable you are. Zoey, your body to me is perfect. I love how high and full your tits are while your waist narrows down to fill back out at your hips. And those long as fuck legs of yours. Do you know how many times a day I'm masturbating with you as my muse? So, no, I'm not covering you because I don't want to see you, but before anything else, I want you to feel good about whatever you, me, or together we do. Got it?"

Watching her struggle tears my heart out but I'm walking on mines with her history. Do I want her? Fuck yeah, but I will not push her at all. She slowly slides her arms in the flannel and closes it with just two buttons midway down.

"Do you know how long it took me to convince myself to come out naked? That you'd be so overtaken you'd ravish me instantly. God, what a moron. I sound like those fucked-up romance books Squirt's hooked on."

I pull her before I sit on the edge of the bed, Zoey in my lap.

"Hey, look at me. Feel this."

Grabbing her hand, I place it over my throbbing erection.

"See, that should tell you the story you need. I'm burning up with want and need for you. Beautiful,

I'm a man and we are visual creatures. Saying that, I just listened to your life's story and, goddamn, it was hard. Probably one of the hardest things I've ever done. And I mean ever, so don't doubt it. I want you with everything I am, Nizhoni. You have the power of when, how, and where. I get why you need it."

She grabs my face down to hers so she can plant a hard closed-mouth kiss on my lips. When she lets me go, I pull her back to me as I nibble, lick, and taste her lips until she moans and lets me in. Then we make out on the edge of the bed like two teenagers. Until I hear her stomach growl, which tells me she's beyond hungry. *Time to feed my woman*, I think to myself.

* * *

Zoey is actually as hungry as I am. We get lucky, the kitchen is almost empty, except for Heartbreaker, who is by herself, sitting at one of the tables eating a bowl of minestrone soup and fresh bread. It smells beyond delicious, so I leave the two women to talk and go to fill up two bowls with soup. I put some parmesan cheese in each bowl then grab a plate, stacking it with the bread and some tabs of butter. Lastly, I manage to put two soup spoons in my front pocket with some napkins.

Making my way back, I can see both women smiling so I'm thinking it's safe to make my approach. When I sit down, I'm surprised that

Heartbreaker doesn't run off like usual. Seems like my Zoey is getting better at sharing her feelings and what she needs. It is a very enjoyable meal with good conversation and some great laughs. When Zoey starts yawning, I know it's time to make our way to her room. Helping her up first, the women hug then Heartbreaker leaves the room just as Hannah enters.

Seeing us she goes directly to Zoey, who puts her arms in front of her.

"Enough, Squirt, with the goddamn hugging. You're gonna ruin my reputation of being a badass motherfucker. Come on, you spent like twenty minutes earlier hugging me. That's enough for the week."

She looks between the two of us, then motions for me to come her way. When I do, she throws herself in my arms while I almost drop her ass. Hearing Zoey growling behind me, I get what's going on. Looking down, Hannah has a mischievous look on her face, so I slightly nod. She crawls up me like a little monkey before wrapping her legs around my waist. Way above the usual area but don't think Zoey even sees that. She yanks on the younger woman's shoulders, who's holding on to me with superhuman strength. I can feel something is about to hit the fan when Tink walks in, takes one look at the situation, and loses her mind, screaming out loud.

"Goddamn it, enough, Hannah. Climb the fuck off of Panther right this second. Zoey, step back, don't kill the dumb little bitch, our parents will lose themselves. Hannah, Momma Diane called, said you need to clean the yard, your dogs have filled it with their shit. Go on, get. NOW!"

Grumbling, she shifts her way down me then stomps out screaming out every swear word and some I don't even know. Zoey and Tink are staring at each other until first one then the other starts laughing like hyenas.

"Fuck, that was hilarious, Goldilocks. Gotta ask, did Momma Diane call you at all? Nope, didn't think so. Squirt is going to be beyond pissed but she deserved it putting Panther in the middle, so to speak."

I laugh loudly as both of them turn to look at me.

"Beautiful, not a bad situation for a man, got to tell ya. A young, sexy, beautiful woman jumps into a man's arms then climbs up him. What is so bad about, ugh. Hey, that hurt, damn it, woman."

I grab my arm where she punched me, and now I understand why Avalanche is always bitching. She can really pack a punch. Son of a bitch, that hurt.

"You know what, seems like the two of you want to talk, think I'm gonna go upstairs maybe watch some television or just relax. Zoey, I'll be upstairs if you need anything. Tink, again thanks for your hospitality. I'll probably be heading back to my ranch in the next day or so. Got my men there but don't like leaving it for too long. Night, ladies."

With that said, I turn but not before I see Zoey's eyes close, and pain hit her face. That look alone almost has me turning around, but today was rough on those two and they need to hash it out. So, I head up the stairs to hit the shower and beat one out before Zoey comes up to bed, putting me right back in my own hurt and misery of a hard as fuck dick. That thought brings a smirk to my face.

THIRTY-ONE
'SHADOW'
ZOEY

Watching Panther walk away hurts my heart. And hearing him say he's going to head back to his ranch, oh shit, that's over an hour with any kind of traffic. What do I do? I can't leave Goldilocks and I don't want Panther to leave me. He makes me feel good and beautiful. I'm actually starting to believe it.

"What got your undies in a bundle, Zoey?"

Laughing at Goldilocks because she never thinks before she spurts out words together.

"For your information, I'm not wearing any panties, so there."

I stick my tongue out at her and she reciprocates right back.

"Zoey, come let's grab a beer and talk for a bit. Noodles is on the phone with Ollie, some ordering problem, and Panther is, well, doing what Panther wants to do. We need to talk, sister."

So over a beer or four Goldilocks breaks it down for me. Explains that she might have been a bit selfish over the years, always wanting me close by. That in her love for me she was afraid, without her, I wouldn't survive day-to-day life. She has a good point though, I'm an adult who has been part of an all-female motorcycle club for years. And to take it a step further, I'm their enforcer. I've done things no one else has ever given a thought to. And I sleep like a baby. That shit never bothers me because those assholes and jagoffs deserve everything I do and more. To me they get off too easy when I kill them because they've been torturing women and children for years.

As we talk it out, what she is trying to say cracks me across the face hard. And as usual, I don't think before I talk.

"Are you kicking me out, you bitch?"

Tink's head jerks back for just a minute before her own temper comes to the surface.

"No, you asswipe, I'm cutting you some slack. Open your eyes, dumbass, you want to be with Panther and for some crazy as fuck reason he wants to be with you too. Poor man must have hit is head hard. Now, just saying if you hit me, I'll grab that cast iron frying pan and split your head open. Stop hitting people, Zoey, it's not nice or even funny. So anyway, yeah, stay here, this is your home. Well, it is for now. Who knows what the future holds for any of us, Zoey.

Things are changing but our club is still going to operate as it always has. Our mission will stay on course until there are no victims to save or I'm dead. So what's wrong with spending time with a man who adores you, while he also puts up with all of your bullshit at the same time? You should be thanking your lucky stars."

Damn it, I hate it when my Goldilocks bitch is right, which is more times than I care to admit. She's glaring at me, waiting for me to admit she's right. Again. I sit here though and just wait, because it sucks big time, she's going to gloat for at least a couple of days to a week.

"Yeah, whatever, Goldilocks, we'll see. He hasn't even told me what's next for us, so maybe he's had enough of all the crazy that is me. Who the fuck knows anymore. So just let it rest, will you? For Pete's sake, it's been a couple of days from hell, don't try to make it any worse than it's been."

With that, we just start to rehash the day and everything that was revealed. She asked me about Sheriff George, and I told her honestly—like I told Panther—I don't know. I'm going to take it one day at a time for now.

When we finally head up to bed, both of us are tipsy. Not sure what I'll find but as long as Panther's still here, I'm good with anything else.

* * *

Staring down at a phenomenally naked Panther, I shift my position on the side of him on the bed so now I'm sitting on my ankles. I know what I want to do, but I can't remember if I've ever done it when it was my choice. Also, not sure if I'm good at it or not. We'll soon find out, I'm guessing. As embarrassing as it was, I even talked to Goldilocks about this and so much more. She was awesome, as usual. Told me to go with what I'm feeling and pay attention to how Panther reacts. Listen for sounds of enjoyment and if there is any discomfort to stop and try something else. She told me generally you can't fuck this up, so we will see.

She also shared that after she was raped by Buck, even though she was a child, when she was old enough, she didn't have sex for a very long time because she was scared and had all these triggers, as she called them. When she finally did have sex, it was like a one-night stand, so she really didn't care how it went, though she mentioned that one time she found a good guy who took his time with her. Played her body like a fine instrument. Problem was he was going through town so no chance of a long relationship. The purpose of her story was to let me know she had an idea of what was going through my head. She told me that maybe I should talk to our new psychologist, who's working with Ollie's sanctuary and spending a few hours a week at our ranch. Goldilocks also let me know that no matter what, or when, she'd always be a phone call away if I had questions or was panicking about anything.

So fast forward, here I am, looking at Panther's beautiful semi-hard cock. He is long and thick though not too thick, actually. I think he's beautiful everywhere. I rub my hands together, so they warm up, I don't want to put him into cardiac arrest. I slowly place my hands on his thick thighs and whisper my fingers up until I reach the base of his cock. Wrapping my hand around him, slowly with firm pressure, I glide up then slam down once, twice, and on the third time when my hand hits his body, my mouth moves over the mushroom head, pulling it in before sealing my lips. Watching his face, I see his eyes pop open in shock at the same time his head lifts to see who or, more importantly, what the fuck is going on. That look in his eyes gives me courage to loosen my lips and slide down as far as I can without gagging. My hand is right there, and as I move back up my hand follows with a tight grip. His eyes close for a second then pop back open, his hands landing on my hair. He's not pressuring or pushing me, just holding my hair out of the way so he can watch. I start to find my rhythm, keeping my lips tight and letting my tongue move over his warm, hard velvety shaft. I can tell he's liking it by the liquid coming from the tip. Also, by the way his hips chase my mouth.

Feeling like maybe I'm doing okay, my hand reaches for his balls. I think my grip is light but from the gruff sound that comes out of his mouth, it scares me. I lift off his dick and try to move away but his hands move to my shoulders, holding me right where I am.

"No, Zoey, don't. You're doing great. Please don't stop. I mean if you want to, that's fine, but I don't want you to. You surprised me, that's all. Didn't expect your hand or the squeeze so I reacted 'cause I was surprised, that's all. I've never been so turned on or hard, so yeah, you're doing just fine. The choice is yours though, so whatever you decide, beautiful."

Hearing the desire in his voice gives me the courage to continue. Doesn't take long for us to get back to where we were. As my head is bobbing, he's moaning like crazy, not holding anything back from me. His hips are now meeting my mouth on the downswing. Suddenly, I feel him swell in my mouth, right before he warns me.

"Nizhoni, I'm very close. If you're uncomfortable just finish me with your hand. Oh God, yeah, just like that, Zoey. Fuck, I'm not going to last, please, yeah."

Hearing the want in his voice amps up my determination to finish what I started. When the mushroom head swells even bigger, the first burst of him hits the back of my throat then it just keeps coming and coming. By the time he's slowing down, I'm used to the unique salty taste of him. When he stops twitching, I move my mouth to the tip of him and pop off just like Goldilocks told me to. He looks at me, shock all over his face for a second, then he smiles the most beautiful smile I've ever seen. Thinking to myself, *I did that. Made that man share his beautiful smile with only me.*

I go to the bathroom, rinse my mouth, and look at my face. It looks serene and happy. I'm so lucky to have found Panther. Feeling so content, I head back to the bedroom to see him lying in the exact spot I left him in. Taking the washcloth, I wipe him down then slip in next to him.

"Zoey, wow. That was beyond, holy shit. And that you cleaned me up... never in my life has a woman taken care of me like you just did. Thank you so much, beautiful. How are you doing?"

Taking a minute or two to try and find my words, I try to clear my head.

"Panther, I owe you a thank-you for standing by me through all of this. It's not been easy, and not going to lie, I know I still have a long road to go. I can finally say I care about you, maybe even love you, though I don't have a clue what that means in a relationship like ours. You not only make me feel desired and beautiful but take your time and give me time to adjust. I've never felt like this before and have not ever had a man look out for me. Please have patience with me is all I ask."

"Nizhoni, it's time I explain to you what Ayóó'ánííníshní means. Woman, it means I love you in Navajo. Zoey, you've gotten under my skin, and I don't want you to go anywhere. We've got the rest of our lives to work through all the baggage we're both carrying. I still have things to share with you. And we need to figure out how to keep what we do because it is important. Maybe I can talk to your club, and we can somehow work together on dissolving some of the circuits. I'm not sure, but one thing I know for certain is, you are it for me. So whatever you want, I want. I'm not a hard person to live with as long as you can respect my way of living as one with the earth. I want you to hear the words and understand them. Zoey, I love you, woman."

His arms crush me to him as his lips show me exactly how he truly feels. My world feels whole now, as I do. The dark past of mine will always be with me but I'm trying to look toward the future like Goldilocks told me to. As Panther keeps me at his side, I close my eyes, enjoying the peace of the moment. That is the last thing I remember as I drift off to sleep surrounded by my man's love.

THIRTY-TWO
'PANTHER'

CHAHÓÓŁHÉÉL NAABAAHII T'ÁÁ SÁHI
DARK WARRIOR WALKING ALONE

Trying to leave the bed with Zoey still sleeping is hard for me. What she did last night showed me how much she's not only trying, but also that she's ready to move forward. Shifting her off my arm, I lift off the bed carefully as my leg is still tender. Placing my pillow in her arms, she snuggles down and relaxes again.

Making my way downstairs, I head to the kitchen to see Noodles is already there. Giving him a chin lift, I make my way to the coffee. Can't start my day without it.

"Morning, brother. You doing good today? I know yesterday was a rough one for both you and Shadow. I'm here if you need anything."

"Thanks, Noodles, appreciate it. Yeah, Zoey and I talked a little last night and have started to clear all the muck out. Like we both agreed that this shit along with us is a work in progress so there's no time frame, we're going to take one day at a time. I appreciate you being cool with us being around here so much. I'm gonna have to get back to my ranch eventually, but we haven't even talked about that. Don't want to put too much on Zoey's shoulders, if you know what I mean."

As we shoot the shit, my mind is on my brother, Avalanche. He texted me early this morning, telling me he planned on stopping here to talk to me. I'm nervous on what he wants to talk to me about. I have a feeling he's got this stupid idea he's a third wheel now that Zoey and I are taking our relationship to the next step. He's in for a big fucking surprise, because I'm not letting him go back home and disappear. That's Avalanche's way, run and hide then just disappear. I need him at my side; we're both stronger when we are together.

When Noodles goes back up to wake up Tink, I walk outside to sit on the porch and enjoy the beginning of a new day. Looking at the land this ranch is on, I can understand the pull of this place for each of the Devil's Handmaidens women. From the little Zoey has shared, they've all come from really bad situations and the club has been their saving grace. And that this ranch is like their reward for finding a way to push it forward. Or that's what one of her sisters said to her one day.

Hearing a vehicle, I look down the road to see a

truck coming in. Yeah, it's my brother, just like him to be here at the break of dawn. I stand and walk down to the driveway, waiting for him to park. Once he's stopped and throws his door open, I move toward him, arms open.

"Brother, welcome. How's your leg doing? Haven't heard anything so hope the old saying that no news is good news applies here. Come on in, want some coffee?"

He just stands outside his truck like he wants to jump back in and drive away. Okay, what the fuck? We've been through so much shit together, no way in hell is he running, tail between his legs, because I now have a woman. One who cares about him too.

"What's going on, nitsaa yikah tsintah? Talk to me so we can work through it. There's nothing that can come between us unless we let it. Don't just stand there, tell me already, asshole."

He fights a grin then moves and follows me into the kitchen for a cup of coffee. When we're both sitting with our full cups of coffee, he leans back, looking around.

"Nice pad, chahóółhééł naabaahii t'áá sáhi. Don't blame you for wanting to move this way. I would too if I had the choice."

"What the hell are you even talking about? I'm not moving here anytime soon. I have a home, duh, just like you do. Our ranch is where we live, brother, and call home. Don't feel left out 'cause you're doing that bullshit to yourself. I need you at my side, nothing's changed between us. We still have a lot of work toward making this world a better place. Don't bail on me when we're not done. I fucking need you, Avalanche."

His head falls forward, hands holding each side of it. Neither of us hear the door open, well, until he jumps when Zoey punches his arm hard.

"Yo, Big Bird, you ain't going anywhere. What the fuck is wrong with you, did you bang your head when we were rolling around in Pops's SUV? Don't go all pussy on me, dude. I like you better when you're full of shit and vinegar. Man up, for Christ's sake."

His head jerks up and he glares at Zoey. His lip curls and, for a second, I worry he might try to hurt her, but unexpectedly he takes a deep breath and pulls her close, his head resting on hers.

"I don't want to get in your way, Nizhoni anii'. This is new for the two of you, don't need a third person when you want to be alone. I get it, so just going to go home for a bit, that's all. No big deal."

Stepping back Zoey glares at Avalanche with that look of hers that has people shitting their pants. Fuck she's pissed here we go.

"Really, Avalanche? Thought the three of us are adults and if we want or need private time, Panther has a huge bedroom. We can have all the time we want. I'm not the type of woman to drop clothes and fuck all over, so no worries there. Don't look surprised, you started us down this bullshit road. And, Big Bird, there's a very lucky woman out there waiting on you, so gotta stick around so we can find her for you. Please don't leave. Let's see if this works. I mean, if it doesn't, build your own house on the property, or fuck, move here, take one of the cabins in back. I know Panther doesn't want you to leave and neither do I. Don't make me beg, asshole, though I'd do it to make him happy. You don't want to see me pissed off, I'm just saying."

Hearing the huge breath he lets out; I know she's gotten to him. That's her way and she doesn't even recognize how good she is at reading people. She moves back in to him wrapping her arms around his waist.

"Thanks, brother, you won't be sorry, promise. Hey, think of all the nights we can play board games and sing karaoke… to start."

The look on his face is worth millions. And through it all Zoey looks so innocent, like she is totally serious. Well, until she bursts out laughing and shoving at him 'til he breaks a smile himself. Zoey walks away to grab some coffee and Avalanche nods toward the door, so I let her know I'll be back and I walk to the front porch with him.

"Panther, really, if I'm too much of a bother, just say so. This is new for you guys, I won't be pissed or put out, promise."

"Brother, listen to me. You're never a bother and your part of the house is on the other side of mine. I mean, three of us should be able to share a kitchen and great room with the screen porch. There are two offices, so that's no problem. Give it and the three of us a chance like Zoey said. If it don't work, then go do whatever you want, but you have the magic with the horses, just like me. So let's get back to what we do best."

When I pull him in, he holds on to me for dear life and it hits me. He really has no one on his side except me. When we were in the military, most assholes tried to pick on him because he's usually quiet and keeps to himself. That comes from growing up a half-breed, as he was called all the time. It makes sense now and I hold on to him even tighter. After we finally break, I see the wet in his eyes but don't say a word. That he cares this much, to be willing to change his life for me, says it all. I feel exactly the same way about him and I'm not ashamed to show him.

Once Avalanche has his head straight and knows he's going to live with us and is heading back toward my ranch, I pull Zoey with coffee in hand, out front. We both sit in a rocker and take in the gorgeous morning.

"Beautiful, we need to talk, make some decisions. First though, I want to thank you for last night. Best night of my life, Zoey. I'll always treasure the memory."

I watch her and can almost see her blush under her tattoo. She is fidgeting too, so I grab both of her hands and place them on my lap with mine on top.

"Panther, I'm glad it was okay. I'll get better, promise. Ask me to kill someone, I can come up with like thirty different ways to do it but talk about sex, and I'm at a loss. Just give me a chance. I'll watch porn and read books like Squirt does, maybe I can learn a thing or two."

Squeezing her hands, the smile on my face is huge.

"You'll watch porn and read books? Gorgeous, no need. We'll figure it out together and if porn is necessary, we'll watch it together. You never know, we might want to practice while watching."

She starts a nervous laugh then leans into me, giving me a shoulder bump. Yeah, it'll work out. Now for the hard shit.

"Zoey, I love being here with you but can't expect Avalanche and the guys to run my ranch. We're coming into our busy stud season and that means long days and nights with lots of work. I'm needed back home. But if you tell me not to go, I'll figure something else out or will do my best to split my time between the ranches. We need to figure out what works best for us."

"Panther, I knew this was coming. I talked to Goldilocks about it and if you're willing to try, and Avalanche is good with it, I'd like to split my time. This will always be my home, but that doesn't mean I can't have more than one place to lay my head. So if we aren't working a mission, I can spend half the week with you and then come back here to do my share of the work. That is until we see how our relationship moves along. I'm willing to try if you are."

Pulling her to me, she lands across my lap with my lips on her beautiful full ones. She's trying not to laugh as I kiss her, but the vibrations are about to burst out of her. Leaning back, removing my lips, she bursts out immediately. I join her, thinking that life has a balance. There can be a ton of shit and bad then one day, out of nowhere, good enters your life. Just have to be open enough to let it in.

Hearing the door open, I try to see who it is but fuck the voice tells me.

"Fuck, get a room will you both? Auntie Zoey, Uncle Panther, I'm too young to see that kind of stuff. I'll have to bleach my eyes now. Yuck. Put your tongue back in your mouth, Auntie."

Laughing, she turns, going back in the house, slamming the door behind her. Zoey cuddles up to me, a sigh of something leaving her. My arms wrap around her and together we welcome the beginning of a new day.

THIRTY-THREE
'SHADOW'
ZOEY

The blood splatter hits me right in the face and I swear up a storm. Had plans to do something after our Chapel meeting. Son of a bitch, they always have to fuck with my plans.

"Are you going to let it go now, or are we going to take it to the ring?"

I look at the new prospect of the Intruders, who looks a mess. When I hit him, breaking his nose, that's what got blood all over me. This asshole isn't going to make another day unless he wises up.

"I'm only going to say this once, she's off-limits to you forever, punk. Got me? Just nod if you understand."

Waiting, I take a glance at Squirt, who instead of looking scared, her face is way pissed off. Great, a young hormonal and horny bitch.

"Okay, times up, do you understand, or do I need

to put a call into Tank, Enforcer, or Wrench? Your choice. One is her dad, the others her uncles, so I think you get where I'm going with this, you little asswipe."

"Hey, she's been chasing me, gagging for it. Why am I the one getting my ass kicked while she stands there?"

Turning, I catch Hannah's eyes then give it to her.

"This is what you want in your life? A pansy ass pussy who would rather you take the beatdown instead of him. You deserve so much more, Squirt, so quit trying to rush it, will you?"

She drops her head but says nothing. I turn back to what the fuck is his name, oh that's right, Dylan something.

"Dylan, times up, and I'm going to put a call into all three of the Intruders and let them determine your punishment. Though being a prospect, you might lose the opportunity to keep going for that kutte. I don't know their rules. Go on, get your ass gone, and I don't want to see you again. Move it… now."

He takes one more look at me then over at Hannah but says nothing. When he starts to leave, I hear a sniffle and wait for it because I know it's going to be my fault, always is, when it comes to my little pain in the ass.

"What the hell, Auntie? I'll never lose my V card if you keep running off the available males around here. Shit, you're worse than Pops is and there aren't that many to choose from we, live in Bumfuck, Montana. Are you done? Can I go?"

"Um, not by a long shot, young lady. How many times have I warned you? Now, unfortunately, punishment is coming your way. For the next two weeks you will not leave the ranch unless you're going to the clubhouse. You're responsible for all dinners and also cleaning the ranch. No, don't want to hear it. Squirt, I tried to tell you, but you know everything, so now suck it up, you pain in my ass. And on top of it all, I have to let Tink know you were at it again. I mean, in the back of the clubhouse you let a prospect put you up against the building, feeling you up. Damn, you're better than that and him. What the fuck is your rush?"

As she bitches about her life, I try to come up with the words for Goldilocks, and then after Chapel finally I get to go home to Panther. That alone brings a smile to my face. The last two months have been beautiful and hard. We are in the process of trying this partial living together arrangement. I don't feel comfortable yet to just up and leave Goldilocks and the ranch. Panther has even talked about selling his ranch and finding one closer to the Devil's Handmaidens property. We'll see what happens.

On the front of our sexual interactions, they are getting easier for me. We've even managed to have sex, or as he called it, make love. Wasn't all that enjoyable at first, but Panther went above and beyond and, in the end, I felt loved. This and me are a work in progress for sure.

* * *

Goddamn, I'm late. Chapel ran over so by the time I got on the road it was already starting to get dark. Now that we are in the winter months in Montana, generally, I'm in a cage not on my bike. It's not safe to even try, so I'm being responsible for a change. I text Panther to let him know that I'll be late, and he replies to take my time, be safe, he isn't going anywhere.

Goldilocks wants me to share with him and Avalanche about our upcoming mission. She thinks they might be some help. I'm bringing some information with me that Raven put together. It'll be up to them if they want to be a part of it or not. No pressure.

Taking the turn off to the ranch, after a very long hour plus drive, my body relaxes when it sees the log house. Pulling my cage into the garage, I shut it off and just take a minute to rest my head. I'm beyond exhausted and all I want is to jump into a hot shower then follow it up with a good night's sleep. Maybe Panther had a long day and will want to get some sleep too. I can only hope.

Getting out of the SUV, I walk to the house when both dogs, Ma'iitsoh and Zhį́'ii, run full force

to greet me. And just like every other time they

rush me, I end up on my ass with two huge beasts licking me to death.

"Oh fuck, Panther said to get them inside the house sorry, Zoey, my bad. Let me give you a hand up you, okay? Damn it, Ma'iitsoh, and Zhį́'ii, come on, get off of her. I said come, goddamn it."

Suddenly, his deep raspy voice sends chills down my spine. That is, good chills as I feel my nipples harden under my jacket.

"Ma'iitsoh and Zhį́'ii, come. Heel, now."

Both dogs immediately get up and go to Panther's side, sitting at attention. I hear Avalanche swearing under his breath, but my eyes are glued to Panther. God, how did I get so fucking lucky? When a hand appears in front of me, I grab it and Avalanche almost throws me across the driveway. Shit, man don't know his own strength.

"Welcome home, Nizhoni, I'm glad you're here. Let's get you settled. We cooked dinner, so maybe a glass of wine to start. Then we can sit down and share our days together. Avalanche, come on, brother, time to eat all that food we spent half a day to cook. And no, don't go there, you're not a bother, so drop that shit already."

As I move toward the door, I thank whoever is responsible for bringing me both men. One to be my other half, the other to be my pain in the ass brother. I'm thankful for both as I turn and shut out the world, and the three of us—along with our dogs—go into the kitchen to eat dinner. Together.

* * *

Want more of Zoey/Shadow and Panther/chahóółhééł naabaahii t'áá sáhi
Goto https://dl.bookfunnel.com/in4k5jv7ke to download a <u>bonus</u> epilogue.

Check out the sneak peek of Taz, Book Three coming May 18, 2023 on the next page.

CHAPTER 1 - SNEAK PEEK

'TAZ'

RAQUEL

This has to be a goddamn mistake. There is no other explanation for something of this magnitude. Fuck, I'm always on top of all of the accounts, how did this happen? Knowing I have no choice at all, a phone call is going to have to go out to my prez and VP. This can have a downward effect on our trafficking side of the business. Especially since we have that lawsuit from that one victim we saved six months ago. What a little bitch she turned out to be. And how this is even an issue but, somehow, she's managed to not only get an attorney but file her complaint in the courts.

Reaching for the phone, I'm dreading this call. Thankfully, God is looking out for me because both Tink's and Glory's phones go to voicemail, so I leave both of them a message to call me back as soon as they get my call. After that, I take a quick minute and try to think how this could have happened. I'm so careful, have all my firewalls and securities on our system and update regularly. Also have a separate off-site storage area. My office in the clubhouse is always shut and locked. Only way in is a fingerprint and eye scans, with the four-digit code only a few people know.

Running my hands through my long rainbow-colored hair, I feel the fingers of my anxiety starting to spread throughout my body. No, can't let that happen. I don't lose control, not anymore. Doing what my psychologist has told me to do whenever I have an episode, I lean back, close my eyes, and take some large deep breaths. After a few minutes I feel the stress leaving my shoulders and can actually take in some air without my chest compressing.

Going back to the banking site I recheck my calculations, and shit, it's the same as before. Somehow there is over seven hundred fifty thousand dollars and change missing from one of Tink's, our president's, private accounts. For some that would devastate them, thinking they lost more than their life savings but for Tink, who inherited a massive amount from her grandmother, it's barely a nut in the barrel. Still, in my mind, that's a whole hell of a lot of money to show up suddenly missing.

Not sure what else to do, I put in a call to the bank manager/vice president. I've been dealing with Cynthia Micks since she started. She's a nice lady, single mom with two young children. Yeah, I had

Raven do a background check because we do a lot of business with this financial institution and need to make sure I know who has access to these accounts.

"Good afternoon. Cynthia, please."

"May I ask who's calling?"

"Yeah, can you tell her it's Taz from the Devil's Handmaidens? Need a word with her."

As I wait for the call to connect, my mind is trying to fix this problem. Last time I checked this account was when Tink informed me she needed me to get some money together for Panther. He's Shadow's man, but at the time all I knew was he was a hot as fuck guy who looked like a woman's wet dream. And I'm up for a good dream every now and then.

My phone ringing has me jumping like an idiot in my chair. Without looking at it, I answer.

"Hey, ya got Taz."

"Sister, it's Glory, what's up?"

"Glory, got a situation, need to talk it through with you and Tink. Can you make your way to my office today? I'm waiting to hear back from our prez, then I can text a time."

"Yeah, I can make it, but remember Tink and Noodles took a few days off. Think they went to Bozeman; I could be wrong. Can this wait or do you want me to still come by?"

Shit forgot all about Tink being gone. Well, this can't wait so guess I have my answer.

"Glory, think we need to deal with this sooner

rather than later, so yeah, stop by whenever. I'm here."

"'Kay, maybe I'll grab Shadow and the two of us will be there shortly. See ya."

Oh fuck, just what I don't need, our know-it-all enforcer getting in my face and up my ass. Guess I'm being rough on Shadow, since she's the reason I'm even here in Timber-Ghost Montana and part of the Devil's Handmaidens MC.

Damn, just the thought of that day when Shadow convinced me to trust her, now I'm truly starting to lose it. That's a joke in itself because I didn't even do anything wrong. I've spent years in the Devil's Handmaidens, trying to rebuild everything in me that he ruined. I thank God daily that I fought tooth and nail to escape. Not only just for me, but also for Teddy, my six-year-old autistic son. I made a promise to Teddy the day he was born that nothing would ever come before him. His father was a total jagoff and was on the verge of spreading his evil to our son when I decided to finally leave. The main reason was, on that day, Slick grabbed our son, shaking him to get him to shut up and stop crying.

Seeing him manhandle our son with absolutely no regrets made my decision so fucking easy. I'd gotten used to Slick's beatings and repeatedly raping me. I thought that it was me, that I did something wrong to upset him. No matter what I did, he would find something wrong in everything I did. I'd make what he told me he wanted, only to have him fling the plate across the room, screaming it was too salty or tasted like shit. I knew in my gut that if I stayed, eventually Slick would kill me and teach our son to be just like him. Or he'd kill Teddy for not being able to be the jerk asshole that he was.

Feeling the beginnings of a headache, I get up and go to the little bathroom off of my office. Grabbing some medication, I close the medicine cabinet and see my reflection in the mirror. Makes me remember how I looked that day I literally ran into Shadow. I'd been driving nonstop since I stole one of Slick's cars. I wanted to get as far away from Wisconsin as I could before getting caught. Teddy was coming down with something so besides stopping to fill up the tanks, I needed some children's medication for him.

When it hit me I left my purse in the car, I turned suddenly and ran smack-dab into the middle of all that is Shadow. Looking up to her face, as she is so much taller than me, I screamed, at the same time took a few steps away from her. She never acted like my actions hurt her feelings. All she did was search my face. I was never sure what she saw but when she patted my shoulders, I felt like someone finally had my back. That thought in itself was crazy because she looked insane. She stood there for a bit before asking me if I was in trouble. When I didn't answer, she told me to stay in Timber-Ghost. When I said I didn't know anyone, she asked me if I could trust her? A woman who has a skull tatted face, asking if I could trust her. And to this day I'm not sure why but I did trust her, and more important, standing with her I felt safe, which I hadn't felt in years. I'd already seen evil so just because she, for some unknown reason, tattooed her face, that alone didn't make her a bad person. Especially after the way she won Teddy over when she met him.

The rest is history. She helped me find somewhere to live, well that's not exactly true. She talked to Tink, and they gave me an opportunity, to this day I don't know why. They offered me a job on the ranch to take care of the place and cook meals. For that they would pay me, give me benefits, and a small cabin behind the main house. I know my mouth dropped open because I wasn't used to people doing nice things for me. When I hesitated, Tink came up to me, grabbing my hand, telling me no one would ever put their hands on me again unless it was what I wanted. How she knew Slick raped me constantly, don't know, but that alone made me say yes.

So Teddy and I became an extended part of the Devil's Handmaidens MC. Momma Diane after just a bit, became Teddy's Grammy and Tank, his grandaddy. We were enveloped into the family fold before I knew it and fuck it felt so good.

When Tink and Glory approached me to prospect for the club, I hesitated. I had a kid to think about but the way they explained it to me, I'd be a member eventually. Mainly I'd take care of the books and banking. When Glory found out I had an associates in finance, she jumped on it. They also offered to send me to school to further that education. It didn't take me long to agree to all of it.

Prospecting with a child was not easy at all. I know the club sisters took it easier on me than other prospects, which I appreciated. When I made it and got my patch and rocker, never was I prouder of my accomplishment. As Teddy grew and got older, his autism became more of a problem. Momma Diane found a specialist in Billings who focused on childhood autism. Teddy was enrolled and went into the city once a week. Everyone took turns getting him to his appointments, which I think helped my son's condition. He became more used to being around all types of folks, and to my utter shock and surprise, his favorite of the Devil's Handmaidens was, of course, Shadow.

So lost in my thoughts, I jump in my chair at the abrupt knock on the door. Oh yeah, Glory found Shadow, I think, fingers crossed. Though when she found Panther, she'd tone down but she's even tougher and surer of herself.

"Yeah, come on in."

"Hey, Tazzy, brought our pain in the ass with since Tink is off and about. What's up?"

Once I get them situated at the small lounge area

in my office, all of us with bottled water, I lean forward and just let it all out.

"I was auditing our club accounts and Tink's ranch and private accounts, and one caught my attention. It's one of Tink's personal ones and I don't have a fucking clue how, but it seems that over seven hundred fifty thousand and change is gone. Before you ask, I've got a call in to the bank manager to find out why I wasn't alerted that such a large amount of funds were removed without my approval. As soon as I saw it, I put the call out first to Tink. I forgot they were gone, then reached out to you, Glory. I've never had this happen, not sure what the protocol is."

Glory leans forward, grabbing for her phone. Shadow is watching me very closely. I've known this sister since I made Timber-Ghost my home so even though she thinks she's all badass and everyone is afraid of her, I'm not.

"Go ahead ask away, Shadow. No, I didn't take the money. First, don't need that amount and, second, if something came up and I found myself in trouble I'd come to the club in Chapel and talk it through. I make more than enough for Teddy and me to live on. Yeah, the new house is much more coming out of my account monthly, but I've been saving for years. And since Tink let me buy the acreage cheap from her, I was ahead of the game before I built my house, thanks to Ollie and his people. So no, Shadow, I didn't help myself to Tink's personal account money.

I'd be a fool to even consider it. And before you go where you're going next, no there's no one in my life who could have used me to get to the accounts. No one, and I mean no one, but Tink has the information for her personal accounts. I'm sure she's let Noodles in since they're planning on getting married, but she's not stupid."

Our enforcer stares at me for ages before she shifts back into the couch, crossing her one leg over the other.

"Taz, I never thought that you took the fucking money. You don't have the ability to be that type of person. What worries me is that someone was able to do this in between your audits. Who knows when you do the audits and on what schedule? I know Tink, Glory, and I know about them, any other club sisters?"

I shake my head because as far as I know, no one knows about my process with the books and accounts. I'm usually left alone since my work is behind a desk. Not like some of the sisters who run the businesses or help out at the ranch, or when we have survivors who are here to recover, some of the club sisters help out with those folks.

Between my job and Teddy, I'm back at school, trying to get my master's in finance. My days are full, as are my nights, with my son and homework. I maintain my duties as a Devil's Handmaidens sister, which means spending some time at the Wooden

Spirits Bar and Grill or helping out at our trucking company. I tend to lean toward the bar and grill since I can bring Teddy with and while he's eating, I can help out with whatever is needed.

Glory is on the phone and I'm only hearing one side of the conversation.

"Hey, Prez, thank God. We have Tazzy, who is so on top of shit and pays attention to everything. Okay, when do you think you'll be back? Yeah, I get it, enjoy your time with your man. I'll tell her and we'll move forward with contacting the bank personnel and doing a dive there. I'll put Raven on it and she can do her geek shit to see if anyone has had their hands in our cookie jar. Will do, thanks, Tink."

"Tazzy, don't worry Tink, like the two of us, know you had absolutely nothing to do with this. We just need to find out who does though. I think the best way to…"

Hearing my phone ringing, I reach into my top drawer and pull it out, looking down. My heart almost stops beating when I see that it's Teddy's school.

"Hey, Glory, got to take this. It's my son's school, hang on."

"Hello."

"Is this Raquel Smith?"

"Yes, it is, what's going on? Is Teddy okay? Please just tell me."

"Miss Smith, Teddy had an episode a few minutes

ago. He started off by being withdrawn when his class started, then got moody with his teacher, which is rare, he loves Mrs. James. When she questioned him, he jumped up and ran to the corner crying. We've emptied the room but he's rocking back and forth asking for you. Can you please come get your son?"

"I'll be there right away. Leaving now."

Slamming the phone down on the desk, I jump up and reach for my sweater then grab my purse, throwing my phone in it. I totally forgot that Glory and Shadow were still here. It's Shadow who asks the question.

"What's wrong with Teddy, sister? Is everything okay?"

"Not sure, Zoey, fuck he's having an episode; something he's not experienced in forever. Maybe it's the new medicine. I'm sorry, I've got to go pick him up. The school is requesting I come get him. Shit, what am I going to do? We have to find out about this banking issue, but I can't just leave him when he's like this. Oh God, my head is killing me. Another fucking migraine is what I don't need right now."

Glory and Shadow stand and walk toward my door.

"Come on, Tazzy, let's go get Teddy. We'll figure it out as we go. Move your ass, sister, your kid needs us now."

Glory puts her arm around my shoulders, walking

me out to a club cage. Shadow comes out with a booster seat since Teddy is so small. Fuck, how does she even know we need that?

"Taz, I've had Teddy in my cage more than anyone else. He's gonna be fine, just breathe. Glory, let's go, you drive."

The school is only about an eight-minute drive from the clubhouse, but we make it there in under five minutes. I jump out of the SUV and jog to the entrance, with my two club sisters behind me. When we enter and go to the office, it dawns on me that Shadow is very unique, especially with her skull tatted face. When the receptionist stands, she shocks the total shit outta me.

"Hi, Raquel, thanks for coming in so quickly. I'll let our principal know you're here. Hey, Glory, Shadow. How's things?"

Glory replies but even though it is polite, it also is very short. What got me is how the receptionist was almost hero-worshipping Shadow. If I wasn't so worried about Teddy, I'd burst out laughing.

The principle walks in, and he doesn't hide his disgust at seeing Glory and Shadow. Well, fuck him silly, he don't know shit.

"Where's my son? I need to see him, make sure he's okay."

"Ms. Smith, he's with the nurse. I'd be happy to show you where that is, and your friends can wait here for you."

He goes to touch my arm when Shadow growls, which makes him jump back.

"No, we'll all be going to get Teddy, Mr. Jerk—oh, sorry—Mr. Jerksy. Lead the way."

As we walk out, I hear the receptionist trying to hold in her giggles. I turn, looking at Shadow, who smirks and winks at me. Oh God, what is going on, she's actually being nice. It has to be Panther being in her life 'cause usually she has been like a devil on wheels.

Walking into the nurse's office, I can hear Teddy crying uncontrollably. I rush to my baby, whose arms come up as soon as he sees me. I grab him, pulling him close, rocking back and forth, trying to calm him down. When his tears are ending, I look down at him to see his thumb in his mouth. Fuck, he's six years old and he only does the thumb thing when he's extremely anxious.

"Baby boy, you okay? Tell Mommy what's wrong."

He looks at me with those big eyes before he looks around me, a huge smile appearing on his face.

"Auntie Shadow, I want you. Come get me from Mommy. Please?"

I'm shocked and even a bit hurt. Shadow comes our way, mouthing "sorry" to me before gently picking up Teddy, pulling him to her chest. His hand starts to trace her skull tattoo and Mr. Jerksy makes a nasty face and says something under his breath. I miss the first part of their conversation but catch the ending. And what I hear makes my blood freeze.

"Teddy, tell Auntie Shadow what's got you all riled up? You know I won't let anything, or anyone hurt you. Come whisper it so it's between the two of us."

My son leans toward her, putting his cheek to hers, so his mouth is at her ear. Unfortunately, Teddy doesn't understand a soft voice, so he talks in his normal one.

"Auntie Shadow, that mean man is back. I don't want Mommy to know, but he was at the fence during our outside time, and he was mean to me. Squeezed my hand really hard trying to drag me over the fence. I'm scared, he looks really mad."

"Who is it, Teddy? I promise Auntie Shadow has your back, little man, you know that. Plus, I've been teaching you how to protect yourself, so you're not a little boy but a tough man who can take care of himself. Now, who is this bast… jerk who's bothering you."

My heart is beating and I'm having a hard time breathing. But when Teddy talks, I feel a disconnect from my body.

"His name is Slick, the man who used to beat up Mommy and would shake me when I was young because I cried a lot. He said he was finally back to claim his family, and no one was going to stop him, if they know what's best for them."

Hearing Glory calling my name, the next thing I feel is Shadow next to me, pushing me down.

"Taz, put your head between your legs. No, Teddy, she'll be fine, don't cry. In fact, I need you to sit right next to your mommy, help hold her up. Taz, you need to breathe in and out. Glory went to get you some water, just take it easy. We'll talk in a bit but, sister, don't worry. You know I won't let that bastard, I mean jerk, get near either of you. Promise. Teddy, don't use the bad word Auntie used kay?"

I start to pray that Shadow is right, and she can protect both of us, because otherwise I'm going to do whatever it takes to put Slick in the ground this time. I'm not the same woman that prick used to beat up that's for damn sure. I'll never give him a chance to hurt me or, more importantly, my boy ever again.

Grab your copy of Taz (Book #3) now!

ABOUT THE AUTHOR

USA Today Bestselling author, D. M. Earl creates authentic and genuine characters while spinning stories that feel so real and relatable that the readers plunge deep within the plot, begging for more. Complete with drama, angst, romance, and passion, the stories jump off the page.

When Earl, an avid reader since childhood, isn't at her keyboard pouring her heart into her work, you'll find her in Northwest Indiana snuggling up to her husband, the love of her life, with her seven fur babies nearby. Her other passions include gardening and shockingly cruising around town on the back of her 2004 Harley. She's a woman of many talents and interests. Earl appreciates each and every reader who has ever given her a chance--and hopes to connect on social media with all of her readers.

Contact D.M at DM@DMEARL.COM
Website: http://www.dmearl.com/

- facebook.com/DMEarlAuthorIndie
- twitter.com/dmearl
- instagram.com/dmearl14
- amazon.com/D-M-Earl/e/B00M2HB12U
- bookbub.com/authors/d-m-earl
- goodreads.com/dmearl
- pinterest.com/dauthor

ALSO BY D.M. EARL

DEVIL'S HANDMAIDENS MC: TIMBER-GHOST, MONTANA CHAPTER

Tink (Book #1)

Shadow (Book #2)

Taz (Book #3)

Vixen (Book #4)

Glory (Book #5)

GRIMM WOLVES MC SERIES

Behemoth (Book 1)

Bottom of the Chains-Prospect (Book 2)

Santa...Nope The Grimm Wolves (Book 3)

Keeping Secrets-Prospect (Book 4)

A Tormented Man's Soul: Part One (Book 5)

Triad Resumption: Part Two (Book 6)

WHEELS & HOGS SERIES

Connelly's Horde (Book 1)

Cadence Reflection (Book 2)

Gabriel's Treasure (Book 3)

Holidays with the Horde (Book 4)

My Sugar (Book 5)

[Daisy's Darkness (Book 6)](#)

The Journals Trilogy

[Anguish (Book 1)](#)

Vengeance (Book 2)

Awakening (Book 3)

Stand Alone Titles

[Survivor: A Salvation Society Novel](#)

Printed in Great Britain
by Amazon